The Billionaire's Touch

THE SINCLAIRS

ALSO BY J.S. SCOTT

The Sinclairs

The Billionaire's Christmas (A Sinclair Novella)
No Ordinary Billionaire
The Forbidden Billionaire

The Billionaire's Obsession

*The Billionaire's Obsession Complete
Collection*—Simon
Mine for Tonight
Mine for Now
Mine Forever
Mine Completely

Mine for Christmas

Heart of the Billionaire—Sam
The Billionaire's Salvation—Max
The Billionaire's Game—Kade
Billionaire Unmasked—Jason
Billionaire Undone—Travis
Billionaire Untamed—Tate
Billionaire Unbound—Chloe

The Sentinel Demons

A Dangerous Bargain
A Dangerous Hunger
A Dangerous Fury

Big Girls and Bad Boys

The Curve Ball
The Beast Loves Curves
Curves by Design

*The Pleasure of His Punishment:
Stories*

The Changeling Encounters

Mate of the Werewolf
The Dangers of Adopting a Werewolf
All I Want for Christmas Is a Werewolf

The Vampire Coalition

Ethan's Mate
Rory's Mate
Nathan's Mate
Liam's Mate
Daric's Mate

The Billionaire's Touch

THE SINCLAIRS

J.S. Scott

Montlake
Romance

Text copyright © 2016 J.S. SCOTT

Published by Montlake Romance, Seattle

www.apub.com

Amazon, the Amazon logo, and Montlake Romance are trademarks of Amazon.com, Inc., or its affiliates.

ISBN-13: 9781503950924
ISBN-10: 1503950921

Cover design by Laura Klynstra

Printed in the United States of America

This book is dedicated to my beloved mother, Jennie. She left this world on August 22nd, 2015, after a long battle with Parkinson's disease. My mom is the reason that I'm writing today. She was a romance reader, and I started devouring romance books very early in life, because throughout my teenage years I swiped her Harlequin Romances after she finished with them. Reading those books started a lifelong love of romance novels that stayed with me and was the very beginning of my desire to write them myself. Mom believed that working hard and being kind to others would take a person a long way in life. She was right, and I'll always try my best to live by the example she set for me.

I love you, Mom, and I'll miss you every day for the rest of my life, but you'll always live on through me and my memories of what an extraordinary woman you were. Thank you for always being my biggest fan and for being so proud of me.

From Your Loving Daughter Who Will Never Forget You,

-Jan

PROLOGUE

Fourteen Months Ago

Miranda Tyler chewed absently on the pen between her fingers, oblivious to the germs she was probably ingesting from the well-used object. She stared pensively at the blank email draft in front of her. Was she really going to do this? It seemed pretty pointless, and yet . . .

Her friend Emily had just gone to try to speak personally with the only Sinclair living in the area, the only man who had the resources to save Christmas for the seacoast town of Amesport, Maine.

It wasn't Emily's fault that all of the funds for the Youth Center of Amesport had been stolen, but Miranda—otherwise known simply as Randi to her friends—knew that Emily was blaming herself completely for the fiasco. Her friend was sweet, trusting, and those traits had gotten her completely screwed. All of the money was gone from the Christmas fund for the Center, stolen by an asshole who Emily had trusted, and now they desperately needed help.

J.S. Scott

Come on, Randi. If Emily can go try to talk to the Amesport Beast, Grady Sinclair, you can find the damn balls to send a stupid email.

Honestly, sending an email off to a generic address in the hopes that one of the billionaire Sinclairs might actually read it and help the town of Amesport *did* seem like a meaningless action. But Randi was desperate, and she couldn't seem to conjure up a better idea, although she badly wished she had one. Her foster parents had left her their home, but her teaching job wasn't exactly lucrative. She got by on what it paid, but she didn't have the kind of funds needed to replace the Christmas money. If she did, she'd give it without a thought. Unfortunately, that wasn't an option.

Once Emily had gone to meet The Beast—aka Grady Sinclair—Randi had sat down at one of the Center's aging computers, trying to find email addresses for the rest of the Sinclair family. *Like the billionaire brothers and cousins are really going to make their personal emails public?* Still, Randi wanted to do *something*.

Emily had been so devastated and desperate. Randi couldn't bear it, and she couldn't sit and do nothing while Emily went to grovel to Grady Sinclair and continued to make everything her fault. In reality, Emily was an amazing director for the Center, a selfless woman who had dedicated herself to the nonprofit organization that was the heart of Amesport life. The Center was a better place since Emily had accepted the job of director.

Just do it! Send the damn email. What's the worst that could happen?

Randi put down the pen she was chewing on and copied and pasted the "info" email address published on the Sinclair Fund web page into her empty draft. She'd found the site during her search—the organization was a large group charity in which all of the billionaire Sinclairs participated. More than likely, her email would end up in the hands of some assistant or secretary. She very much doubted that any of the Sinclairs were really hands-on with the charity. But maybe one of the

2

employees would have a heart and pass the emailed info to one of the bosses. It *was* almost Christmas.

Dear Mr. Sinclair:

Randi paused after typing the generic greeting, figuring that was as good a start as any, since every one of them had the same last name. She quickly wrote the shortest email possible, explaining the crisis and practically begging for their assistance. When she finished, she breathed a sigh of relief. She hated groveling for anything; it rubbed her the wrong way. But she loved Emily, and there was very little she wouldn't do for her real friends.

Grady was the only Sinclair who lived in Amesport, and Emily was currently approaching *him* personally. With his reputation for being a jerk and a recluse, it had taken a lot of guts for Emily to seek him out on the secluded Amesport Peninsula.

Her eyes darting to the clock on the wall, Randi realized that Emily was probably just now arriving at Grady's mansion. Grady's brothers Evan and Jared each had a home on the same cape right at the edge of town, as did their sister, Hope. The mansions were currently empty and rarely, if ever, visited.

Plenty of people gossiped about the Sinclairs, especially about Grady, but nobody really *knew* any of them. Honestly, Randi couldn't remember an occasion where she'd actually *seen* any of the other Sinclairs come to Amesport on vacation. Jared had overseen the building of his siblings' homes on the exclusive peninsula, but she'd never *seen* any of them.

All of the Sinclair men have to be stiff-necked snobs! They certainly have never frequented any of the local businesses, or people would know them.

Randi dearly wished she had found information on the Sinclair sister, but Hope was rarely in the media and apparently not active on social media. Grady's cousins, Micah, Julian, and Xander, had little connection to the town, but some of their heritage was here. So she'd try to appeal to their sense of family.

As she read the hastily written note to check for errors, she hesitated on how to sign the letter. Writing from her email at the Center, she could be anonymous, a worried citizen. Everyone in the town of Amesport had access to email here in the tiny computer room of the Center, and Randi had her own free email address she'd created only for business here. She rarely utilized it except for sending progress reports to the parents of the students she helped tutor after hours as a volunteer. Unfortunately, she was fairly certain most of the parents didn't even bother to read her correspondence.

She ended up simply signing the email: *A Concerned Resident of Amesport.*

Hitting the "Send" button with a heavy sigh, she watched as the letter was sent off into cyberspace, wondering exactly *who* would read it. *Probably an assistant who would delete it without another thought.* The Sinclair Fund was an enormous charity. They were in the business of raising funds for large nonprofit organizations, not giving them out to a small town in crisis.

Randi signed herself out of her email for the Center and shut down the computer. She'd promised Emily she'd watch over the activities here while her friend was approaching Grady Sinclair to try and raise the funds they needed to save Christmas for Amesport and the surrounding villages. Unfortunately, Christmas wouldn't be very merry if they couldn't get the funds back for presents for needy children and the annual Christmas party. For some of the kids, whatever they got from the Center would be their only gift, and the food provided at the Christmas party their main Christmas dinner.

Randi pushed the dreary thought from her mind as she looked at all of the decorations around the old building. Emily had brought life into the aging structure, even though the tired Center desperately needed maintenance. Colorful wreaths and Christmas decorations were everywhere, hung with love for the season by its employees and volunteers.

Peeking into the area where the senior citizens held their bingo sessions, Randi's stomach rumbled at the enticing smells coming from the room. She'd come to the Center, straight from her teaching job at the local school, to tutor a few students who were struggling with their studies, and she was starving.

Sneaking quietly into the room to snatch a few chicken wings and some cake without being detected by some of the sharp old ladies was never easy, but she was up for the challenge. Snatching food had become almost an art for her in her early teenage years.

After a nervous week of checking for an answer with no return message, Randi completely forgot about the email she had sent in desperation . . . until she finally got a reply . . .

Two Months Later . . .

Evan Sinclair might have laughed at the ridiculous email he'd just finished reading—if he was actually the type of man who found humor in anything . . . which he didn't. Ever!

He stared at the email, frowning as he read it for the second time. What kind of person would have the gall to ask a charity raising big money for cancer research, abused women, and the several other urgent causes that the Sinclair Fund actually helped, for money? And it wasn't even for a good cause, in his opinion. It was for a small coastal town that needed Christmas funds. Did the author of the missive really think he was some sort of friendly elf to grant her Christmas wish?

Hardly!

Evan didn't believe in Christmas. If there was a modern-day version of Scrooge, it would be him, except he wouldn't ever have the apparent epiphany that old Ebenezer experienced. In fact, the holiday *did* irritate him and always would. It meant a disruption of business, and scheduling meetings around the frivolous, commercialized season. It hadn't been a pleasant holiday when he was a child, and he abhorred it almost as much as an adult.

Normally, none of his brothers or cousins looked at the mailbox for the Fund, and they certainly didn't answer letters personally; they had employees for that. But the email had caught his eye when his assistant had written to him about a complaint a big donor had mentioned over the quality of assistance he was getting via email from the website. Evan had logged in to the mailbox from home to evaluate how some of the inquiries were being handled. They couldn't afford to lose important donors, and especially not people who donated millions.

He could hardly miss the subject line "Help Us Save Our Town" as he scrolled through old emails.

Intrigued, he'd opened the missive.

Now, he was scowling at the correspondence in front of him. The email's author was anonymous, the email address generic, simply signing the short explanation and plea for help with "A Concerned Resident of Amesport."

He should have dismissed it, especially since he knew his brother Grady had already solved the problem well before Christmas. In fact, Grady was now a town hero in Amesport because he'd donated the needed funds. He had also gotten himself engaged and then married to the Center's director, Emily.

Christmas is over. Leave it. Grady solved the ridiculous situation, getting himself injured in the process.

Evan wasn't crazy about the outcome, especially the fact that his younger brother had thrown himself into the line of danger to resolve the whole debacle and rescue his new bride. But Grady seemed happy enough since his nuptials with Emily, even though, in Evan's opinion, he'd married with far too little thought and way too much haste.

The entire holiday season had passed . . . thank God. Unfortunately, the audacity of the person who had sent the correspondence still annoyed him.

He frowned as he read the email again, still wondering about the author. It was a well-written account of the situation at the time it was composed, but it was still presumptuous. He hated the fact that the words were trying to play on his sense of guilt, duty, and family. If there was one thing that Evan did, it was watch out for his family. As the eldest in his broken family, he considered everything that happened to his siblings his business, his responsibility.

Uncharacteristically, he forgot about *why* he was in the mailbox for the Sinclair Fund in the first place. He switched gears and signed up for an anonymous email address on one of the numerous free sites that offered them, and decided to reply to the inquiry. The email had been appropriately ignored previously by employees, and probably should have just been deleted. For the sake of the charity, he didn't want the sender to know exactly who was replying. He just wanted the author to understand that the Sinclair Fund wasn't an appropriate place to seek a donation for a trivial problem. He could reprimand the person, discourage future emails of the same nature to the Sinclair Fund, and no one would ever know.

He copied and pasted the original email from the mystery author before replying.

Dear Concerned:

How else could he start the return email? He wasn't even sure about the gender of the person writing, but he would place a hefty bet on the writer being a female. Women seemed to get ridiculously sentimental over certain holidays.

He promptly shot out a reply, closed the window for the free email site, and forgot all about the issue as he returned his attention to the Sinclair Fund mailbox to see if his donor actually had cause for complaint. Evan didn't even think about the annoying email again . . . until he got an answer several days later.

Randi gaped at the rudest email she'd ever received, her mouth actually opening and closing like a fish out of water that was struggling to take a breath.

> *Dear Concerned:*
> *I'm curious as to whether you really expected to receive an answer to your email sent before Christmas. Did you really think one of the Sinclairs was going to read your email, then actually provide funds for a town that isn't even on the map, and for such a ludicrous reason? We are trying to help solve pressing concerns in both our nation and the world with the Sinclair Fund, not masquerade as Santa Claus. I think it would have been much more appropriate for you to address your email to the North Pole.*
> *However, it is my understanding that you and the citizens of Amesport did get your Christmas wish. Wasn't this issue completely resolved by Grady Sinclair?*
> *Sincerely,*
> *Unsympathetic in Boston*

"*Unsympathetic in Boston*? Oh, my God! What a jerk!" Randi scowled at the computer screen at the Center, completely taken aback by the response to the email she'd sent two months earlier. After so long, she'd completely given up on getting an answer.

The only reason she'd signed in to that email address at all was to contact a parent of one of the children she was tutoring, and she'd been stunned to find that she finally had a reply to the email she'd sent to the Sinclair Fund.

She checked the date and realized her plea had only been answered a few days ago. *Why now?* She'd pathetically checked every single day for over a week after writing her email to the Sinclairs, desperately hoping somebody would respond. And so they did . . . *after* Christmas had passed, and with the snottiest comments imaginable!

Randi's temper started to slowly simmer as she continued to gape at the snooty response, unable to believe that an employee of a charity would respond so bluntly. Maybe the problem *did* seem small to them, but it was important to her town.

"Condescending asshole," she whispered to herself even as she wondered at the question in the email, about the situation being resolved. Truth was, the crisis *had* been more than adequately fixed. Emily was now married to Grady Sinclair, and the Center was not only thriving, but undergoing some major renovations.

She closed her email, shut down the computer, and stood up, deciding she'd do progress reports tomorrow. She was too pissed off to do them now.

"*Not on the map?* Amesport?" she mumbled under her breath as she picked up her jacket from the back of the chair. Luckily, she was alone in the computer room, so it didn't matter that she was talking to herself. Nobody was around to listen. While Amesport was no Boston, it *was* a thriving seacoast town, a place where tourists flocked in the summer to enjoy the beauty of the ocean and a multitude of water sports.

"Write to Santa Claus my ass!" She yanked her coat on and picked up her purse from the desk before exiting the room, her brain still trying to process the fact that a Sinclair employee had been that rude. It hadn't been necessary. The person could have politely declined. Or better yet . . . ignored the email like they already had for months now. After all, Grady *had* rescued Christmas, and her request was two months old. What would possess someone to answer an old email with that much arrogance and condescension?

She paused as she opened the door, remembering the last line of the reply:

Wasn't this issue completely resolved by Grady Sinclair?

"How do they know about that? Why do they care?" she pondered quietly as she pulled the door completely open. "If this person thinks my email was stupid, what does it matter whether Grady helped the town or not?"

Pushing aside the fact that someone had tried to make her feel ridiculous and small, she wanted to make sense of the last comment in the email. Did this person really expect her to verify the question?

Taking a deep breath, she did her best to ignore her negative thoughts and to reason without anger. She really *shouldn't* answer the email. Emily was her friend, so she should tell her about the rude employee. Randi had actually come to like and respect Emily's new husband. But something in her gut wouldn't and couldn't leave the situation as it stood. She wasn't about to go running to Grady just because she could now call him a friend. The email address had been weird, a free service that was unlikely to be traceable. If she was the victim of a bad joke, or an unhappy person, she'd fire back. Some idiot in an office somewhere wasn't going to insult her and her beloved town without *some* kind of answer.

The Center was quiet as she exited the front doors. Very little was happening tonight, except for the few men still left in the building working on improvements. Randi shivered as the bitter-cold wind did a full-frontal assault, reminding her that she hadn't bothered to zip her jacket. Tugging the ends of the material together, she sprinted for her vehicle, smirking evilly as she decided on just how to reply to her churlish prankster. She was a teacher, a woman with an education. If there was one thing she was good at, it was finding mistakes and stating facts.

So, that's exactly what she did the very next day.

Two Days Later . . .

Evan wasn't sure why he even bothered to check his bogus email address. It wasn't like he had nothing better to do. He was in his downtown offices, and he had an important meeting in less than fifteen minutes. Checking his notes and making sure he had all of the documents he needed should be his priority at the moment. Nevertheless, he was drumming his fingers on the oak desk in front of him, waiting for the free email page to appear. It came up after a wait he considered way too long, even for a free service, and he logged in impatiently.

This is a waste of time. I have work to do. Why do I even care if some presumptuous person in Amesport answered my email?

He knew for a fact that Grady had more than rescued the Center and the town of Amesport. Evan didn't need an answer. Still, he wondered if there *was* an answer to his question, and if the sender of the email had felt appropriately sorry they had sent a letter to a worthwhile charity for help with such a small issue.

Frowning as the annoyingly slow mailbox appeared, he noticed that he did indeed have mail. Clicking the mouse efficiently, he deleted the junk that was a prerequisite to signing up for the free service. He hesitated uncharacteristically as he saw that there actually was a response from the same generic email that he'd written to a few days earlier. A haughty, dark brow rose as he saw the subject line:

Proof that Amesport is On the Map!!

Intrigued, he clicked on the response.

> *Dear Unsympathetic:*
> *Had I known that all of the Sinclair Fund employees were as heartless and arrogant as you appear to be, I would have definitely written to Santa Claus instead. In the future, I'll direct all urgent email to the North Pole.*
> *You're also uninformed. Amesport certainly is on the map and is a popular tourist destination in the summer. The town appears quite clearly. Please see the attached.*
> *P.S. Grady Sinclair is a wonderful man with a heart, and the issues with the Center are completely resolved. Luckily, there is someone affiliated with the Sinclairs who actually has a heart.*
> *Sincerely,*
> *No Longer Concerned in Amesport*

Evan read the email again, strangely amused by the less-than-pleasant response. It wasn't often that anyone addressed him with anything less than complete reverence. It was oddly . . . refreshing.

He clicked on the attachment, staring at it for a moment before he truly understood exactly what it was. It was a map of the Maine coastline, with the town of Amesport circled in red and blown up so that it was prominently displayed with a handwritten caption.

The town of Amesport certainly is on the map. It appears quite clearly.

Evan looked from her comment to the oversized area of Amesport circled in red. Then, Evan Sinclair did something he almost never did . . . he laughed.

CHAPTER 1

The Present

"We should be landing soon," Micah Sinclair mentioned casually as he glanced out the window of Evan's private jet. "It's been a while. I'm sure you're eager to see Hope and your new nephew."

Evan lifted his eyes from his laptop and looked at Micah, realizing the two of them had barely spoken during the flight. When his cousin had asked to hitch a ride with him to Amesport from New York City because he'd lent his own jet to his brother Julian, Evan had thought he'd welcome the company. Micah had a residence in New York; Evan didn't, but was there quite frequently on business, so they met whenever possible.

As the eldest of the Sinclairs, Evan had the most in common with Micah. They were both just entering their midthirties, and, unlike his cousin's younger brothers, Micah was obsessed with business. Granted, his business was extreme sports, but he took his bottom line and his responsibilities to his siblings seriously. As the oldest in their immediate families, Evan and Micah understood each other when it came to what everyone else called "meddling" in the business of younger relatives. He and Micah preferred to call it "guidance," and neither one of them had ever felt guilty about checking on family. Maybe some people would actually refer to how they handled things as spying, but Evan preferred to think of it as checking on the well-being of his relatives.

Evan shrugged. "It's been over six months since I've seen them, and I want to meet my nephew. I saw pictures. He looks bald. That can't be normal. No Sinclair has ever been hairless. Our grandfather died with a full head of hair." Their grandfather had lived to a ripe old age, and his hair had been gray as long as Evan could remember, but he hadn't had a single bald spot on his head.

Micah chuckled as he fastened his seat belt in preparation for landing. "He's not bald. His hair is blond, and it's thin. He's a cute little guy. Hope sent me a picture to my cell phone."

Evan checked his seat belt and leaned back in the leather seat of his private aircraft, frowning at Micah, who was seated across from him. "He looked bald to me. And he's not *cute*. He's handsome. He's a Sinclair."

Micah's laughter boomed in the cabin of the aircraft. "God, you're an arrogant prick! But I like that about you. I always have."

Evan smoothed down the lapel of his custom suit and straightened his tie before replying. "I'm sure the traits are easy to recognize since you happen to have the same attributes."

If Evan was totally honest—which he wasn't going to be—Micah probably wasn't quite as uptight as he was, but he wasn't going to admit *that* to his eldest cousin.

"Why do you always dress like you're going to a business meeting or a funeral? Sometimes I wonder if you even own a pair of jeans," Micah queried, sounding more curious than teasing.

Evan shot him a condescending look, unwilling to admit that he didn't, in fact, own a pair of jeans or any other casual clothing. "I'm perfectly comfortable in a suit." Well, at least that was the truth. If he was dressed for business, he felt more in control. His attire reminded him of his goals. He didn't want to be sidetracked into something frivolous or unimportant.

Eyeing the guy for a moment, Evan had to admit that wearing a pair of jeans and a button-down green shirt didn't lessen Micah's aura of power. But Micah was different, normal. He was an expert at several of the sports that he sold state-of-the-art equipment for, and he had no reason to be anything other than self-assured. He might think that Micah was certifiable for participating in some of the extreme sports that he excelled at, but Evan couldn't deny that his cousin was good at them. Really good. It took intense concentration and focus to do the stunts Micah was capable of performing, and he took his business just as seriously.

"I heard they named the baby David," Micah said conversationally as the plane continued to descend for landing.

Evan inwardly released a sigh of relief that Micah had dropped the teasing. It wasn't something he was entirely comfortable with, even from family.

He nodded as he answered. "David was a friend of Hope's who was killed while chasing tornadoes. An extreme meteorologist. They wanted to pass the name on to their son."

Evan admired the fact that Hope was paying tribute to a good friend who had died trying to collect weather data, but he sure as hell hoped that his nephew didn't decide on the same line of work as his mother or his namesake. Maybe it was a good thing that Evan hadn't known that Hope was chasing tornadoes and every other form of extreme weather before she married Jason Sutherland. However, it still ate at him that he'd failed his only sister, hadn't protected her from the horrors she'd suffered early in her career. She had hidden her involvement in her dangerous endeavors well, but he should have been better, more involved in her life. He was her oldest brother, and he should have kept her safe. Evan hated failing at anything, but what had happened to Hope was his deepest regret and his greatest defeat. He still hadn't forgiven himself; he was pretty sure he never would.

"I can't believe that our sweet little Hope was such a wild child," Micah mused, his voice sounding slightly awed.

"It was her career," Evan answered unhappily. "It's not like she was out seeking thrills for no reason." He didn't like her being referred to as *wild*. She wasn't. Not usually. As Micah had already mentioned, Hope had been a very sweet child and a quiet teenager. Evan had thought she was just carrying on in the same manner in Aspen, living a very sedate life free of media attention in the Colorado Rockies. In reality, she'd been roaming around the world photographing extreme weather events.

I don't really know her. I don't really know any of my siblings anymore.

If he wanted to be honest—which he didn't—he had never really known them at all. They'd spent very little time together as children or adults. Evan hated the fact that there was distance between himself and his siblings, but now that they were all grown and happy, he wasn't certain how to fit into the Sinclair family or how to fix the situation, or even if he wanted it to *be* fixed. Too much time had passed.

Maybe I feel distant because I'm not happy or content like they are now? We have nothing in common.

No. That wasn't quite right. Evan had always *needed* to maintain his distance in order to keep his secrets. Now, he wasn't sure he could or would ever truly be close to any of them. He was fairly certain that all of them saw him as more of a pain in the ass than a brother, simply because he interfered in their lives from time to time. But he was okay with that. As long as they were all safe and happy.

"I still think she's pretty ballsy," Micah said with admiration. "And her photography work is incredible."

"It is," Evan answered simply. He was proud of all of his siblings, and Hope's talent was truly astonishing. His home in Boston was filled with as many of her photos as he'd been able to acquire after he'd found out about her secret career path.

Hope was currently working on her nature shots, but Evan loved the very photos that had caused her harm: her extreme-weather photography. Some of them were very tangled and dark, breathtaking in their intense ferocity. Evan knew little about photography techniques, but he didn't need to know much about taking pictures to recognize that the shadowy images struck a chord in him that resonated through his entire being. Hope's creations reminded him of his own life, and the uncertainty of life itself.

Neither man spoke as they came to a rather bumpy landing on the runway of the small airport located outside Amesport, each seemingly lost in his own thoughts. Evan noted that his car and his driver, Stokes, had already arrived, the Rolls-Royce waiting just beyond the area where the plane would come to a stop.

"Do you want to stay with me?" Evan offered sincerely. Both Micah and Julian were coming for the party Hope was hosting, which she was calling The Amesport Midwinter Ball, though Evan knew it was really just a reason to get the entire town together to see her new son. It was being held in the Youth Center, and he had no doubt everyone invited would be there.

He unbuckled his seat belt as the plane came to a stop, damn glad he didn't have to attend yet another marriage ceremony. It seemed like the only reason he usually came to this town was to be in a wedding. If he had to stand up one more time with Randi Tyler, he was likely to lose it. Luckily, he had no more brothers to marry off, his sister was already married to Jason, and he'd never again have to stand across from Randi and pretend he actually liked her as she took his arm with a false smile on her face while he led her down the aisle. Hopefully he could avoid her almost entirely on this trip. It wasn't like he saw every resident in Amesport on each visit. The town was small, but it wasn't *that* small. Unfortunately, Evan doubted that he'd be able to avoid Randi completely. She was friends with Hope now, and would inevitably show up at the party.

"Naw. I'm good. Jared is putting me and Julian up in his guest-house. Now that Mara doesn't need it for her business anymore, it's empty. Julian won't be coming in until tomorrow. He can't stay long—now that he's been nominated for an Academy Award, he thinks he's busy." Micah smirked as he stood and retrieved his suitcase from one of the spacious closets on the plane. "He's shooting his next movie in a month, and the award ceremonies are in just a couple of weeks. I guess he's been bombarded for interviews."

Evan knew that Micah might be teasing but was actually really proud of Julian. Honestly, Evan was proud of him, too. Julian had tried never to use his power as a Sinclair or his inherited money in his pursuit of stardom. He'd played the small parts, worked his way up in the movie industry. When he'd finally landed a leading role in a film after years of struggling, he'd done it by the merit of his own talent. Being nominated for an Oscar was proof that he'd really made it because of his own abilities.

"I hope he wins," Evan grumbled as he gathered the rest of the things he'd need while in Amesport. He didn't need much. His assistant had sent all of the necessities to his home here a while ago.

"Me too," Micah admitted as they headed closer to the door of the aircraft, pulling on his dark-blue ski jacket. Evan donned his black wool dress coat.

"How's Xander?" Evan didn't want to ask the question, but he felt compelled to know how his youngest cousin was doing.

Micah shrugged a little too nonchalantly as he moved toward the exit. "The same. I never know from one day to the next what to expect with him now. He's not coming for Hope's party."

"Is he on or off the wagon?" Evan asked cautiously as he followed Micah's lead.

"On for now," Micah replied with a heavy sigh. "But I'm not certain how long it will last."

Evan's heart sank, and he hurt for all of his cousins. After a tragic incident several months ago, Xander had abruptly quit his successful career as a musician and had been spiraling downhill ever since. He was drinking heavily, and was addicted to the very drugs that were supposed to help him. It reminded Evan of a period in Jared's life that he didn't even want to think about.

"I'm sorry to hear that, Micah." He really *was* sorry, because he could relate. It was hell wondering if your brother was going to make it through the challenge of facing life again, or if he was going to keep going down until he hit rock bottom and stayed there. Worse yet, would they all get the news that Xander had fallen all the way and would never be getting up again?

"I hate feeling this damn helpless to do anything else. He's been in rehab, and he refuses any further help. I don't know whether to give him time, or wrestle him into a safe place where he can't hurt himself," Micah told Evan huskily, his voice vibrating with sorrow.

"I know." Evan followed Micah down the stairs of the plane and clapped him on the back as they reached solid ground. "You've done all that you can do. Xander has to want to stay clean."

The bitter-cold Maine winter wind blasted them both mercilessly as they exited the sleek aircraft, but Micah's expression stayed grim, as though he was thinking too much to even feel the brutally frigid air. His dark-blond hair ruffled in the breeze, but he seemed totally oblivious to his surroundings. "Have I done everything I can?" he asked quietly, almost as though he were talking to himself rather than Evan.

"You have," Evan replied staunchly. There was no reason for Micah to feel otherwise. "Let's get to the car. I'll give you a lift to the Peninsula."

"Thanks," Micah acknowledged gratefully, nodding at Evan like he was silently thanking him for his support, even though neither one of them would voice their emotions aloud. "My car is already at Jared's place."

Evan watched as Micah jogged toward the Rolls, shaking his head as he thought about the mess Xander was in at the moment. Thank God those days of worrying about the sanity of a younger brother were over for him, and Jared had finally healed. But Evan couldn't help but have sympathy pains for his eldest cousin. He'd been where Micah was now, and it had been pure hell just dealing with Jared's alcohol binge. He couldn't imagine adding drugs into the mix.

"Welcome to Amesport, sir," his gray-haired chauffeur told him in a monotone voice, a sound that always greeted Evan in nearly every city he visited. His driver was dressed just as he always was: a gray suit and tie, his silver hair seemingly immaculate even though the wind was blowing. He took Evan's small suitcase and his laptop from his hands and put both in the front seat.

"Stokes," Evan acknowledged with a single nod as the old man opened the back door for him.

Micah didn't wait for Stokes to move around to the other side. He slid through the open door and scooted over on the backseat, making room for Evan. Stokes closed the door firmly after Evan had taken his seat, and the elderly man stoically took his place behind the wheel and put the vehicle in motion almost immediately.

Evan silently approved of the way Stokes handled the expensive vehicle, even in blowing snow and poorly cleared roads. The chauffeur had been with Evan for years and knew exactly what his boss wanted. Evan always wanted to reach his destination with as little drama as possible. Usually, he'd be working in the backseat—like Micah had started doing as soon as he'd gotten settled in the car. Stokes got him safely from place to place, so he was generally unconcerned about traffic, the roads, or what was happening outside of the vehicle, but Evan knew he wouldn't be able to concentrate on work today.

He was too worried about whether or not he'd see *her.*

Why do I care? She's really not worth the wasted time I spend thinking about her, or wondering why we can't seem to be together without irritating

21

each other. So what if we see each other at the party? We're two grown adults. We can be civil for a short period of time.

Not that he and Randi had ever accomplished being nice to each other in the past, but Evan vowed that he wouldn't let her bait him this time. He wondered once again—he thought about the subject way too often—why he and Randi Tyler couldn't seem to get along without throwing insults at each other. He never lost his temper to the point of bellowing, like some men did, but he'd come close with the she-devil he'd been forcefully paired with three awkward times. First it was Grady's, and then Dante's, and finally Jared's wedding. Every experience had been a lesson in patience.

She'd decided he was arrogant and bossy.

He'd decided she was bitchy and impatient.

Strangely, Randi didn't seem impressed by his wealth or his status as a Sinclair. She'd started out treating him like a friend, teasing him like she did with her friends and all the other Sinclairs. That had made him uncomfortable, so he'd ignored her. In turn, she'd either snubbed him or insulted him every single time he saw her, after the first time.

"She's overly sensitive, unpredictable, and emotional," Evan muttered under his breath, relieved when he saw that Micah was apparently answering emails on his phone and hadn't heard him. Randi Tyler was everything he disliked in a woman, but for some reason he was still highly attracted to her. It was perplexing, confusing. He didn't like her, but his cock certainly did. Her personality might annoy him, but there was never an encounter with her when he didn't want to pin her to the wall and fuck her until he was completely sated. It was a situation he'd never experienced before, and he didn't like it. He'd never had such a volatile reaction to a woman, and it wasn't comfortable.

I can just avoid her, not react to her taunts.

The problem was, he never knew whether he was going to get the cold shoulder or if she'd decide to throw insults at him. Honestly, he preferred she did neither. He rather missed the way she had treated him that very first day . . . like a new friend. It had been . . . nice. But he hadn't quite known what to make of her behavior then. He hadn't been able to form the words fast enough to react to her friendly behavior. She'd taken his silence as disapproval—which it really wasn't. Evan just hadn't been certain how to respond to her, especially since she gave him an instant case of blue balls that never went away whenever he was near her.

Sometimes I wish I could do everything with Randi all over again from the beginning. It would have been nice to have another friend. But nothing has even changed between us, and it's a little too late to try to start over again. Besides, I'd still want to nail her. Having a friend you wanted to fuck could become a problem.

The disagreeable female *did* have a killer smile. Too bad he'd never seen it directed his way again after their first meeting.

Evan only had one real friend, a female he'd shared much more than he should with, but had never met in person.

Have I passed her on the street in Amesport, or even talked to her?

The woman he'd been corresponding with from Amesport, formerly known as *A Concerned Resident of Amesport*, still remained a mystery to him. He'd tried his best to figure out who she was, because his curiosity had finally overridden his agreement with her not to share identities. Now, he wished he'd never agreed to her suggestion to not reveal their real names. It had made sense at the time, at the beginning of their correspondence. He wanted to meet her now, though she still didn't know that he was wealthy—or a Sinclair. She had always presumed he was an employee of the Sinclair Fund, and he'd never corrected her assumption. In fact, he'd lied, verifying to her that he was just an employee several times. He'd rationalized the falsehood by telling himself she didn't want to know his identity, and by sharing what his position was in the company, he'd reveal who he really was. Part of him wanted to remain a mystery to her, just a man instead of a billionaire from one of the most prominent families in the world. But as they'd continued to correspond for over a year, his desires had slowly changed. He wasn't sure how they'd communicate face-to-face, but he'd really like to find out.

At one time, he'd wondered if the woman was his now sister-in-law, Mara. His mystery emailer had started signing her letters simply with the initial "M."—and Mara had been in Dante's wedding. However, it hadn't taken him long to realize that Mara was head-over-heels in love with Jared, and that she wasn't his secret letter writer.

Would I have fought my own brother for Mara if it was actually her?

Evan shook his head slightly as he watched the town of Amesport pass him by on the way to the private peninsula where his house was located. Jared deserved to be happy, and Evan would never have stood between his brother and a woman who brought him that much happiness. Luckily, he'd felt nothing for Mara except a platonic fondness that he still had for her today. She was perfect for Jared, and Evan had pushed and tested his younger brother to the limit to make him see that he needed to snap up Mara before someone else did. If his tactics had been a little deceitful, it hadn't mattered. His actions were a means to a happy ending for Jared.

He released a pent-up breath he didn't realize he'd been holding. Evan's hand itched to check his email on his cell, see if he had an email from his . . . friend.

I won't. I can't. I don't need to be checking email several times a day like I'm obsessed. She's my friend, but that doesn't mean I have to open that mailbox like a madman, pathetically hoping for a reply.

Absently, he fingered the stone keychain some crazy elderly woman had sent him several months ago with a note attached, telling him he needed the stone to clear his blocked paths to happiness. He should have thrown the Apache-tear rock away. Apparently, according to the letter that accompanied the gift, she'd stocked up on this particular crystal since she'd decided that every one of the Sinclair men and their prospective mates needed one. He'd met . . . what was her name? "Beatrice," he whispered gruffly, remembering the senior citizen he'd met at Dante's—and then Jared's—wedding. She seemed harmless enough, but she was definitely "touched" or suffering from some sort of dementia.

For some unknown reason, he'd never gotten rid of the stone. In fact, he kept it on his person almost all of the time. Maybe it was the novelty of actually getting a gift from someone, or just the fantasy that the supposedly mystic woman had woven around the nature of the stone.

I'll find Beatrice in Amesport and give it back.

It was the least he could do. Even *he* wasn't hardhearted enough to offend a woman of advanced life experience by throwing away her gift. Maybe she could peddle it to someone else.

Surprisingly, he realized they were already moving through the gate to the Peninsula and getting close to the long driveway leading to Jared's home. The miles had sped by, but his mind was elsewhere.

Damn! He'd meant to check out the progress Jared had made on restoring Mara's old home and shop as he passed it by. It had been a mess after the fire that had almost taken Mara's life. He'd looked forward to seeing it nearly restored, but had missed the chance by being lost in his own thoughts.

Later. It's not like I won't see it while I'm in town.

The former shop sat directly on Main Street.

"We need to drop Micah off at Jared's," Evan told Stokes in a firm voice.

"Yes, sir," the chauffeur answered appropriately.

Micah was dropped off quickly and efficiently, Stokes never missing a beat once he had instructions. Evan waited as they approached his home on the Peninsula, forcing himself not to look at his phone for messages. If there was one thing Evan had in excess, it was control. His life ran in a very orderly fashion, just the way he liked and needed it to be.

The only two things that had even thrown him off-balance were his correspondence with the mysterious M.—and Randi Tyler. His pen-pal-type relationship with his mystery woman had been easier. He was drawn to her and her personality, but he had been able to remain anonymous, and he didn't have the same visceral, gut-wrenching reaction to M. as he did to Randi. Maybe some of his desire to meet his email friend was curiosity, the need to find out if he'd feel the same reaction to her as he did to Randi if he met her in person. In some ways, it would really suck if he did. Then he'd want to nail two women who didn't feel the same way he did.

Once they arrived at his home on the Peninsula and he was settled in, Evan finally checked his email, because it was the appropriate time to do so. He seated himself in a recliner in the living room, his laptop on his long, stretched-out legs as he connected to the Internet.

His heart raced just a little, and he felt the dampness of sweat on his forehead as the free email service took its damn time to appear. He might not have the visceral physical reaction to M. that he experienced with Randi, but he was always anxious to hear what she had to say. And then . . .

Nothing!

There were no new emails in the inbox.

Is she okay? She usually answers right away. What if she's hurt? What if she's still mourning the loss of her foster mother and is really depressed? I should be there for her. She's listened to me complain a thousand times.

M. always listened to him as a person and not a boss, which was why he valued the relationship so much. It was unique to talk to someone like a normal person.

Disappointed, but determined not to let an absence of any new emails bother him, he turned his attention to work just like he always did, trying desperately to lie to himself that it didn't matter that she hadn't yet responded.

CHAPTER 2

Dear M.,
I can't pretend that I understand your sense of loss regarding your foster mother, but I do understand your mixed emotions. I think it's probably quite normal to want to see an end to her suffering, yet mourn your loss of her at the same time.

It's moments like these that make me wish we had never promised to remain strangers. I'd like to help, but I'm not certain I know exactly how. All I can do is send you virtual support and let you know that my thoughts are with you right now. You're not alone.

Sincerely,
S.

Randi sighed as she read the entry from her pen pal, feeling just a little bit better after reading his words. The email was short, but somehow comforting. Whatever S. said in his messages, she always sensed that he was sincere.

Her foster mother, Joan Tyler, had passed away not long after the beginning of the new year from heart failure, and Randi knew she'd be mourning the loss of the last person on earth who would love her unconditionally for a very long time. Her foster father, Dennis, had died a few years ago, and Joan had never been the same after his death. Her heart problems had escalated, and she'd been declining since Dennis's death. Sometimes Randi wondered if she'd actually finally died of grief rather than advanced age.

Joan and Dennis had been in their early seventies when they'd brought Randi to Amesport, and both foster parents had lived a long, happy life—well into their eighties. Knowing that still didn't lessen the pain of losing them for Randi, or make her wish any less that she'd had more time to spend with them.

Nothing had prepared Randi for the deep emptiness she'd experienced since her loss. Dennis's death had been heartbreaking; Joan's had been unbearable. She wasn't sure if the uncontrollable ache she felt every time she thought about her would ever go away.

Looking at the note, she smiled sadly. Her correspondence with S. was more like a continual conversation. Their entries often weren't long, and sometimes they wandered into subjects that weren't really important, but that was part of the fun of having a secret friend.

I still can't believe that I've befriended a person who started off as such an asshole!

Her buddy, formerly known as *Unsympathetic in Boston*, *had* been a jerk in the beginning, but what had started off as what she assumed was a practical joke soon turned into a conversation, and eventually mutual admiration. Randi felt a connection to the author of these emails that made her laugh and cry, and were sometimes so thoughtful—like his email in front of her—they made her melancholy.

She shared mostly thoughts and emotions, something that was easier when she could be anonymous. She suspected he'd felt the same way in the beginning. Lately, he'd been hinting at the possibility of the two of them meeting in person.

"Do I ever really want to meet him? Do I ever want to reveal my identity to him?" she whispered to herself as she stared at the screen in the Center.

Yes.

No.

Oh hell, she didn't know. She'd shared more with S. than she'd ever shared with anyone about her true thoughts and emotions. They never shared details. About the only few facts he knew about her were that she was in her late twenties and that she had been fostered by a loving, elderly couple when she was fourteen, a life-changing event that had brought her from California to Maine.

The only information she knew about him was that he was male, worked for the Sinclair Fund, was entering his midthirties, wasn't married, and seemed to be around a computer when he probably should be out dating. He'd captured her interest when he'd simply replied to her snide return email, complimenting her intelligence and humor, telling her she'd made him laugh, like it was a very rare occurrence for him. She assumed it was something he didn't do often.

He's listened to me through my grief, trying to understand my pain and fix it. Somehow, he always seems to know I feel alone now.

Dennis and Joan had brought her into their home fourteen years ago, and she'd felt the sense of actually being "home" for the first time in her life. She'd only left Maine for college, returning home with her teaching degree. The Tylers had been so proud of her, so encouraging. They'd never been able to have children of their own, and they didn't have close family. They weren't rich, but they'd been happy together for almost sixty years. Randi hoped she'd find a love like theirs some-day. "Everything I am, I owe to them," she said softly as she clicked the "Reply" button on her friend's thoughtful email.

> Dear S.,
> Sorry it's been a few days since your email and I haven't answered. I've finally tackled the task of going through my foster mom's things. She wouldn't want them to be wasted. I've donated as much as I can, and kept the things that are sentimental. Everything feels more final now, and I still feel alone in my parents' empty house. But thank you for your kind words. I don't feel as conflicted any-more. I'm glad the suffering is over, though the loneliness remains. I try to just focus on my job, and appreciate my friends. I think it will just take time.
>   Speaking of parents, are yours still alive? We've never spoken much about family.
>   Hoping you're staying warm in this incredibly cold winter!
>   M.

Randi sent the email, hoping she hadn't crossed the invisible line that she and her pen pal had drawn by asking for personal details. She'd shared her situation with her foster parents willingly, though she'd left out the particulars. They shared thoughts and feelings, but never details.

He had recently said he sometimes wished they could meet face-to-face. Sometimes Randi wanted that, too, and more often than not she wanted to know more about the man who had been her confidant through some very difficult times.

"The mysterious man in my life," Randi murmured under her breath. "What's his first name? Starting with S?" *Stewart? Sam? Sylvester? Scott? Seth?* Randi had gone through the list many times. None of those names had ever quite fit.

Her heart accelerated as she saw an answer pop into her mailbox almost immediately. She clicked on the mouse to show his response.

> Dear M.,
> I'm glad you're feeling a little less conflicted, but sorry you are feeling so alone. Please let me know what I can do to help you. I know we've never met in person, but you've been more of a friend to me than anyone else in my life in the past year.
> Are my parents living? Yes . . . and no. My father died when I was in college and I haven't seen my mother for many years. She doesn't want anything to do with me or my siblings. The last I heard, she was living with a guy in Europe, probably trying to forget about my deceased, alcoholic father. He wasn't a pleasant man. Perhaps that's too much information, but it's the truth.
> I'm not in Boston at the moment, but I haven't gone to a warmer climate, unfortunately.
> Hope you manage to stay warm, too.
> Sincerely,
> S.

Randi had to read the email twice, surprised that S. had shared so much personal information. Then again, maybe she shouldn't be shocked. She'd certainly poured her heart out to him about her foster parents over the last few months. Maybe he felt more comfortable. She hit "Reply," somehow knowing he was waiting for her response. Sometimes it played out that way. They had a back-and-forth discussion when both of them happened to be on the computer at the same time.

Dear S.,
Where are you now?

She didn't bother to sign the reply because they were in conversation mode at the moment. He answered within a minute.

Maine. And can I just say that it's pretty damn
cold here.

"He's here," Randi whispered, tracing her finger over his answer on the screen. His reply could have been creepy, since she lived in the state he was visiting, but it wasn't. Whatever his reason might be for visiting Maine, it wasn't because of her. He'd always known what town she lived in, and she'd been writing to him for over a year. "Don't do it, Randi. Don't ask him to meet up. He's probably here on business or fundraising. Most likely in some rich area where donors can be found," she reasoned to herself quietly. Her fear of meeting an unknown male overrode her desire to see him, no matter how much she'd like to know him in person.

Randi typed back a quick reply.

Why are you here? BTW . . . there's a storm
coming. I hope you don't get stuck here.

His response came back quickly.

I have family in Maine. I'm just visiting. And no, I didn't know we were expecting bad weather. But it's not a problem if I have to stay here a little longer. I have a place to stay.

It made sense. He was in the area for a family visit, and he hadn't said a word about meeting her in person. Seeing each other face-to-face would be as unlikely as it was inadvisable. With a major storm coming their way, they could hardly meet. She answered him for the last time, knowing she needed to get moving.

I have to get going, but I hope you have a good time with your family. Maybe we can talk if you get bored during the storm.

She moved her mouse to sign off the Center's computer, but she saw a reply pop back into her mailbox almost instantly.

Hot date?

Randi laughed aloud, glad there was nobody else in the Center's computer room at the moment. It was Friday night, and the two of them often caught up and went into conversation mode on date nights, razzing each other because they were both alone when most single people like them were out on the town. Unable to resist answering, she typed a response.

Actually, I do have a date, but whether it's hot or not is still in question. A high school friend of mine wanted me to meet her brother. She

*thinks we'd get along well. We're meeting up
in a few minutes. So I have to go. Talk to you
soon. Stay safe during the storm.*

She really *did* have to go, so she shrugged her jacket on as she stared at the screen, almost wishing she didn't have a kind-of-a-date with Liam Sullivan, her friend Tessa's brother. She knew *of* Liam, but she'd only said a handful of words to him in the past. After months of Tessa's nagging, Randi had finally agreed to have coffee with him at Brew Magic. If she didn't move her rear, she'd be late.

She didn't really expect a reply from S. since she'd basically said good-bye, but she got one anyway.

*You have a date with a local guy on a Friday
night? I think I'm jealous. I hope you have a
lousy time while I'm sitting here alone working. Be careful and email me when you get
home.*

Randi smiled at the computer screen. She was used to her mystery man's quirky humor. But the demand that she email him was . . . different. He didn't know that she never sent him an email except when she was volunteering at the Center. It was more out of habit now than the concern about him tracking her down. It was kind of sweet that he was actually concerned about her safety.

Okay.

She sent the one-word email and forced herself to shut down her computer. She'd have to sprint down the street to Brew Magic or Liam would think she'd stood him up. From what she'd heard, he was a pretty nice guy, and she didn't want to hurt his feelings. How could he not be nice? He'd given up a promising career to move back to Amesport to watch over his deaf sister. Not that Tessa would accept any help. Her friend didn't think she was any different just because she'd lost her ability to hear.

Randi was meeting with him mainly to get Tessa off her back; she had a feeling Liam had agreed for the same reason. Her friend Tessa might be deaf, but she was a master at manipulating people. She could be like a dog with a tasty bone when she wanted something, and she wanted her brother Liam to be happily settled with a woman of his own. Tessa loved her brother, but he was incredibly protective since she'd lost her ability to hear. Since Liam blamed himself for Tessa's condition, he'd moved from California back to Amesport several years ago.

He gave up a career he loved to look after his sister. I know he's a nice guy, but I've just never really felt a connection with him.

The few times she'd met up with Liam had been at his and Tessa's restaurant, Sullivan's Steak and Seafood. Randi knew a lot about Liam because Tessa talked about him a lot, but they had only spoken to each other in passing.

Maybe there will be something more if we have a private chat . . .

Randi was an optimist, and more than anything else she wanted to feel loved. Sure, she'd had boyfriends, but they'd never amounted to a serious relationship. She liked sex as much as any other female her age, but she was burnt out on meaningless relationships that involved nothing but sex. There had to be something more. She'd seen it between her foster parents, and she saw it every day between her married friends and their spouses. Unfortunately, she'd never experienced that white-hot connection with anyone except the one man she couldn't stand: Evan Sinclair.

Don't think about him. He's an arrogant, insufferable asshole.

She shuddered as she thought about how hard she'd tried to get to know Evan in the beginning, only to be soundly rejected. Obviously, a lowly teacher in a small town wasn't worth him putting out the effort to even be polite. It wasn't like she'd wanted to jump his bones. Well . . . maybe she *had* wanted to, but at the time she was just trying to be nice to a man she knew she was going to have to deal with for Emily's wedding. She had managed to shrug off the first snub during Emily's nuptials, thinking maybe Evan was just having a bad day. But when he'd responded the same way when Sarah and Dante had gotten married and the two of them had found themselves paired once again, Randi had finally realized that Evan simply didn't like *her*. By the time Mara and Jared got married, Randi had completely ignored him except for the necessary superficial smiles and robotic motions she'd made as a bridesmaid to Evan's groomsman. Since all of the married Sinclairs had wanted to be paired with their wives, Randi had ended up being a bridesmaid by default, as Mara's best friend's broken leg hadn't completely healed in time for her to be part of the ceremony. She didn't regret having been a bridesmaid so many times. Through the ceremonies, she'd made an incredible circle of female friends who had been there to support her during the last few dark weeks. Unfortunately, those friendships had come at the price of putting up with Evan Sinclair.

Too bad he's such a self-involved dick, because he's majorly hot. I wish I could figure out why I'm so damn attracted to him when I can't stand him.

She was still contemplating what it was about Evan that irritated her when she left the building. The Center was busy as Randi exited, deciding to walk down to Brew Magic instead of taking the time to clean the snow off her car. Friday night saw a lot of activity at the Center, especially since Grady had married Emily and so many new programs and changes had occurred.

Shoving her cold hands into the pockets of her jacket, Randi gripped the Apache-tear crystal that Beatrice had given her months ago when she'd stopped by the elderly woman's store, Natural Elements, to chat. Beatrice had been friends with Randi's foster mother, and she'd stopped into the eclectic shop whenever she had the chance to update

Beatrice on Joan's medical condition. It was on one of those visits that Beatrice had made her prediction and handed Randi the crystal along with her predictions.

Joan will pass in the winter, but you'll open a new chapter in your life soon after with a man who needs you even more than you need him. He'll be your soul mate, and you'll finally become a bride instead of a bridesmaid.

Randi shook her head with a sad smile, remembering the certainty on Beatrice's face that day.

Picking up her pace, she trudged quickly through the lightly falling snow on the sidewalk. It wasn't that she didn't believe that supernatural talents *could* exist, but she didn't take the elderly woman's words too seriously. She'd known Beatrice since she'd moved to Amesport as a teen. Some of her predictions were eerily accurate, some of them weren't. Randi's rational mind was telling her that the accurate predictions Beatrice made could simply be coincidence. They had to be flukes. Randi was open-minded, but she had to draw the line at somebody knowing her future. She believed in people deciding their own fate or destiny. Anything else was just . . . chance.

She waited for traffic to clear before she sprinted across the street, her boots sliding in the snow as she stopped breathlessly in front of Brew Magic. She ignored the sensation that the crystal in her pocket appeared to warm beneath her fingers, before she jerked her hands from the warmth of the fleece compartments to hastily attempt to right her damp, wind-tossed hair.

"Beatrice's stone is *not* magic, and her prediction is nothing more than nonsense," she told herself forcefully as she brushed the snow from her head and tried to make herself presentable to go chat with Liam. "Things like that don't happen to women like me. I make my own luck and my own future."

Considering her past, Randi *was* happy with her life, even though she was still grieving for Joan. She had a good education, a good job, and friends who meant everything to her. If she was lonely sometimes now that her foster mother was gone, she'd get through it. Her earlier childhood had taught her that life was tough, and wishes didn't often become reality. Dennis and Joan coming into her life had been her miracle, if there was any such thing. She didn't need any more than what they'd given her: a home for a homeless girl with no hope for the future.

Randi tried not to remember that Beatrice had predicted that Dennis and Joan would still have a child, even after all hope of Joan getting pregnant was long gone. Before her foster parents had left on vacation to California, Beatrice had reminded them of her prediction, saying her spirit guides had told her that they'd find their daughter while they were on their Southern California sightseeing tour.

Joan had been a firm believer in Beatrice's gift of premonitions. Being a realist, Randi had always been on the fence.

"Beatrice runs about fifty-fifty on her predictions," Randi whispered to herself. "She was right about Jared and Mara, so she's due to be wrong about mine."

Chastising herself for standing in the brutal weather contemplating a silly rock, Randi hurried into Brew Magic, determined not to regret the fact that she'd had to cut her conversation short with her pen pal because of her prior engagement.

She tried not to think about what S. was doing right at the moment as she searched the crowded coffee shop for Liam.

CHAPTER 3

Evan waited impatiently for his turn at the coffee shop in Amesport, having stood in line for almost ten minutes before arriving at the front of the queue. He wasn't used to standing in line, and *his turn* was usually immediate. He was wasting time, and that annoyed him. He didn't squander time that he could be using for work, and he didn't spend any evenings so distracted that he stopped the dictation he'd been doing on an important financial report to find a diversion.

He'd ended up driving himself to Brew Magic for a nonfat mocha coffee with no whipped cream, a beverage he'd come to tolerate after Jared kept dragging him into the coffee shop to get his fix. If Jared was here, he wouldn't be sparing the whipped cream or the fat. Evan's younger brother liked his coffee with every available evil known to man, usually accompanied by several of the calorie-, sugar-, and fat-laden pastries that Evan could now see gracing the shelves of the racks behind the glass.

"Can I help you, sir?" A friendly teenager stepped up to assist him as Evan became the next person to place his order.

He quickly told the smiling girl what he wanted, feeling uncomfortable in the cramped, busy space. People were vying for tables to sit and sip coffee, probably to get out of the frigid temperatures outside. People milled around him as he waited for his coffee to be blended.

What am I doing here?

Unfortunately, Evan knew exactly why he was there. After finding out that even his pen pal had a date, he'd been restless. For some unknown reason, he'd been annoyed that she was actually going out on a date. He hadn't been teasing when he'd told her he was jealous. He *was* envious of the man she was out with tonight. Somehow, he'd become addicted to her words on the screen, and he wanted to know what she was doing. Was she having a good time? Was the guy she was seeing a decent sort of man?

Christ! This is ridiculous. I don't even know her, and I'm worrying about her.

The problem was, she'd become a friend to him, and Evan Sinclair didn't have very many friends. He had people who catered to him, told him what he wanted to hear. But those people didn't like *him*; they liked his money and power. He had acquaintances with the same status he had, but all of them were too busy to actually strike up a real friendship. They were connected by business, and business was a priority for all of them.

I like her. And she likes me as a person. She has no idea who I really am.

Just the fact that his mystery writer liked him as a person without knowing his identity was a novelty, and it made him covet her attention. Okay. Yes. He was greedy and selfish, but it was the first time he'd wanted something just for himself.

I should have told her that I wanted to meet her.

He'd had the chance when he'd admitted he was in Maine, but then he'd have to tell her that he was in the same town she lived in, thus having to reveal his identity. If he didn't, she'd think he was some kind of crazy stalker. Why would an employee of the Sinclair Fund be in Amesport? It would be way too much of a coincidence that he just happened to have family in this town. She might be alarmed, afraid of him.

Grimacing at the thought of his email friend being fearful of him, he picked up his coffee at the pickup window and carefully made his way through the crowd and out of the shop. He was going to get into his black BMW, which he'd bought to keep at his Amesport house, and he *was* going to get back to work. He could have called Stokes to drive him into town, but the elderly man had already gotten himself settled into Evan's guesthouse. He didn't want to disturb his driver after he'd probably already gone to bed. Stokes might seem invincible and unflappable, but he wasn't a young man anymore. Evan had found the keys to the vehicle he'd never used before and had driven himself.

Every Sinclair home on the Peninsula had a guest home, but some were bigger than others. Evan's was relatively small. Maybe Jared had rightly guessed that Evan would never have friends visiting here. That was a depressing thought.

"Dammit!" The curse was followed by a collision with Evan's back that nearly took him to the ground on the slick sidewalk. He quickly regained his footing, and then swung around to see a guilty-looking Randi Tyler right in front of him.

Evan's cock hardened instantly, and his entire body tensed, a reaction he had anytime he saw Randi—an automatic, carnal response that completely annoyed him at the moment.

He glared at her as she informed him contritely, "I spilled most of my coffee on the back of your coat. I'm sorry."

He didn't speak as he observed her flushed cheeks and her breathless state. Her dark hair was loosely held to the back of her head by a hair clip that Evan was secretly itching to remove. Even though she had apologized, there was no fear in her beautiful hazel eyes as she met his pointed stare directly. She looked sorry, but she wasn't afraid of him like most people usually were. She never had been.

"It's one of my favorite coats," he muttered huskily, not knowing what else to say. It was indeed one of his favorites, but it didn't matter if it was stained. He had another one just like it in his closet.

Evan saw a flash of irritation in her beautiful eyes, their color so vibrant in the dim light that they reminded him of a rich milk chocolate. Her eyes changed from deep brown to a greenish tint in different lighting, but the ring and flecks within the iris remained exactly the same. No matter what color they appeared to be, they were always frustratingly gorgeous, just like the rest of her. Framed by long, velvety black lashes the same color as her hair, her gaze was nearly mesmerizing him.

"If the stain doesn't come out, I'll pay for it," she told him, sounding annoyed as her chin rose stubbornly.

He highly doubted her teacher's salary was going to cover one very expensive custom coat. "It's just coffee." He shrugged, but he was feeling far from nonchalant. Randi made him edgy and out of sorts. He could be charming when he had to be for fundraising or business, but he couldn't seem to find the right words to say to a woman like her—maybe because he'd never met anyone quite like her before.

Evan nearly flinched as she licked a smudge of chocolate from her lips and held up a gooey chocolate pastry she was holding with a napkin underneath the bottom. He continued to stare at her intently as he watched her eyes close and her tongue lap up the remaining sweetness from her plump, succulent lips before retreating back into her mouth.

"I'm afraid I smudged chocolate on it, too," she informed him solemnly, her eyes open again.

"Not a problem," he told her in a clipped voice, knowing he'd probably let her stain every item of clothing he owned if he could just sit and watch her eat the rest of what looked like a slightly dented éclair.

One thing he'd noticed about Randi in the past was when she ate, she looked like she was having an almost orgasmic experience. She wasn't shy, and she dug into food like she thoroughly enjoyed every bite. The pleasure she found in food showed on her face and her expressions. Evan found that odd, but fascinating.

"Hold my coffee," she insisted as she hastily shoved the cup she was holding into his empty hand. "I have napkins." She dug into the pocket of her jacket and pulled out a wad of disposable paper, moving behind him to swipe at the stain on his coat. "What are you doing out here in the common population? I thought you despised anything that took you away from your business."

"I slum it with the commoners occasionally," Evan shot back sarcastically, automatically. Her snide comment had triggered his defenses. He glanced down at her coffee, noting that it had a double helping of whipped cream, and it looked anything but nonfat.

Throwing the napkins in a nearby trash can, Randi stood in front of him once more, her eyes shooting daggers at him. Strangely, he preferred her anger to her indifference. He had no idea why.

She took her coffee back and proceeded to take an enormous bite of her éclair as though daring him to say something about her eating junk. "Send me a bill," she told him, her gaze challenging him.

"I don't think that will be necessary," he told her in a sedate voice, with a calmness he wasn't really feeling. "Maybe you could just be more careful in the future."

"Me?" Her expression turned to one of astonishment. "I wasn't the one who stopped right outside the door. The place is busy. You could have kept moving when you knew that people were coming in and out."

Evan looked behind him, realizing he *had* actually stopped right outside the door. "You could have watched where you were going," he argued, annoyed that she had a point. They'd moved away from the constant traffic to and from the coffee shop, but his abrupt stop *might* have caused her to run into him if she'd been in motion. Not that he'd admit he might be partly to blame. People watched the people in front of them where he came from, which was mostly large cities. If they were in traffic, the car in the rear would have the responsibility of stopping before it crashed into the back of the car in front. It should work the same way with people.

Randi finished her sweet treat and wiped her fingers with another napkin before depositing it into the trash, ignoring him. Finally, she replied, "I'm sorry. I'm human. I make mistakes."

Apologetic words might be coming from her mouth, but Evan knew she was mocking him. "Perfection can be hard to achieve," he told her mildly, knowing his arrogant statement would rile her.

She turned her back on him and began walking down the sidewalk, calling over her shoulder, "Send me a bill, Mr. Perfect. I'll take care of my horrible aberration."

He watched her navigate her way through the snowy walkway, wondering where in the hell she was going. Where was her vehicle? "Wait!" he called impulsively as she started to disappear in the dark. He followed her as she hesitated but didn't turn around. He caught up to her at the curb. "Where did you park? It's dark."

"This is Amesport, not New York City. I'm fine," she told him as she started walking again, navigating normally even in the dim light. "Why are you out here, anyway? The weather sucks, and it's going to get worse. It's brutally cold, and I'm sure you have more important things to do."

Evan fell into step beside her. "I didn't feel like working," he admitted reluctantly. "Why are you still out in town?" He knew she was a teacher and got off work in the late afternoon.

"I was working at the Center and I wanted a coffee before I went home," she said, her tone defensive. "And I was craving that éclair that I smashed on your coat."

"I noticed you still ate it," he observed.

She snorted. "It was *your* coat. I don't imagine it was anything other than squeaky clean."

She was poking fun at his attire.

Don't let her get to you. Ignore it.

"Is your car at the Center?"

"Yes. And I'm perfectly safe. You don't need to follow me."

Evan felt his level of irritation rise, pushed to the limit. "Isn't it rather ignorant to believe that bad things only happen in big cities?"

"In my experience, they usually do," she answered quietly. "We have all kinds of visitors here, but other than the incidents with your brothers at the Center, nothing much has ever happened here in Amesport."

"That doesn't mean that it couldn't," Evan argued, the thought of anything bad happening to Randi strangely unsettling. Hell, Grady and Dante had both been injured here in Amesport by some pretty nasty men. It happened. Amesport was a tourist town. There could be all kinds of temporary crazies running around the town.

She turned to him suddenly and stopped, looking up at him in the muted illumination of the streetlights. "Look, I don't feel like fighting with you right now. Catch me tomorrow, or any other day, and I'll spar with you. But I'm tired. I've had a long day. Can you just go back to your car now and leave me alone?"

Evan looked down at her. Even without much light, he could see the dark circles under her eyes, and weariness in her expression.

They were right across the street from the Center where her car was parked.

"I won't say a word if you don't," he told her uncharacteristically. For some reason, he didn't want to see her look defeated. If they couldn't speak without zinging each other, he'd stay silent to see her to her vehicle.

She turned without uttering a sound, crossing the street and shooting him a doubtful look as he followed.

True to his word, Evan didn't say anything as he fell into step beside her. He wanted to ask her why she was weary, but he assumed she'd done a full day at work, and then had come to tutor as a volunteer at the Center. Obviously, if she was out this late, her workday had been long. However, he sensed there were other factors, but they were none of his business, and he didn't want to start another verbal sparring match with her.

I feel like it's either fight with her or pin her against the wall and fuck her until she's out of my system.

It didn't matter that they were out in the frigid open air. His cock was at attention, begging him to pick the second option.

Unfortunately, she hated him, and Evan didn't think fucking her senseless was going to be an option.

He wrapped his fingers unconsciously around the crystal in his pocket, wishing he could find a way to communicate with Randi. What was bothering her? Why did she look so tired? He wanted to strike up a reasonable conversation, but he was afraid of putting his foot in his mouth . . . again. The moment she put him on the defensive, he struck out verbally. It was always this way with her.

"We're here. This is me," Randi said breathlessly, pointing toward a vehicle covered in snow, one of the few cars still in the parking lot.

She dropped the remainder of her cold coffee into a trash receptacle close to her vehicle, and Evan did the same. He'd never really wanted the beverage anyway.

"Give me the keys," he demanded.

Surprisingly, she reached in her pocket to hand them over. She pulled them, causing something else to drop to the ground. Without thinking, Evan bent and picked up the object. He held the item in his hand for a moment, stunned. "You have one of these, too?" he asked hoarsely.

"The Apache tear. Yeah. I got it from Beatrice. She thinks I'm going to meet my soul mate." Randi reached for the stone and hurriedly shoved it back in her pocket. "I like her. I didn't want to hurt her feelings."

Evan took the keys she was dangling in front of him and opened the door of the vehicle. It was hard to tell exactly what kind of car it was when it was covered in snow, but it appeared to be a small SUV. He started it quickly and grabbed the snow brush in the backseat to clear the slush and ice off the body and windows of the car.

"I can do that," Randi insisted, trying to take the brush from his hand.

"I'm sure you're perfectly capable, but let me," Evan requested evenly. "There's no reason for you to do it since I'm here." He made short work of removing the snow and scraping the ice as he watched Randi eye him curiously.

She crossed her arms and observed his movements as he worked. "You're a gentleman underneath all of your bluster." The statement was almost accusing.

"I'm not chauvinistic," Evan said carefully. "I employ plenty of smart women, some of them smarter than my male employees." He put the snow brush back in the car, closed the door so the windows would finish defrosting, and turned to face her. "But I'll admit that I have a hard time watching a woman do physical work when a stronger body is around."

She frowned as her eyes drifted over his tall, muscular form. "I have a hard time arguing with the fact that you're bigger and probably stronger. But it doesn't mean that you have to always do the physical work."

Evan looked at her petite figure. Logically, she couldn't argue their difference in size. At a little over six feet tall, he towered over her. She might be the athletic type, but he worked out every day, and he was a hell of a lot stronger. "I have very little opportunity to do anything physical except in a gym. I have employees who do most things for me. I don't mind, and cleaning your car is hardly strenuous." He hesitated before he inquired in what he hoped was a casual voice, "Can I ask you a question?"

She lifted a brow before asking, "What?"

"Does Beatrice give out these stones to everyone?" He pulled the crystal from his pocket and held it out to her.

Hesitantly, Randi reached out and took the rock into her own hand. She turned it over and over a few times before handing it back with a perplexed look on her face. "Hardly ever," she admitted. "You got one, too?"

"She mailed it to me with a letter a few months ago, telling me I was going to be married within six months," he answered reluctantly, slipping the Apache tear back into his coat pocket. "I think she might be demented."

Randi laughed, and a bolt of pleasure raced through Evan's body at the husky, sultry sound.

"She's not crazy. She's just a little eccentric. Sometimes her predictions actually do come true."

Evan shook his head. "She's destined for disappointment with me."

"I was thinking the same thing," Randi admitted, reaching for the door of her rapidly defrosting vehicle. It was a deep-purple SUV that somehow suited her bold personality. Evan could finally see the make and model clearly.

"Randi?" he questioned huskily.

"Yes?" She turned and looked at him, her expression no longer hostile.

"Don't worry about my coat. I have another one." It wasn't what he really wanted to say, but he couldn't exactly tell her what he was thinking. She was likely to apply a knee to his balls, and he rather liked them intact.

"I told you to send me a bill if the stain doesn't come out. You might try the dry cleaners here. They've done miracles with some of my clothes. Stains are a job hazard for teachers," she told him amiably.

It was her smile that made Evan snap. Her eyes were warm and happy, her lips curving into a beautiful expression of joy when she talked about her profession. But the grin was aimed at him, and Evan couldn't possibly resist seizing the moment. He'd never made an impulsive move in his entire life, but he couldn't seem to control his mind or body when she smiled at him this way.

He stepped forward without debating his options first, pinned her body against her vehicle, and without a cautionary thought in his head, he kissed her.

Evan groaned as his lips crashed down on hers, knowing that he'd just made a mistake that would probably cost him his sanity. Her body stiffened as he wrapped his arms around her, one hand threading through her hair to protect her head and keep it exactly in a position that allowed him complete access to her mouth. An unfamiliar sense of male satisfaction moved deep in his gut as the clip holding her hair fell to the ground and the dark strands tumbled around her shoulders.

She tasted like chocolate and coffee, and Evan savored the delectable softness of her lips beneath his. Out of control, he demanded access instead of asking. Finally, she became pliant beneath him, letting him in, and he inwardly released a sigh of relief as she wrapped her arms around him and met his marauding tongue stroke for stroke. Evan felt himself drowning in sensation, and it definitely wasn't the cold of the surrounding environment. Every instinct he had was to claim the woman in his arms, make sure she remembered the heat that raged between them as they kissed each other like they were ravenous for each other. His cock strained for release as Evan explored Randi's mouth demandingly, his body overheating from the way she returned his embrace enthusiastically.

She was panting by the time he finally lifted his head, both of them desperate for air. It took Evan a few minutes before he could manage to release her. He continued to hold her in his arms, saying nothing, their heavy, ragged breathing the only sound he could identify, the cloudy spirals of their every breath visible in the frigid air around them the only thing he could see. Slowly, reluctantly, his hand untangled from her silky hair and he finally stepped back.

"We can pretend that never happened," Randi squeaked in a pan-icked voice.

The hell they could! Evan knew he'd probably have wet dreams about what else could have happened if they weren't in the middle of the brutal cold in a damn parking lot. "I'm not certain I can," he con-fided gruffly.

"We can," Randi chattered optimistically. "We can't stand each other. It's just some crazy physical thing."

It was definitely physical, but it wasn't crazy or random. He'd wanted to bury his cock so deeply inside Randi Tyler with an uniden-tifiable primitive instinct he couldn't explain since the moment they'd met, and he had a feeling that impulse wasn't going to go away. Not after he'd tasted her, felt her willing response. She wanted him, and knowing *that* changed the entire game they'd been playing since the first time he saw her.

She might not like me, but she feels the same chemistry that I do.

"Do you have an escort for Hope's party?" He ignored her sugges-tion that they pretend he'd never touched her. He had kissed her . . . and they had both enjoyed it.

"No."

"You'll go with me," he decided, pulling his cell phone out of his pocket and handing it to her. "Call your phone so you have my number. Call me when you get home safely." He didn't like the way the wind was starting to kick up and the snow was coming down more steadily now.

She looked dazed as she dialed her own phone number, letting it ring in her purse so his number would show up before handing it back to him. "Evan, I don't think—"

He put a finger over her lips. "Don't think about it. Just go with me."

She nodded slowly as though she was still in a pleasure-induced trance. Evan decided he liked that look on her. He was determined now to see what she looked like as she came, screaming his name, his cock deep inside her, her body shuddering in climax.

She would look exquisite, and Evan was more than eager to share that experience with her. Maybe it would resolve the knot of longing that seemed to be pulling tighter and tighter in his gut right now.

Turning and walking away from her took almost superhuman strength, but he did it anyway. He wasn't giving her a chance to think, a chance to change her mind. He paused to pick up the clip from her hair before he moved away from her and stuck it in his coat pocket.

He ambled slowly toward his car, satisfied when he saw her vehicle plow through the snowy parking lot and exit the Center.

What in the hell just happened?

Evan picked up his pace after he saw the taillights of Randi's car disappear into the night, still more than a little shocked at his own behavior. He didn't give in to urges or impulses, but tonight . . . he had.

He didn't regret it. Sexual tension like he'd never experienced before had been smoldering between him and Randi Tyler since the moment they'd met. Now that he knew that she was just as attracted to him as he was to her, he understood the real truth.

She was wrong. They didn't hate each other. What they were both feeling was desire in its most carnal form. He'd tried to ignore it because any loss of control scared the shit out of him. Maybe it unsettled her, too.

What would be the harm in spending some time together? Maybe they could fuck each other until the attraction was out of both of their systems. It was bound to happen if they acted on their fantasies. Evan had never been with a woman more than once before he got bored and was ready to go back to work. He didn't do relationships. He sought out women who wanted the same thing he did . . . sex for one night to scratch an itch. Most of them were successful women who were busy with their own careers or businesses. Those arrangements had always suited him just fine.

Evan released a masculine sigh as he finally reached his vehicle, admitting to himself that exorcising the lust he had for Randi could take more than just one night.

In fact, it could take a very, very long time.

Strangely, he was good with that.

CHAPTER 4

The Amesport Midwinter Ball was cancelled and rescheduled for the following weekend because the area had been struck by a major blizzard.

Randi sighed and looked out the window of the small home that she'd inherited, glad that she now had five more days to try to find a way out of attending the ball with Evan.

Why in the hell did I let him kiss me? Worse yet, why did I enjoy it so damn much?

She'd been asking herself that very question for the last two days—since he'd rocked her world with the demanding, possessive, scorching-hot embrace that hadn't left her mind since it happened.

Dammit! I don't want to be attracted to Evan Sinclair.

Tired and let down because Liam hadn't shown up at their meeting place, the last thing she'd needed last Friday was to literally run into Evan Sinclair as she was leaving Brew Magic.

Why him? Anybody but him.

She'd only found out after arriving home that evening that Liam had the flu. He hadn't had her cell-phone number to contact her, and he hadn't been able to reach Tessa. He'd sounded horrible in the message he'd left on her home phone, and she didn't doubt for a moment that he really was sick. She'd quickly sent a text to Evan—because calling him seemed too personal—that she'd arrived home safely, and then a message via email to S. so he didn't worry.

For the last two days, she'd been pretty much snowbound. The flakes were coming down faster than they could be cleared from the roads. She lived ten miles from town on a tranquil five acres of land that nobody really cared about. Dennis and Joan hadn't been anywhere close to being able to afford waterfront property, but Randi hadn't minded not living right on the beach. It was too crowded in town, too busy with tourists in the summer. She loved having her own space to breathe.

Letting the curtain she was holding fall back into place, Randi turned back toward the small living room. So much of her parents still remained in the house, but Randi liked it that way. She'd kept as many items as she could that had belonged to them, wanting to somehow keep them with her even now.

Her heart clenched as her gaze fell on a picture of all three of them, a family, huddled together on the beach soon after they'd brought her to Amesport. Dennis and Joan had been the parents she'd never had, even though they were more appropriate in age to be her grandparents. It hadn't mattered to Randi. They'd filled up an emotional void she had carried all her life. Now, it was like the gaping dark hole was back, and nothing could ever fill it in again.

She tore her eyes from the photo, knowing that eventually the pain would ease. There would probably come a time when she felt nothing but joy looking at pictures of her saviors, but that day wasn't today.

"I need to shower." Her golden retriever, Lily, lifted her head off the floor to look at Randi with soulful, curious eyes. "I stink," Randi told her dog, watching as Lily cocked her head as though she understood.

Randi had spent the morning working out and meditating, so her yoga pants and T-shirt were damply clinging to her body even though a snowstorm raged outdoors.

Lily trotted along behind her as Randi shed her clothes, throwing them all into the hamper as she arrived in the bathroom.

"We need food for both of us," Randi announced as she turned on the shower and looked down at Lily's prostrate body on the rug beside her.

She hadn't stocked up enough on food, and she was hungry. Lily was down to the last of her dog food. Randi would need to clear out her driveway with the old ATV and plow in the garage, and then hope her small four-wheel drive could get through the snow on the road. Another storm had developed behind the one they were experiencing now, so the weather was only going to get worse. Even though the snow was still falling, it might be the only break she'd get for the next few days. If the weather predictions were correct, the next storm would be just as bad as the first.

Feeling less gloomy after her shower, Randi went into what used to be her parents' bedroom. It was now a home office, since she couldn't bear to make their room into her bedroom. Not now. Maybe not ever.

It's only noon. I have time to check my email.

Of course, she was rationalizing. The sooner she got outside to plow, the faster she could go get food. But she hadn't checked for a reply from S., and she'd love to know what he had to say about her email to him last Friday.

Sitting down at the small desk, she opened her laptop and waited for her email to boot up.

> *Dear M.,*
> *I'm sorry you got stood up. Oh hell . . . I'm not really that sorry. I never want anything to happen that hurts you, but I really was envious of your date. Maybe he'll stay sick for weeks so you can't reschedule.*

*I did end up getting stuck in the bliz-
zard, so I'm still in Maine. I'll be here until the
weather clears, so talk to me. What stupid
thing did you do tonight if your date never
showed up?*
Sincerely,
S.

Randi glanced at the date on the email. He'd answered back only a short time after she'd emailed him two days ago. She'd been too restless to sit, so she'd kept herself busy and hadn't checked her email since she'd sent her note on Friday.

She had told him it had been a long day, and that she'd done something stupid. Randi wasn't certain she wanted to fess up to exactly *what* she'd done.

I kissed Evan Sinclair. Okay, he kissed me, but I kissed him back. I don't want to want him. I don't want to be attracted to him at all.

"I can't stand the guy. Why did it feel so amazing?" she asked Lily, who was now on the floor next to her feet. She smiled as Lily's head came up and she let out a huge yawn. "Human problems are boring stuff to you, huh?" Randi guessed that her problems weren't much of an issue to a creature who lived for food, belly rubs, and playing fetch.

Toying with her computer mouse, she contemplated how much she wanted to share with her email friend. Finally, she decided to just tell him the truth.

Dear S.,
*Have you been attracted to someone who
you don't even like as a person? I haven't,
at least not until recently. I didn't think that*

*something like that could even happen. How
can you want to be intimate with someone
you don't even like?*

Randi let the question hang there for a moment before pressing the "Send" button. She talked to her friend about many things, but they'd never gotten quite this personal. But she'd found that being anonymous had allowed her to talk about any number of thoughts and feelings openly. In many ways, she had developed an indescribable connection to S. over the last year. She didn't think there was much she couldn't tell him.

She wasn't really surprised when a reply popped into her mailbox a few moments later.

*Dear M.,
I thought your date stood you up. Who are
we talking about?*

She smiled and quickly typed a response. Somehow, she'd been almost certain he'd start talking to her. What else was there to do in the middle of a Northeast blizzard if you still had an Internet connection?

*Dear S.,
He didn't actually stand me up. He was sick.
I'm talking about someone else I've known for
a while. I've always thought he was attractive,
yet I don't like him. How does that happen?*

He wrote back.

Dear M.,
I'm not certain, to be quite honest. But I do
know that two people can irritate the hell out
of each other and still desire each other. I've
had the same experience myself recently.

Randi was slightly taken aback and wasn't sure how she felt about her longtime email buddy wanting another woman. He'd kept her company during some of her darkest times, and it stung a little that he had other women in his life. She'd always assumed he was alone, like her, and that was one of the reasons they'd connected so well with each other.

She shrugged. He was a nice guy, and it wasn't like she wouldn't date if the opportunity came up with somebody she could connect with and liked. It made sense that he had women in his life. She'd just never considered the possibility. They always laughed about being alone on date nights.

Dear S.,
Glad to hear it's not just me. I have noth-
ing in common with the guy, and he's totally
obnoxious. Yet I find him physically attractive.
Weird, huh?

It took a minute to get his response.

Dear M.,
Not really weird. However, I think you should
stay away from him. You deserve someone
who adores you, and he sounds like a jack-
ass. Don't settle for anything less.

Randi sighed as she stared at his answer. Why couldn't there be a man in her life as nice as her pen pal?

> Dear S.,
> Maybe I'm a raving bitch? Sometimes I am, you know.

She laughed at his return email.

> Dear M.,
> Impossible. I don't think you have a mean bone in your body except when it comes to agreeing to meet me.

Randi sighed. It wasn't that part of her didn't want to meet the mysterious S., but she knew she never would. Deep down, she wasn't certain that he really wanted to meet her, either, even though he said that he did. Being anonymous was what made them such good friends. Randi never wanted to lose that connection. Meeting him wasn't worth the risk of losing a valuable friendship.

> Dear S.,
> That just goes to prove that you don't know me well. I'm off to stock up on dog food and junk food to ride out the next storm. Stay warm.
> TTYS,
> M.

She waited for him to sign off.

Dear M.,
Be careful. Even if you are in a small town,
the roads are bad everywhere. Let me know
that you got back safe.

After reading his note, she shut down her computer. He had no idea that she lived outside of the city limits, and getting back in was more difficult for her than the average citizen of Amesport. She was actually starting to like his protective instinct. It was nice to know someone cared.

"Want to go for a ride?" Randi waved toward the door as she rose from her seat at the desk. Her dog vaulted up immediately, her tail wagging at the prospect of sitting on the ATV with her owner while she plowed out the driveway.

Randi smiled as Lily whined enthusiastically and ran for the outside door. Her pup knew what the word *ride* meant.

Trying to push all thoughts of Evan Sinclair from her mind, Randi got busy trying to accomplish her tasks before the weather got worse.

CHAPTER 5

"Tell me again exactly *why* we're here?" Hope asked Evan as they passed down each aisle of the supermarket closest to the Peninsula. She was dropping things into the cart as Evan navigated it down the aisle with the junk food.

"Because you told me that Randi lives outside of town, and she might need supplies," Evan answered his sister calmly, even though he'd explained himself several times. "There's a second storm coming in, according to the weather report."

What if she can't get into town?

What if she lost power and she's all alone out in the country?

What if she doesn't have enough to eat?

Hope tossed a bag of chips and some dip into the cart, then stopped and propped her hands on her hips. "Since when would you care? I talked to Randi this morning to see if she needed anything, and she said she was fine. The power is still on, and she was getting ready to go out and clear the snow with her plow. She just mentioned possibly needing to come into town. She's lived in Maine for over fourteen years, Evan. Believe me, Miranda Tyler knows how to get through snow."

"Miranda?" Evan looked at Hope, confused.

Hope went back to throwing food in the cart. "Miranda is her full name, but everybody calls her Randi," she clarified.

"She didn't grow up here?" Evan asked casually. He'd always assumed that Amesport was her hometown.

He reached down and removed the chips and dip from the cart to put them back. It was pure junk, with very little nutritional value.

"Hold it!" Hope said firmly. "Put those back. You asked me to come here to help you pick out what Randi likes. Those are her favorites."

Evan peered into the cart, frowning. "Does she eat anything healthy?"

Hope's laughter rang out merrily in the crowded store. "Not often, and not much you would approve of. She's a junk-food junkie, but she's a runner, so she burns the calories as fast as she puts them in her mouth." She snatched the items from Evan's hands, dropped them back into the cart, and added some bagels.

"So her family moved here when she was an adolescent?" Evan knew he was digging for information, and so did his sister. Hope had been giving him perplexed looks ever since he'd asked her to leave the baby with Jason for a short time to help him go to the store.

He'd spent most of the weekend catching up with his family. Travel was easy within the Peninsula because they all lived in the same general area. They also had a plow on private contract, and the road and their driveways were constantly being cleared.

Micah had been right about baby David. He really wasn't bald. The infant had very light hair, and he took after his dad . . . a lot. But Evan could see many of Hope's features in the baby, too, and his heart had swelled with unexpected pride the first time he saw his new nephew. He wasn't a man who thought much about babies, but David was one of their own, and his protective instinct had kicked into gear almost immediately after seeing the innocent baby. Evan knew he'd be busy in the years ahead making sure his nephew was on the right path. Not that he didn't trust his sister and Jason as parents, but Hope hadn't exactly picked a safe career choice. He wouldn't interfere, of course, but he'd check in often on the first of the new generation of Sinclairs to see if his nephew needed . . . guidance. Technically, Evan knew David was a Sutherland, but it didn't matter what his last name was; he had Sinclair blood and Evan considered him a Sinclair, his baby sister's child and Evan's first nephew.

Evan looked at Hope because she still hadn't answered his question. His sister looked unusually disconcerted. He cocked an eyebrow at her and she looked at him carefully, as though she was contemplating how to answer.

Finally, she said carefully, "No. She wasn't born here. Randi moved from California to Amesport when she was fourteen."

"With her parents?" Evan didn't think it was that unusual to change locations. People did it all the time for various reasons.

"With her new parents," Hope admitted. "Randi was sort of a foster child to the Tylers."

"Sort of?" How could somebody be "sort of" a foster child? They either were fostered or they weren't, no matter how long of a time they remained with their foster parents.

Hope shrugged and gave Evan a pleading glance. "It's Randi's story to tell. I've told you what I'm comfortable revealing. The Tylers were elderly, but they gave her a good home."

Her name is really Miranda.

Her foster parents were elderly, now most likely deceased.

She loves junk food.

Evan stopped walking abruptly, alarm bells screeching loudly in his mind. It couldn't possibly be . . .

"Did she lose her foster mother recently?" Evan held his breath, his jaw clenched tightly. What were the chances?

Coincidence. Highly unlikely. There was no way that Randi was . . .

"Yes." Hope looked at Evan suspiciously. "How did you know? Joan passed away over a month ago. Randi was completely devastated."

"Fuck!" The expletive shot out of his mouth like a cannonball. "There's no damn way!"

Hope reached out and grasped his arm, smiling at the people staring at Evan, as though she was trying to tell them everything was fine. "I think you're scaring the other customers. What's the matter?"

"Nothing," he replied in a husky voice, looking down into Hope's concerned expression. "Everything," he admitted reluctantly.

He felt like he'd just taken a forceful punch in the gut by a heavyweight.

He had no doubt in his mind that Randi Tyler and his mysterious M. were the same woman. It was no coincidence. The chances of two women in Amesport losing an elderly foster mother just a short time ago were just too far of a stretch. "Let's finish," he told Hope in a milder voice, edging the cart forward.

Hope gave him a dubious look, but she continued putting items in the cart while Evan tried to process the information he'd just discovered. The more he thought about it, the more it made sense. Randi did a lot of volunteer work at the Center, and she *was* good friends with Emily.

"So is Randi seeing anyone?" Evan asked curiously as he watched Hope carefully place a sugar-filled cake into the basket. The entire cart was loaded now. Randi could probably survive a very long siege if she had to, even if the majority of the items weren't all that nutritious.

Hope shot him a sideways glance and shook her head. "No serious relationship. Tessa has been trying to get her to go out with her brother, Liam. The two of them own Sullivan's Steak and Seafood. They have the best lobster rolls in town."

"Never heard of the place," Evan muttered.

"Liam's quite successful with the restaurant. He's also a nice guy. He'd be perfect for Randi when they finally get to meet for a real date. I hope she finds someone. She deserves a nice guy in her life."

Over his dead body. He might not be the nice guy Hope had wished for, but it didn't matter. "He's not perfect for her," Evan told his sister hurriedly, his voice sounding slightly raspy. "She needs somebody who understands her."

"And that would be . . . ?" Hope left Evan to fill in the blank.

"Me," he growled in a low voice only Hope would hear.

"You two hate each other," his sister answered, her tone confused.

"I don't hate her. I never have," Evan admitted, following Hope as she pulled the shopping cart around the corner and went down the pet-food aisle. "I just don't know what to say to her."

Hope motioned to a bag of dog food that looked big enough to feed a horse. "Can you get one of those and put it on the bottom?"

Evan hefted up the bag and slid it onto the bottom rack. "Does she own a damn kennel full of dogs?" he grumbled as he pulled himself up to his full height again.

Hope snickered. "No . . . just Lily, her golden retriever. But her dog runs with her, and Lily is very active. The bag isn't that big." She hesitated before she added, "That's another thing . . . You don't like dogs." Letting out an exasperated sigh, Hope turned to face him. "You're going to tell me what's going on the minute we leave this store."

"I'll think about it," Evan told her evenly, not sure how much he could say. Hell, he hadn't even been able to put everything together himself yet, or reconcile the two women as one.

"You'll do it or I'll call Randi myself and find out," Hope threatened ominously.

"Don't," Evan asked hastily. "I'll tell you." If Hope started digging, it could mean trouble. He didn't know if Randi had ever told his sister about her email correspondence, but it wouldn't take much for the two intelligent women to figure everything out.

Hope nodded and started pulling the cart toward the checkout. "Good. I was pretty sure you would." Her voice sounded smug.

When did his sweet baby sister get this bossy and manipulative? Evan must have missed her transition from kind younger sibling to tough negotiator somewhere over the years.

He was silent as he followed Hope to check out the groceries, still shaking his head in shock.

He liked M. and he always had.

He was incredibly attracted to Randi—aka Miranda—but he didn't exactly like her. Maybe he knew that he definitely didn't *hate* her, but to say he was actually fond of her was stretching it, even though his dick definitely adored her.

If he put the two women together as one single female . . . he knew he was completely and totally screwed, and not in a good way.

Evan didn't say another word until they got back to Hope's vehicle, and then he didn't have a choice but to spill the whole story.

Unfortunately, once he started spilling his secrets to Hope, he couldn't stop.

"Oh, Evan," Hope said softly, bringing her palm to her brother's face. Tears were pouring down her cheeks as he finally finished his last story about his childhood. "Why did you go through so much all alone? We could have helped you, or at least been there to support you. You didn't have to face all of your challenges alone."

He shrugged. "I'm the oldest. It's my responsibility to take care of all of you."

Hope's heart had broken as she'd realized that Evan had faced so many challenges when he was so young, and still did because of his issues. "We're all grown up now, Evan. We don't need you to take care of us anymore, but we'll always love you and need you as our brother."

Evan grasped her hand and turned his blue-eyed stare her way. For once, the way he was feeling was actually revealed on his face. He looked solemn and remorseful, and Hope already knew why.

"I failed you the worst, Hope," he uttered hoarsely. "When you needed me the most, I wasn't there."

Her tears fell harder until she could barely see his face, her vision blurred. How could he blame himself for her past? She'd been an adult, made her own decisions. From where she was now, she didn't regret her past, because it had brought her to Jason and her beloved son. Regardless, the horror she'd suffered in the past had nothing to do with Evan. She'd intentionally covered her tracks, and she hadn't expected him to save her from anything. She'd wanted to do things on her own.

"I didn't want you to know, Evan. I didn't want anyone to know. I was free for the first time in my life, and I loved it at the time. Nothing you could have done would have made me stop, and it's not your fault. I was an adult and it was my life." She needed to find a way to get her lug-headed brother to understand that he wasn't responsible for every bad thing that happened to any of them in their lives. If he could, Evan would bear the blame for every wrong in the Sinclair family, but it couldn't continue. "It wasn't your fault," she repeated, hoping he'd believe it in time if she said it often enough.

"Our father was an asshole, and our mother didn't give a damn about any of us. Somebody needed to protect all of you," he said defensively.

"Who was there to protect you? You were just a child, too," Hope said softly, keeping her hand in Evan's as he lowered her arm, resting his hand on the leather seat of the car.

"I don't think I was ever a child," Evan answered abruptly.

Sometimes Hope wondered if he ever *had* been just a kid. It seemed like he'd been born in a suit and tie, ready to be an adult. But he hadn't always been an adult, and nobody had been there for him during his childhood. Now that she understood why Evan was the way he was, she knew that she had to try to fix it. Her heart ached with sadness at the unfairness of the situation, and his insistence on always being the strong protector. He'd always been distant, but she'd felt him pulling away from his family, and he needed them. The truth was, they needed him just as much. The entire Sinclair family needed to finally heal from the wounds of their upbringing. "I think you need to tell Grady, Dante, and Jared." All of them worried about Evan and the distance he'd put between them. She understood why, to an extent, but it needed to end. He was mistaken in thinking he wasn't wanted anymore. Not that he'd said that, but Hope could sense it. Every one of them loved him, whether he could accept that affection or not. Yeah, sometimes Evan was a jerk. But looking back, he had been a protector to each one of them at one time or another. Right now, Hope's heart ached that none of them had realized that Evan had experienced his own unique challenges.

"I don't know if I can," Evan shared quietly. "They're all happy now."

So they no longer needed or wanted their eldest brother?

Hope's heart clenched because Evan didn't feel like he had a purpose anymore, now that they were all grown. He'd tried to be a surrogate father to them all for so long that he didn't know how to be just a brother. "We still need you, Evan. We love you. You don't need to be perfect anymore."

"I'm as close to perfect as any man can be," Evan grumbled disgruntledly. "It's impossible to be completely faultless."

Hope burst out laughing. Tears were still rolling down her face as she realized that some things about her eldest brother would never change, and she really didn't want him to be someone he wasn't. He was a product of his upbringing and his own experiences in his life. Evan was a good man, but he needed a woman who would help him laugh at himself occasionally.

Randi would be perfect for him, but the situation was definitely precarious at the moment. After everything she'd learned about Evan today, the last thing she wanted was to see him brokenhearted. Oh, not that he'd admitted that he was anything more than strangely attracted to Randi right now, and that he'd come to like her through their correspondence when he'd thought he was talking to someone else. But Hope could see all of the signs. She had a husband she'd been in love with most of her life. It wasn't difficult for her to recognize Evan's attraction as a little more than what he'd described.

"Just shut up and hug me, Evan," she insisted, smiling through her tears.

He turned away from the steering wheel and held his arms open for her. "Of course, if that's what you need," he agreed readily.

I'm not the only one who needs it.

Hope threw herself into his sheltering embrace, knowing he needed a hug just as badly as she did. He held her close and she rested her head on his shoulder, hopeful that someone special like Randi could help heal Evan's hidden pain. He'd been the rock of their family, the sibling who had always been there for every one of them. As Hope squeezed him tightly, she knew it was beyond his turn to begin healing the wounds of his childhood. She planned on doing everything in her power to make that happen.

"So do you have any suggestions?" Evan asked hesitantly.

Hope knew he was talking about his situation with Randi. As she pulled back from his hug and swiped at her damp face, she told him firmly, "Plenty of them. We need to make another stop on the way back to the Peninsula. We have to get you to loosen up a little. You can drop me off afterward and then run out to Randi's place with the groceries. I'll call her so she doesn't try to make the trip into town. Take my vehicle, and have the plow run in front of you on the way out there. It's a small, two-lane highway going out to her place. It can get pretty bad."

Evan gave her a suspicious look, but he didn't say another word. He shifted the large SUV into gear and asked her where she wanted to go. She gave him directions, and he followed them silently. For once, Hope didn't feel awkward because of the distance he was trying to create, or his silence, because she understood that Evan was far from indifferent.

So much of the *Evan* they saw on the surface was nothing more than a façade. There was no question he was arrogant, but he was so much more.

"Turn right at the light," she instructed, wondering how difficult he was going to make her effort to get him some casual clothing.

"When did you get so bossy?" Evan asked gruffly, but he slowed the vehicle to make the turn.

Hope smiled at his comment and answered, "I've always been that way. You just never noticed because you were so much bossier."

He didn't answer, but she could see the corners of his lips start to turn up.

She leaned back in the heated leather seat contentedly with a grin on her face. Evan was nearly smiling. It might not seem like much to most people, but for her, it meant a hell of a lot.

CHAPTER 6

Randi lost her power around two o'clock in the afternoon, just as she was getting ready to leave for town.

Hope called her cell phone just a few minutes after to let her know she'd picked up supplies for her and they were on their way.

"My power is out," she told Hope unhappily as she stuffed some clothing into her backpack. "I'm going to need to come into town anyway and wait out the storm. My generator isn't working."

Randi had made that unfortunate discovery soon after the power had gone off. Being rural, she lost power more often than they did in town, and it was slower to come back on. She should have checked the generator before winter, but Joan had been so sick that it had slipped her mind. "I'll get a room at one of the inns for a day or two. The hotels and inns should have openings. It's off-season right now."

"No, you will not!" Hope's declaration came fiercely across the phone communication. "You can stay with us. We have plenty of room, and we have a whole-house generator even if the power goes out."

"You have a new baby—"

"And you have friends. Lots of them," Hope said firmly. "Get your butt over here. Tell Evan to bring you home with him. He should be there to drop off your groceries any minute."

"Evan?" Randi stopped short of stuffing her underwear inside her pack.

"He's bringing the supplies personally. He was worried about you."

"Evan?" Randi repeated, having a difficult time imagining one of the richest men in the world delivering groceries, much less just because he was concerned about her being caught in a storm.

"He's not so bad, Randi," Hope replied softly. "Maybe he can't always express himself well, but he does have a heart."

Randi could hear the fondness radiate through Hope's voice, and she could hardly tell Evan's sister that she thought her brother was an arrogant jackass. "It was a nice thing for him to do," she admitted reluctantly, wondering at the same time what ulterior motive Evan had in doing her a favor. Men like Evan Sinclair didn't just do menial jobs for anybody who needed something. He had to have a purpose. She supposed all sisters wanted to think their brothers had a heart, but Randi certainly hadn't seen any sign of one existing in Evan yet.

"Do me a favor?" Hope requested.

"Of course," Randi agreed readily. She adored Hope, and she'd do anything she asked.

"Give Evan a chance."

Okay . . . she'd do anything except *that*. "We don't like each other, Hope. We rub each other the wrong way. We're too different to be friends." It wasn't like Randi hadn't tried, and she still couldn't forget the scorching-hot kiss they'd shared a few days ago. However, getting involved with a heartless billionaire like Evan would be a big mistake. In spite of having some basic and incredibly strong physical chemistry, they couldn't be together for more than a minute without arguing or just plain ignoring each other so they didn't fight.

"Things aren't always exactly what they seem," Hope hedged.

"Are you saying your brother isn't an asshole?" Randi asked bluntly, wondering if Hope saw a way-different Evan than she did.

"No," Hope admitted with humor in her voice. "He is an asshole sometimes, but maybe he has his reasons. You know what our childhood was like."

Randi's heart clenched as she heard a trace of vulnerability in Hope's voice. She often met with the Sinclair wives, along with her friends Kristin and Tessa, and all of the women had become pretty close. They all shared most of their secrets, and Randi knew how stifling and depressing Hope's upbringing had been. What would it have been like to be the eldest child of Hope's alcoholic, neurotic father? Obviously, Hope's parent had put some pretty high expectations on his eldest son. "I know," she finally answered as she continued stuffing articles of clothing into her bag. "I'll try to be nice to him. I promise," she vowed, optimistic that she could hold her temper for more than a few minutes. The guy was bringing her supplies through a major blizzard. Even if he did have ulterior motives, Randi was grateful. Too bad she'd lost power and had to go into town. It would essentially be a wasted trip for Evan.

"Good. I'll see you soon," Hope said, sounding satisfied.

Randi said good-bye to Hope and clicked the "Off" button on her phone, dropping it onto the bed.

"Looks like we're going for a longer ride, Lily," she informed her dog.

Lily was lying on the bed next to Randi's backpack, watching her mistress carefully, trying to surmise what was about to happen.

At the mention of a ride, Lily bolted to her feet and leapt agilely and happily off the mattress to the carpeted floor, whining her doggy joy.

"I'm glad you're happy," Randi told her pup as she closed the zipper on her pack. She wasn't exactly thrilled about leaving her home, even if it was for just a day or two. She jumped as she heard somebody hammering on her front door.

Evan?

Her heart skipping a beat, she tried not to picture him pinning her body against her vehicle and kissing her breathless.

"Coming," she yelled as Lily began to bark.

She opened the door and every bit of air left her lungs in one enormous *whoosh*, a sound she couldn't conceal as she looked at the man on her doorstep. There was Evan Sinclair in his fancy wool coat, looking as handsome as ever, and she had the same breathless reaction to him that she always did. He had a cream scarf tucked into the neckline, but his head was bare. "I need to unload some stuff," Evan said bluntly, his windblown dark hair whipping around in the brutal storm.

Randi was mute for a moment, her gaze lost in the depths of his blue-eyed stare.

"Um . . . no need," she finally informed him, hating her own body for its volatile reaction to Evan. "I have to go into town. I lost power."

"You don't have a generator?"

"Not working," Randi replied. *Just like my brain right now.* Sweet Jesus! The weather might be frigid, but she was suddenly roasting in her jeans, sweater, and ski jacket.

Evan reached out and took the backpack out of her hand, an item she'd forgotten she was clutching.

"Let's go. The roads aren't good, and the second storm is about to hit. I don't think they'll be passable for much longer," Evan demanded. "I'll take the groceries with us. You'll need them."

Randi snapped out of her haze of lust, telling Evan quickly, "I just need to get my car out of the garage."

"You're not driving. I have a vehicle twice the size of that miniature SUV of yours, and I barely made it through. Let's go. For once, no arguing. We don't have the time." Evan's eyes drilled into hers, his stern expression demanding she relent.

I don't have to argue with him. What he's saying makes sense. He's been on the roads; I haven't.

What Evan suggested was perfectly logical. She just wished he wouldn't say it in such a high-handed way. It made her want to go on the defensive immediately.

"Fine," she answered briskly and went to get the rest of her winter gear and her laptop. She had promised Hope she would try to be nice.

Randi scooped up only what she'd need for the next day or two and put Lily on her leash.

"You're taking the dog?" Evan frowned at her as she met him at the door. He'd stepped inside, but just barely. Just enough to close the door and prevent the heat from escaping.

Randi gaped at him. "I have to take Lily. How would she eat? How would she drink? How would she stay warm?"

Evan gave her a puzzled look, but he took her laptop and the leash from her hand, after slinging the heavy pack to his shoulder to let her lock up. Randi could feel how much the wind had strengthened since she'd plowed out the driveway. "It is getting bad," she yelled at Evan as she locked the front door.

Taking Lily's leash back from Evan, she sprinted with him to Hope's large SUV, letting him grasp her hand as they trekked through ankle-deep snow that had fallen or blown into the driveway. It hadn't been that long since she'd cleaned it, and it was already starting to pile up again.

Breathless from the shock of the wind and cold once she settled into the luxurious SUV, she leaned back against the leather, relieved. It was her first winter alone in Dennis and Joan's home. She hadn't been looking forward to experiencing it without power for a few days. Being there was both a comfort and a trigger for her melancholy moods when she was missing them. Without power, she'd started feeling downright gloomy.

"Thanks," she told Evan as he put the vehicle in motion, and Lily found a comfortable position sitting between her legs on the floorboard.

Evan frowned at Lily as she whined and squirmed with excitement before focusing his attention on the road.

"You don't like dogs?" Randi asked just to make conversation. She might only be ten miles out of town, but it was going to be a long ride, since the roads sucked. They looked like they'd been plowed, but the wind was blowing a massive amount of snow, making visibility a nightmare.

"I wouldn't know. I've never had one," he answered flatly.

"Cats?"

"I've never had any type of animal," Evan said shortly. "I travel too much."

Randi's heart sank, remembering that Hope had once told her that her father had hated animals and hadn't allowed any of the kids to have a pet. She sank her fingers into Lily's silky coat. "Well, Evan, this is Lily. She was my college graduation present from my foster parents. She's four years old and is generally very well behaved. She just gets excited because she loves to go for rides."

"Will she need to go to the bathroom?" Evan asked, sounding concerned.

Randi chuckled at his serious tone. "No. She can hold it. Just keep moving or we might get stuck." She hesitated as she looked at the road in front of them, the visibility so bad that she could barely make out the road. "Can you see okay?"

Evan shrugged his broad shoulders. "Not great. But I'll get us home safely."

His voice was so calm, so certain, that Randi relaxed. She doubted there was anything that Evan Sinclair wasn't capable of doing well. She was glad she wasn't driving. She could probably get through it, but she'd be white-knuckled for the whole drive. Bad weather rarely bothered her, but this was an epic blizzard, even for the East Coast. "I'm surprised that they actually plowed way out here."

"They didn't," Evan answered. "We sent the Peninsula plow out before the SUV. You never would have made it into town. I can't believe you were even going to attempt the drive."

"I guess I forgot how bad the roads can get out here. It's my first winter in the house since I went off to college." Randi had moved back in with Joan last summer, giving up her small apartment in town to take care of her. "Joan needed help, and I couldn't leave her alone anymore. She was forgetting to take her medications, and she wasn't eating very well."

"Your foster mother?" Evan questioned. "Hope told me she passed away not long ago."

Randi nodded, even though Evan was focused on the road. "I miss her. I miss both my foster parents." She buried her fingers in Lily's fur, stroking the dog more to comfort herself than Lily.

"I'm sorry for your loss," Evan said in a husky voice.

"Thanks," she finally answered Evan's expression of sympathy, not certain what to make of him at the moment. His comment was probably the nicest thing he'd ever said to her.

She stared at him in profile, unable to ignore his strong, capable fingers gripping the steering wheel and the rugged handsomeness of his features from a sideways view. He had a small amount of dark stubble on his jaw, but that only made him hotter, more approachable. Randi was willing to bet that the coat—identical to or the same as the one she'd spilled her coffee on—cost more than her monthly salary. But he somehow seemed . . . different today.

Why?

Even though the SUV was large, she could smell his masculine scent, and the fragrance made every female hormone in her body take notice. She'd always loved Evan's essence, ever since the first time she'd had to stand beside him at Emily's wedding.

He doesn't seem like he has a stick up his ass today!

He was still arrogant, but he seemed more . . . relaxed. Her eyes traveled down his body, noting that he was actually dressed in a pair of jeans and was wearing boots instead of shoes. Granted, they looked like they were expensive black leather, but they were more casual, lace-up boots rather than his usual sleek, custom-made shoes. Those were gone today, as were his usual suit and tie. The whole package made him seem more . . . human, and eminently more touchable.

Randi was silent as Evan navigated the roads, not only to let him concentrate, but because desire was burning so fiercely in her gut that she couldn't really even make conversation.

It had always been this way for her. She'd always wanted Evan Sinclair with a savage intensity that she constantly had to fight.

She didn't understand it.

She didn't like it.

However, it wouldn't go away, even when Evan was being a complete ass—which had been almost constantly from the moment they'd first met.

It's just physical. I haven't gotten laid for a long time.

Truthfully, she hadn't had sex with anybody since college. During the six years it had taken to get her master's degree, she'd had some casual flings and a couple of boyfriends. Since returning to Amesport she hadn't wanted to start a relationship unless she knew it could be something permanent. She'd had her wild days during college. She was yearning for something solid, something other than empty sex.

Establishing her career had come first, and once she had started tutoring and then caring for Joan, every minute of her day had been busy.

Randi rationalized that because it had been years since she'd had decent sex, it was perfectly normal to be attracted to Evan. He was definitely the hottest guy she'd ever seen.

Feeling more at ease after justifying the passionate urge she had to jump Evan's bones, she sighed.

"Tired?" Evan asked curiously.

"No. Just glad we're getting close to town." Starting to see familiar territory, she realized they were on the edges of Amesport. "If you could drop me off at Hope's place, I'd appreciate it. She offered to put me up."

"I can't drop you off there." Evan dismissed her request patiently as he navigated toward the Peninsula.

Randi gaped at him. "Why?"

Evan was silent for a few moments before answering. "Because you're staying with me."

CHAPTER 7

Don't panic. You can do this for a day or two. It isn't a big deal.

Randi released a heavy breath as she watched Evan shuck his coat and scarf, getting an eyeful of what a perfect ass in a pair of jeans actually looked like. Holy shit! Evan Sinclair's butt was a work of art, and his broad shoulders in the cream-colored fisherman's sweater he was wearing seemed enormous.

He's not that incredibly built. He's not. He really isn't.

Evan turned around suddenly, lifting a brow at her as he saw exactly what area her eyes were glued to. Jerking away her gaze that was now trained on his crotch, she actually blushed.

"I can't do this," she protested weakly . . . again.

She'd argued with Evan about staying with him at his place, but he'd serenely pointed out that Hope's cat, Daisy, hated dogs. She'd forgotten about Daisy and just about everything else since Evan had picked her up. It was like her IQ score had taken a sudden hit, and she couldn't think of anything intelligent to say when she was in Evan's presence.

"Of course you can," Evan argued. "There's plenty of room."

I can't be trusted to be alone with you, and it has nothing to do with space.

"It isn't the size of the house," she admitted, unzipping her jacket and shrugging out of it.

"Is it because you know I want to fuck you?" Evan asked evenly.

Randi's eyes grew wide the moment Evan made his blunt admission.

Moving forward, Evan took the jacket from her hand and hung it up in the entry closet beside his, talking as he performed the task. "Miranda, I think we're both uncomfortable with each other because all we want to do is fuck each other senseless."

Randi couldn't seem to form any words, still shocked at his straightforward confession. The Evan she was familiar with wasn't a guy who said something like that. Generally, he didn't say much at all.

He continued, "Maybe we should both put it out there and deal with it." He turned and pierced her with a dark look. "I want you. I always have."

He motioned toward the living room and Randi automatically moved into the next room, even though it was pretty dark. "You can't stand me." She could barely keep herself from stammering as she flopped into one of the leather chairs in front of a fireplace, stunned.

Evan flicked a switch, starting the gas fireplace so the room was dimly illuminated before seating himself across from her in a matching chair. "I never disliked you. I don't even really know you."

"You ignored me," Randi protested, remembering how humiliated she'd felt when she'd gotten the cold shoulder from Evan.

He shrugged. "My dick was hard. It wasn't easy to ignore my attraction to you, and it showed."

"But I was nice to you, I wanted to be your friend because your brother was marrying one of my best friends." She still remembered how crushed she'd been when Evan had ignored her efforts to be nice to him at Emily's wedding.

"I was an asshole. I generally am," he told her nonchalantly.

Randi opened her mouth to speak, but how could she argue with him? He was declaring himself an unpleasant person already. Closing her mouth, she fixed her eyes on his expression, trying to figure him out. Was Evan really a jerk, or was he just painfully blunt? Either way, he was usually not a pleasant person to be around. Yet she found him intriguing. He was a mystery to solve, a puzzle to put together. If he was in the mood to talk, maybe she could dig for a little information to figure him out.

Lily had been exploring the enormous mansion since she'd pranced in the front door. Now, she was head-butting Randi's arm.

"She needs to go outside," Randi told Evan as she rose to her feet. The last thing she needed was Lily leaving her mark on one of the plush, expensive area rugs in Evan's living room.

"Is that how you know?" Evan asked curiously as he strode across the room and opened one of the French doors that led to a patio.

"Yes. She's pretty adamant when she really has to go." Randi eyed the patio doubtfully. "Is there a place for her to go?"

"Any place outside of the door is preferable," he said, deadpan.

Randi walked onto the covered patio and opened a small gate leading to the beach. Lily sprinted out into the snow. "She can't poop on the patio."

"It can be cleaned up. It doesn't matter. It's not like I'm going to use it right now, and it's probably warmer than it is beyond that gate."

Laughter burst from Randi's mouth because she was unable to contain it. Evan had said some of the oddest, most surprising things today. And she was fairly certain he probably meant them. "She's used to going all the way outside."

Randi left the gate propped open and slipped back through the door. "It's cold." She was shivering as she closed the door, knowing Lily would come back when she was finished.

Evan blocked her escape route with his body. His touch was gentle as he slipped his fingers into her hair and tipped her head up to look at him. "I'm sorry if I hurt your feelings, Miranda. At Emily's wedding, I really didn't know what to say, so I didn't say anything."

Randi looked up at him and shivered as she fell into his dark, liquid blue eyes. He was looking at her like a predator that hadn't had food in weeks, his gaze devouring every inch of her face. His intensity at the moment made her edgy, and his unexpected apology threw her off balance. This wasn't the Evan she was used to, the Evan who either ignored her or threw out condescending comments.

His body pressed closer, his free hand resting against the door beside her face.

"I forgive you," she said in a rushed voice. "Just don't kiss me again."

If he lays those lips on me, I know I'm toast.

His unique, masculine scent surrounded her, sinking into every pore of her skin, intoxicating her. If he tasted her, she'd never be able to resist him.

"Why?" he asked huskily. "Don't tell me you don't want this, Miranda."

His tone was entreating, almost pleading with her to acknowledge the smoldering heat between them. Her heart skittered as he pressed his lips to her temple, leaving a hot trail of breath along the side of her face.

"I can't," she said painfully, knowing she wanted him to kiss her worse than she'd ever wanted anything else in her life. "And nobody calls me Miranda."

"You can," he cajoled. "And I prefer Miranda. It's a beautiful name."

"I hate it." Randi's chest was heaving as Evan's lips trailed lightly to her ear, his heated breath on her sensitive skin making it difficult for her to draw a breath. "Only my real mother used that name."

"Maybe you could learn to like it again if there was a man saying it while he was making you come harder than you ever have before," Evan suggested hoarsely in her ear.

Oh, sweet baby Jesus. Randi was afraid she'd probably learn to love her full name again under those circumstances. All thoughts of her birth mother gone, the only thing she could think of was the mental picture he'd just painted.

Him . . . in the heat of passion, groaning her name like she was a goddess, pounding into her as she experienced the most divine climax of her life. If his fierce expression was any indication of how he pleasured a woman, he'd strip away every defense she'd built up over the years and leave her begging for more. She felt helpless to resist this seductive side of Evan she'd never seen before.

Reaching behind her, he opened the door to let Lily come back in, and then he closed it quickly and flipped the lock, surging forward as he made the motions.

His engorged cock pressed against her pelvis, and she bit her lip to stifle a moan as she felt the size and strength of his erection against her body.

"Kiss me," Evan demanded as he moved his hands down her back and cupped her jean-clad ass with both of his large, strong hands. His fingers gripped the flesh and pulled her molten core into his hard form. "You asked me not to kiss you, so you have to kiss me."

Randi's willpower broke as she looked up and saw the longing in Evan's eyes. It was an echo of exactly what she was feeling, and she could no more resist him than she could stop breathing. Wrapping her arms around his neck, she speared her hands into his coarse hair and yanked his mouth down to hers. She needed his touch more than she wanted to resist him, and as his lips collided with hers, Randi completely forgot why she was even trying to fight the urge to devour him.

He sprang into action the moment she kissed him, taking control as he demanded her complete surrender. Tasting. Teasing. Commanding. Evan's tongue swept into her mouth, wiping away every doubt she had as he conquered her mouth with his own, leaving her breathless and mindless as he finally surfaced, his teeth catching her bottom lip and nipping at the flesh as though he wanted to mark it.

His lips were suddenly everywhere, and Randi's hand left his hair and wrapped around his neck as she felt herself being lifted off her feet. She landed on something soft—she assumed it was the couch—but she wasn't about to turn her head away from his mouth to look. She was too obsessed with the feel of his body against hers to give a crap what she'd landed on.

For some unknown reason, she felt safe letting Evan take control of her body while it burned for his possession. She knew he was feeling the same insane desires that she was experiencing right now.

Randi nearly whimpered as her body lost contact with his. Opening her eyes, her breath hitched as she saw Evan in the firelight, whipping his sweater over his head and pulling it from his body like he wanted it gone right that second. Randi blinked, stunned by the sight of his muscular chest and defined abs, covered by an abundance of bare skin that she was suddenly itching to touch.

"You're beautiful," she breathed softly, still dazed by his passion.

His eyes were like blue flames, his solemn, unwavering stare fixed on her as he tossed his sweater on the floor. Evan didn't speak as he kneeled beside the couch and sat her up, pulling her sweater over her head. She helped him, tossing the garment to the side, and reached for the front clip of her bra.

"Wait," Evan insisted, fingering the silky material and tracing her hard, sensitive nipples through the bra. "This is sexy. I want to remember you like this. I want to remember everything."

His deep voice was so reverent that the vibrations tremored down her spine and left goose bumps over her skin. "I need this, Evan. Please. This doesn't have to mean that I like you, or that I expect anything. You don't have to like me, either, in the future. But I want this now."

She was usually overly cautious, and not likely to be so needy under usual circumstances. But she was tired of fighting her unrelenting attraction to this man, so tired of grieving her loss, and so damn weary of feeling so empty inside.

"You don't have to like me," Evan growled. "Just let me make you come." He tore the bra from her upper body with a strong tug. The lacy garment was delicate, and it gave to his superior strength.

Yes. Yes. Yes.

Even as Randi mourned the loss of her favorite bra, she moaned as he freed her breasts from their confinement.

In one smooth move, Evan slid onto the couch and between her thighs. She yanked him down, gasping as their heated skin collided. It was both torture and bliss. Her nipples grew impossibly harder as they abraded against his muscular chest.

Wrapping her arms around him, she moved her hands over his shoulders and down his back, touching every inch of bare skin she could find. He felt hot, hard, his skin was like velvet beneath her fingers.

He grasped her hair and pulled her head back, his lips and tongue trailing boldly over the vulnerable flesh on her neck. "I. Need. This. Too." His voice was raspy and desperate.

His words echoed in her mind, and her body ignited as he boldly admitted that he wanted the same thing she did right now, needed it with the same urgency.

She longed to just let him take the lead, satiate her need, but she had to tell him one thing before she completely lost control.

"I don't do oral sex," she warned him. It wasn't that she *wouldn't*. She actually *couldn't*. She'd tried to overcome her fears with a college boyfriend, and it hadn't been a pleasant experience.

"Fine," he answered sharply, sounding like he couldn't care less what she was willing to give him as he rose to pull off her boots and unbutton her jeans.

Desperate and panting, she helped him. After kicking her feet out of her jeans, she reached for him again, but he stood and tore off his own denims. Randi sighed as he lowered his boxer shorts in one smooth motion and stepped out of them.

Backlit by the fire, Evan was gloriously naked and exquisitely made. His cock was long, thick, and so rock-hard that she wanted desperately to have him inside her. She reached out her hand to touch him instinctively, but he grasped her outstretched fingers. "No." His tone was insistent.

He moved back between her thighs, draping one of her legs over the couch and placing the other over his shoulder.

"These match," he observed, rubbing his thumb over the red silk of her panties.

"My favorite set," she panted helplessly, trembling as his finger traced her wet pussy though the material. Her body was ready to incinerate, and he hadn't even started to fuck her. She moaned as he slid one finger under the elastic and lightly touched her clit. "Oh, God. Evan. Please." She desperately needed him inside her. Now. "What are you doing?" Why was he waiting?

"You said you didn't do oral sex. I was assuming that you were talking about performing it and not receiving it. I hope so, anyway." He yanked at the panties, and they gave way just like the bra. "Because I really need to taste you, Miranda." He tossed the panties on the floor as his head dove between her thighs.

She squealed as he claimed her pussy with one long flick of his tongue, the sensation so incredible that her breath seized as he started to consume her, feasting on her vulnerable flesh like she was his only sustenance. Randi raked her hands through his hair, fisting it hard as her body rocked in crazed response to his lips, teeth, and tongue, all of them working together to drive her crazy.

Her hips lifted, and she ground her pussy against his mouth, desperate. "Evan. Please." It was like her body was roaring to life, and it was hungry for more.

Finally, he centered on her clit, his teeth biting gently at the bundle of nerves, his tongue flicking quickly against the quivering flesh.

"Yes," Randi moaned, lost to everything except Evan's touch.

The possessive, dominant way he consumed her left her mindless. It was as though he had only one goal in that moment: to make her come. His laser focus on his task and the obvious enjoyment he received from the carnal act was overwhelming. Evan was like a force of nature that was absolutely relentless.

She climaxed screaming his name, her hips bucking against his hungry mouth as her body trembled with relief.

Her heartbeat was thundering in her ears as he climbed up her body, her breathing still ragged. "Fuck me, Evan," she pleaded. While her body was sated of the need to come, she still felt empty. She needed to touch him, watch him experience his own pleasure.

"I plan on it," he answered gutturally.

Randi tried to reach for his engorged cock again, but he pushed her hand away as he grabbed a condom from the floor. He must have removed it from his pocket before he'd torn off his jeans. Now, he rolled it on like a madman.

"If you touch me, I won't last," Evan growled as he lowered his body over hers.

"I don't care," Randi murmured as she wrapped her arms around his neck and stroked the warm, sleek skin on his shoulders. She wrapped her legs around his lower back.

"Well I sure as hell do," Evan grumbled as he claimed her with one smooth thrust of his hips. "Jesus, you're tight," Evan groaned as he buried himself to the root of his cock.

"Oh, God." It had been so long, and Evan was built big. His entry was both pain and ecstasy. Randi could feel his body tense as he waited for her to adjust to his size, staying still as he remained deeply buried inside her. "Don't wait. Fuck me, Evan." Her muscles relaxed and let him in. The pain had only lasted a second, and then there was only the fullness of him and the exquisite pleasure of having him deep inside her.

"Can't. Wait." Evan started to move with a tortured groan.

Randi felt her whole body start to vibrate, and her belly tightened as Evan started to retreat and pounded back into her as though his life depended on it.

Reality receded and there was only Evan and her as their bodies strained together, Randi feeling like she wanted to crawl inside of him and never come out. His scent surrounded her, intoxicating her. His cock was pummeling her, and his damp flesh was abrading against hers, but it wasn't enough.

"Harder," she pleaded, needing more.

Her nails scored his back as she tried to get him closer.

"Fuck! That feels good," he growled, thrusting himself deeper, harder.

Carnal desire swept them both into its clutches as their bodies slapped together in a hard, fast, and hot rhythm that had Randi writhing beneath Evan in one big whirlpool of longing.

"Come for me, Miranda. Come *with* me," Evan commanded right before his mouth closed over hers.

The coil in her stomach unfurled just as Evan's body began to tense, the feel of his hot mouth invading hers, putting her over the edge. She grasped his tight ass, wanting to hold him inside her as he groaned into her mouth.

She climaxed in a stormy sea of desire that nearly swept her away; the only thing anchoring her in place was her mesmerized gaze on Evan as he pulled his mouth from hers with a guttural, feral groan. He threw his head back, the cords of the muscles in his neck flexing and tiny beads of perspiration were trickling down his face as he found his own release.

In that single moment, as one, they splintered apart, and Randi knew she'd never forget exactly how Evan had looked when they did.

Consumed by passion, he was a sensual, glorious sight that was worth remembering.

He only rested his weight on top of her for a moment before he lifted himself from her to get rid of the used condom.

She missed the feel of him the moment he left her. The scorching heat of his body against hers was sublime, and filled some of the dark, empty places that had resurfaced after her loss.

He returned even before she'd completely caught her breath, lifting her from the sofa and flopping into a recliner with her on his lap. She snuggled against him, getting drunk on the scent of Evan and sex. They were both damp with exertion, even though the storm was probably still raging outside the walls of his massive home. He stroked her hair like she was special to him, and she brushed a stray lock of hair from his forehead.

Her mind tried to berate her for what had just happened, but she pushed the negative thoughts from her brain. She refused to regret what she'd just done. Evan had filled some of the lonely places inside her, and made her body sing with sensation. She'd never had sex remotely as good as she'd just experienced, and she wasn't going to hate herself for enjoying it so much with a man she didn't even really like. Life was too short for those kinds of regrets. She was going to relish exactly what she had right now, right this moment, and to hell with the future.

"I have a problem," Evan said remorsefully.

Randi giggled at his serious tone. She was starting to get used to his somber demeanor. She was starting to think that his personality wasn't all arrogance, and that he sometimes said things seriously because he never had the opportunity to laugh. "I thought we just took care of your problem."

He shook his head. "Not that. Another problem."

"What?" she asked curiously, pulling back to look at his face.

His gaze met hers, and she noticed a slight, endearingly naughty twinkle in his eyes. "I think I'm starting to like you."

His tone was morose, but Randi knew he was trying to tease her. His attempt was adorable and sweet, since she knew instinctively that what he was trying to do wasn't easy for a man like Evan.

Randi burst out laughing and hugged him to her chest. She sobered and tried to mimic his serious tone, but knew that she failed miserably. "I think I like you, too."

CHAPTER 8

Dear S.,
I'm sorry I didn't write earlier, but I lost power at my place. I had to come into town for a day or two until the storm passes. I live about ten miles out of town. I hope you're safe and warm.

Dear M.,
I hope you're okay. Do you have a friend to stay with in town?

Dear S.,
Not really a friend. Actually, I'm staying with the guy I was telling you about, the one you thought I should stay away from. Before you warn me away again, he's not so bad. In fact,

I think I like him. He was kind to me last night and took me into his home. I think maybe I misunderstood him.

Dear M.,
Then definitely don't dump him. Maybe you should try to understand him a little better. And yes, I'm staying very warm. I met someone who helps chase away the cold.

Randi hesitated as she saw her pen pal's answer. He met someone? How did she feel about *that* exactly? She cared a lot about her mysterious S., and she wanted him to be happy. She'd known all along that they'd never meet, and she couldn't be selfish and wish him to be as miserably alone as she was, just so he could write to her forever.

Dear S.,
I'm happy for you. So I guess you won't be alone on date nights anymore?

Dear M.,
Don't know. It isn't really date night yet.

Randi laughed out loud. It was only Monday.

Dear S.,
Here's to hoping you won't be writing to me on Friday. I hope she's good enough for you.

Dear M.,
She's way too good for me, actually.
So what about you? Are you going to be
available on date nights in the future?

Randi sighed and stretched her sore body in the recliner, holding her laptop on her thighs. She'd put some of her muscles into positions the night before that hadn't been tested that way in years.

Evan had taken her up to his bed, where they'd explored each other's bodies at leisure, leaving them both spent when they'd finally fallen asleep.

She'd woken up this morning to find him gone. After showering, she'd come downstairs looking for her laptop and her clothes. She'd found both, and was now sitting in the recliner she and Evan had shared the night before, talking to her mysterious S. while she waited to see where Evan had gone.

Wherever he was, he must have taken Lily with him. Her dog was trained to come when called, and Randi had looked everywhere. "Maybe he took her for a walk," she muttered to herself, still perplexed about where he'd gone.

Dear S.,
Inevitably, I'll be available.

Dear M.,
What about your guy? I think you should get
to know him better. Maybe you misjudged
him initially. You did say he was nice to you.

Randi hesitated, knowing she couldn't say much about Evan. Whoever her mysterious letter writer was, he probably worked for the Sinclairs.

Dear S.,
He's just visiting. It's not really a serious
thing.

Dear M.,
Maybe it could become more?

Dear S.,
Unfortunately . . . no.

Dear M.,
Why? I thought you were starting to like him.

Dear S.,
Long story. We come from two completely
different worlds.

Dear M.,
What if he wants more, and he doesn't care if
you're from separate planets?

Randi chuckled at his comment.

Dear S.,
I don't think that will become an issue. It's
just a fling for us, a way to get over some-
thing that's been between us for a long time.

Evan might desire her, and maybe he'd even come to like her, but
she wasn't deluding herself about the possibility of a schoolteacher with
her jaded background and a billionaire having any chance at a lasting

relationship. Evan would be off to do business again, and she'd go back to her job after the storm was over.

> *Dear M.,*
> *I'm here if you want to talk about it.*

Randi took a deep breath, tempted to tell him everything. But she couldn't. There was still so much about her personal life that he *didn't* know, and his connection to the Sinclairs was uncertain. She might share her emotions with her mystery guy, but there were still some things she didn't dare write about.

> *Dear S.,*
> *Thanks for always being here for me. It's*
> *always meant a lot. Good luck with continuing*
> *to stay warm. I'm off to find my dog. I can't*
> *figure out where she went. We'll talk soon.*

Randi signed out of her email and off the computer, closing the lid and setting it on the floor. She tried desperately not to feel a pang of regret at the news that S. had a new woman in his life, and obviously one he cared about. While she *wanted* to be happy for him, she'd come to rely on his friendship, advice, common sense, and compassion in the last year. There had been times that she'd felt connected to him by something even deeper than friendship, but she had no idea exactly what it was. At times, it was almost as if they were kindred spirits, understanding each other on a level a little different than friendship. Unfortunately, she'd probably never know.

She had wanted to meet him, but a streetwise woman with her background had more sense than to believe that meeting a stranger she knew only by email could be anything other than dangerous. In fact, it could end up being a disaster of epic proportions if they didn't connect well in person. They'd both lose a friendship that they'd come to depend on in the last year.

"Oh well, it doesn't matter anymore. He has his woman now," she whispered quietly to herself, hoping the unknown female realized what a wonderful guy she had. If she didn't, Randi would kick the crap out of the unknown female herself. She might have never met him face-to-face, but he'd spent enough lonely nights with her, comforting her after she lost Joan, that she knew he had an enormous heart.

Randi yawned as she rose from the chair.

I need coffee. Bad.

She wandered through the massive house, searching for the kitchen, noting that although the house and furnishings were beautiful, they seemed . . . unused, cold. It was likely because it was rarely used, and there wasn't really a personal feel to the residence.

Wondering if she should continue to search for Lily, she was surprised when Evan came through a door in the kitchen that she hadn't seen before. Lily was right behind him.

"Hey, sweet girl," Randi crooned, squatting down to let Lily give her morning doggie kisses. She cuddled the enthusiastic dog as she looked up at Evan. "Good morning," she said cautiously, flushing as she remembered all that had happened between them the night before.

"It's much better than good now," Evan remarked huskily, his eyes devouring her.

Randi acknowledged that Evan looked as hot in casual clothing as he did in a suit and tie. Even though he was dressed in another pair of butt-hugging jeans and a green sweater, he still exuded power. It was an aura he carried with him no matter how he was dressed.

"I was worried about Lily," Randi told him as she stroked the dog's golden fur. "I didn't know she had turned traitor on me. I thought you didn't like dogs."

Honestly, she trusted her dog's judgment, and apparently Lily had weighed in on Evan's side. Her canine was looking back and forth between them, her glances at both of them completely adoring.

"I never said I didn't like dogs. Just that I never had one. She's nice. I took her outside to use the facilities," Evan said properly. "And then she followed me downstairs to my office."

Lily licked her cheek one last time before Randi stood up.

"Why does she do that licking thing? I fed her, but she was still doing the same thing after I gave her some food. I thought maybe she was hungry, but I guess not." He looked honestly perplexed.

Randi laughed. "She's showing affection. She likes you."

She found the coffeemaker and the individual capsules to put inside of the machine. She popped one in, closed the lid, and touched the button to brew after finding and placing a mug underneath the spout.

"Does her owner still like me today, too?" Evan asked carefully, wrapping his arms around her waist from behind.

Randi turned and slid her arms around him. "Depends. Are you going to kiss me?"

"Yes. Yes, I think I am. I don't think I can stop myself. You look beautiful today," Evan answered, his eyes stormier than the weather outside.

Randi shivered in anticipation as Evan started to lower his head. She wasn't wearing any makeup, and her long hair was still damp from the shower. Dressed in a pair of jeans and a sweatshirt, she was pretty sure she was a mess, but Evan didn't appear to care.

She nodded her head and smiled. "Flattery helps," she teased.

The corners of his lips started to curl into a slight smile, and he was just lowering his head when he sniffed . . . loudly.

"What's that horrible smell?"

One whiff and Randi knew exactly what was stinking up the kitchen. "What did you feed Lily?"

"I wasn't sure how much or when you feed her, so I just gave her some leftovers I had from yesterday. She seemed to like them, and I thought they would tide her over until you woke up." Evan looked worried. "Please tell me I didn't do anything wrong."

He looked so concerned for Lily's well-being that Randi wanted to laugh, but she didn't. "Please don't tell me you fed her beef."

Steak was the worst, but hamburger wasn't that great, either. Lily loved either one, but they both had too much grease and never seemed to agree with her sensitive digestion.

He nodded immediately. "Steak. But she seemed to really enjoy it."

Randi's worst fear realized. "Oh, she loves it. But if she eats more than a bite, she gets very . . . gassy."

"I fed her a lot. She'll get sick?" Evan's voice rose.

Hearing the panic in his tone, Randi held up her hand. "She won't be sick. Beef isn't going to kill her. But she'll be farting the whole day like this."

He looked totally unfazed by that news. "That's okay, then. I just hope she isn't uncomfortable. I didn't know."

Randi wrinkled her nose as a new round of stink bombs exploded in the kitchen. She watched as Lily walked over to Evan and plopped right next to him, looking up at him with hero worship in her soulful brown eyes. Evan probably didn't know he'd gained her undying affection once he'd given her the first piece of steak. Rather than walk away from the stench, Evan bent down and stroked the dog's head, looking relieved.

"I'm sorry, girl," he crooned in a deep, soothing voice.

Randi quickly doctored her coffee with cream and sugar so she could escape the stinky kitchen, realizing that the way Evan treated animals was just one more reason to like him.

Dammit!

CHAPTER 9

"Fuck! Evan never mentioned his childhood to any of us. No wonder we hardly ever saw him." Jared Sinclair's grip tightened around the mug of coffee he was holding. "Why didn't he tell us?"

"Maybe because we were all too involved in our own problems to notice that he had his own challenges. It was easier for him to just stay quiet," Grady observed from his position on the leather couch. "He's always been the one to take care of us, and I'm betting that he's not used to talking about his problems with anyone. I'm not saying it's fair. It's just not comfortable for Evan *not* to be in a position of control."

"No shit," Jared admitted, possibly because he was remembering the dark times in his life that he might not have survived if not for Evan.

Micah Sinclair felt just a little remorseful himself as he remembered a few jests he'd thrown at Evan, trying to take his pompous eldest cousin down a few notches. He liked Evan, he even understood him a little since he was an eldest son too, but he could never resist a poke at the arrogant, stuffy side of him. No doubt Evan *was* arrogant, but maybe not quite as much as Micah had previously believed. Oh hell, honestly, his cousin definitely *was* a cocky bastard, but not quite for the reasons he'd imagined.

He looked at the three men sitting with him in Jared's living room, all of them pretty somber about Hope's earlier revelations regarding the things none of them had known about Evan. The women had retreated upstairs to finish up plans for Hope's party. The guys were still trying to make sense of Evan's silence.

Hope had said that Evan had never asked her not to share, and she thought that everyone should know about the issues he had dealt with while he was growing up. Micah was pretty sure Evan's omission didn't mean he had wanted his sister to tell the whole family about his problems. In fact, knowing Evan, he never wanted anyone to know at all. Micah could relate to feeling that way. But Hope had taken a chance and shared what she knew about Evan because she cared about him.

Hope just wants all of her family back together and whole after what they experienced earlier in their life.

Micah knew how she felt. Right now, his own immediate family was so torn apart that he was pretty sure nothing would or could put them back together again.

Looking at how far his cousins had come to being a complete family again, Micah envied them. He rarely saw Julian because he'd been in Hollywood for so long trying to make a name for himself. And Xander . . . his youngest brother seemed to have a death wish; it appeared that he simply didn't care if he lived or died.

He mourned the days when all three of them had been close, thinking no amount of distance would ever tear them apart. Admittedly, distance hadn't been the only thing that had separated them; one nightmare tragedy was the biggest factor. They'd all handled it differently, and separately. The one who had come out of it the worst was Xander, and Micah still wasn't sure his youngest brother would recover from his emotional and physical wounds.

Looking around the room, he noticed that the men, and now their brother-in-law, Jason, were deep in conversation about how they could help Evan. Grady and Jared were in a heated conversation, with Jason throwing in his occasional opinions. Dante was out handling calls and checking on the elderly in the community because he was a police detective, and the force here in Amesport was fairly small. Micah had no doubt that it would be even more chaotic if Dante were here.

Micah stood, knowing he had to get back to the guesthouse to make a couple of calls. He'd decided to stay until the party on Saturday night, but he still had to conduct business while he was away from his company.

A big part of him wanted to stay, wanted to keep talking to his cousins. He'd felt more relaxed being here with his extended family than he'd experienced in a long time. But he had responsibilities to his own siblings, and he couldn't ignore them any longer.

Julian had delayed his arrival since he couldn't get through the bad weather, but he should get here by Friday night. Even so, Micah knew he wouldn't share many of his burdens with Julian, who was finally accomplishing everything he'd ever dreamed about in the film industry. He deserved his time to bask in the limelight without worrying about his family right now.

Bidding the guys good-bye during a rare moment of silence, Micah ducked out the sliding rear door and sprinted to the guesthouse, the cold wind whipping around him as he covered the short distance to the smaller house.

Closing the door quickly behind him as he entered to block out the wind, he leaned against it, still in awe of the winter storm they were experiencing.

It should make him feel gloomy or at least a little bit on edge. Instead, it exhilarated him, made the adrenaline pump through his body just a little harder. He was a risk-taker, an adrenaline junkie. Although he'd stopped some of the crazy things he'd done when he was a little younger, he still took calculated risks. For him, there was no better feeling than accomplishing something that had previously been considered impossible.

Pulling the sweatshirt over his head, he moved toward the bathroom, knowing he really needed a shower. He'd popped over to Jared's house because Hope had asked him to come over for a few minutes so he could join the conversation about Evan. He'd grabbed coffee next door, but he hadn't had a chance to shower before he went to the big house.

He turned on the water and stripped off the rest of his clothes, wadded them into a bundle, and shot them across the bathroom, raising his arm in victory as they all landed squarely in the hamper. "Two points," he announced to himself, grinning as he opened the shower door and stepped into the enclosed space.

Tempted to linger because the hot water felt so incredibly good, Micah forced himself to make short work of showering so he could get to work. Punching the rounded handle that shut off the water completely when he was done, he turned to push the door open, but ended up stopping short before shoving the shower entrance open.

Completely nude, water dripping from his body, Micah stood stock-still as he heard someone singing very close to the shower.

Who in the hell is that?

Listening closer, he noticed the voice was a clear soprano, and that she was slightly off-key. It didn't seem to matter to the songbird. Her voice got louder and surer of herself as she reached a crescendo in the composition.

What. The. Fuck.

Was somebody crazy trying to rob the house? How many cat burglars struck during a blizzard and sang badly at the tops of their lungs?

More curious than afraid, Micah pushed slowly on the door and slipped silently out of the shower.

She was there, right in front of him, her shapely ass in the air as she cleaned the toilet. He was looking directly at her rear end, as her back was to him.

He grabbed a towel off the bar. "Could you wait until I'm finished?" he rasped, wondering what had possessed her to start cleaning the bathroom with him in the shower. He didn't know her. Micah never forgot a great ass, and he didn't remember ever seeing someone with hair that spectacularly blonde. It was made up of several different shades, from honey to platinum.

She didn't respond, never hesitated at the sound of his voice.

Micah got irritated as he quickly dried his body. "Did you hear me? Jesus, woman. Are you hard of hearing?"

Pissed off at her lack of response, he reached forward and grasped her upper arm and swung her around. "I've been trying to talk to you. Don't ignore me. Are you fucking deaf?" He couldn't figure out her intentions, but they couldn't be good.

Strangely, he was disappointed when she stopped singing and started screaming, her eyes focused on his mouth.

"Stop it. I'm not hurting you. *You* broke into *my* home."

She stopped shrieking after the initial shock of seeing him wore off and stared at him from the top of his head to his toes, her eyes growing wide as she perused his nude body thoroughly.

Having no problem with being naked, he let her look her fill before he wrapped the bath towel around his waist. "What in the fuck are you doing here? What do you want?" Women always wanted something from him.

She looked at him for a moment before speaking carefully. "Yes, as a matter of fact, I am *fucking* deaf." She signed to him as she spoke, probably out of habit. "I didn't know you were here. I couldn't hear you."

Micah looked at the smoked glass of the shower and realized that she hadn't been able to detect his presence. Looking at her directly so she could read his lips, feeling like a dick, he answered, "I'm sorry I scared you. Why are you here?" He signed the words as well as spoke them aloud.

One of his best friends was hearing impaired, and although he was a little bit rusty, Micah knew sign language fairly well.

"I clean here. Jared pays me to keep up all of the homes on the Peninsula when they aren't occupied. My brother and I own a restaurant in town, but it's slow in the winter. I do this on the side." She removed her rubber gloves and placed them in a bucket on the floor, and then held out her hand. "I'm Tessa Sullivan."

Micah took her offered hand and held on to it a little longer than he should have, his eyes trained on her delicate features and beautiful, curly hair. God, she was gorgeous, now that he could see her clearly. "Micah Sinclair. Jared's cousin."

For some reason, now that he could see her face, she looked familiar, yet he knew they'd never met. He wouldn't have forgotten her if they'd met before.

"I'm sorry. I didn't know you had made it in before the storm. I usually clean the bathrooms first, or I probably would have seen your belongings. Are you the daredevil or the famous movie actor?" She pulled her hand away and smiled at him, a genuine grin that didn't have a trace of deception or pretense. "I haven't seen the movie that made one of Hope's cousins a star yet."

For once in his life, Micah found himself dumbfounded. Her unguarded smile made his cock spring to attention, and he had a sudden urge to take off her clothes and bend her over the bathroom vanity to relieve the throbbing his dick was experiencing at the moment. He wanted to absorb all of the warmth he could sense in her smile.

He felt like a complete jerk for having yelled at her. Of course, she hadn't heard him—or his irritation at her presence. "Extreme sports," Micah corrected, getting more turned on as she stared innocently at his mouth.

Of course she's looking at my lips. It's her only way of understanding me.

Micah didn't consider himself a daredevil anymore at all. In truth, he never had. He still took some risks, but his main focus now was on business. Extreme sports were lucrative, and his business provided the best equipment for people in their fields. He took pride in the fact that he made some dangerous sports safer.

She nodded to acknowledge his correction. "You're the thrill seeker. I've heard a lot about you and your brothers from Mara."

"It's a profession that's made me very rich," Micah answered brusquely, annoyed that he was actually defending his business.

Why do I care?

He didn't. Not really. He'd been called worse for some of the things he'd done in the past, and her expression wasn't making a mockery of his company. Still, having her dismiss what he did was pissing him off. He wasn't sure why . . . but it did.

"Is there a Sinclair who isn't rich?" she asked, a twinkle in her eyes.

"There's probably plenty of them, but none with our DNA," Micah admitted, still staring at her like a horny teenager.

She snorted, a sound that was probably actually a laugh. Micah smiled because, coming from her, the noise was enchanting.

"How did you get here?" The weather was horrible, and he didn't like the idea of her on the road when it was so brutal outside.

"I drove. I'm deaf, not stupid or incapable of performing simple tasks." Propping her hands on her hips, she stared at him stubbornly.

"That's not what I meant. In case you haven't noticed, there's a blizzard outside," Micah informed her sarcastically, only realizing after he made the statement that she wouldn't hear the censure in his voice.

She shrugged. "I've lived here all my life, and I have an apartment near the Peninsula. I knew the roads would be okay here since the Sinclairs have their own plow service."

"And you call me the daredevil," he grumbled, not quite understanding how she could see to drive on the roads right now. She was right. The road was constantly being cleared, but the visibility was almost zero.

"I know the roads here like the back of my hand. I could probably drive them blind."

She was already driving them deaf, and he shuddered at the prospect of her being on the roads at all right now.

"It's not safe to be outside right now," he told her irritably.

"I'm not outside right now," she returned reasonably.

"I'll go get dressed, and then I'll drive you home. The house is fine. You don't have to clean right now." Having her around would distract the hell out of him.

"It's fine. I'll go." Tessa hurriedly gathered her cleaning products and shot out the door.

Micah sprinted to his bedroom and pulled on a clean pair of jeans and an old sweatshirt. He was taming his hair with his fingers as he walked back out to the living room.

Everything was quiet; the only sound he heard was the whistling of the wind.

"Tessa," he bellowed angrily before realizing that she wouldn't hear him. "Fuck!"

Micah tugged on his boots and raced outside via the front door. There were no unidentified vehicles in Jared's driveway.

Tessa was gone.

CHAPTER 10

I have to tell her. I will tell her—very soon.

Evan sat in his downstairs office with Randi's champion farter dog, wondering *when* in the hell he was going to tell her that he was her mystery emailer. He wanted to, he needed to, but what if they couldn't communicate as well face-to-face as they did via email?

What if she panicked? What if she thought he was a jerk for not telling her that he, S., was actually Evan Sinclair long ago? Maybe she'd feel betrayed that he hadn't corrected her assumption that S. was just some person who worked for the Sinclair Fund. Okay . . . maybe he'd even lied to let her keep thinking he was a normal guy. He'd lose both of them, his best friend and the woman he wanted more than he'd ever wanted another female in his life. Okay, yes, they were the same person, but that made it all the more difficult for Evan to tell the truth. There was twice as much at stake.

Evan had already blended the two women together, seeing so much of the Randi he was getting to know in person in her mysterious emails.

Heaving a frustrated sigh, he leaned back in his comfortable office chair and put his hand on Lily's head, stroking her silky fur without even thinking about it. Randi had fallen asleep on the couch after working on some things for her teaching job, and Lily had followed him down to his office. He was beginning to become accustomed to having a dog in the house, and, to his surprise, he was starting to like Lily's company. It was funny how the animal seemed ecstatically happy just because she got affection and food. Really, dogs were fairly easy to please.

Evan didn't want to admit he'd spent far too long just watching Randi sleep, fighting the temptation to touch her, move to the couch and strip off her clothing so that he could slake the frustrated, animalistic urges he kept experiencing to claim her—hard and completely.

"I'll tell her pretty soon," he whispered huskily to Lily. The dog looked up at him, her eyes dark and serious as she cocked her head sideways as though she understood. "Is she going to be pissed?" he questioned the canine as Lily looked at him with an empathic gaze.

Fuck! I can't believe I'm talking to a dog.

Evan knew he had it pretty bad if he was using a golden retriever as his advice counselor. But he was way out of his comfort zone right now, and he was uncertain as to what the hell to do.

He could talk to his brothers, but they'd probably give him hell, and rightfully so. When they were wooing their women, he hadn't exactly been there for them and sympathetic. He'd been the one to try to discourage both Dante and Grady from marrying so quickly, and he'd been a real bastard to Jared when Evan had actually wanted him to get together with Mara.

Hope had told him to fess up to Randi immediately and see where things went from there. She said if they already had good communication, things would evolve.

He hadn't taken his sister's advice, holding off on telling Randi the truth. The longer he procrastinated, the harder it was going to be to blurt out the secret. He knew it, but his concern about her reaction held him back.

Maybe the sexual part of their relationship had developed too quickly, but Evan couldn't regret the most earth-shattering night of his life even if he tried—and he didn't want to. He and Randi had been circling around each other with sparks flying since the first time they'd met. Honestly, he'd thought that maybe once they'd fucked each other senseless, the gut ache he had every time he saw her would go away.

It hadn't.

Now he was pretty sure he had a full-blown ulcer eating away at his stomach every time he looked at her.

Opening his desk drawer, he pulled out a roll of antacids and popped several of them into his mouth. The way he'd been popping the chewable pills since he'd found out he was going to have to see Randi again, he really needed to think about buying stock in the company.

"She's so damn beautiful," he shared with Lily quietly as he swallowed the chalky substance that he hoped would take away the burning ache in his chest and his gut.

Snapping out of his fixation with Randi long enough to shut down his computer, Evan decided he wasn't going to be able to work. He was too damn distracted. He'd go check out the weather and see if Randi was awake. It was getting to be late afternoon and she still hadn't eaten anything.

He stood and brushed down the soft denim of the jeans he was wearing. Really, the casual clothes that Hope had bought for him after they'd visited the supermarket weren't all that bad. In fact, he was pretty comfortable. The sweater was warm, and it was nice not to have a shirt and tie around his neck. Granted, it felt strange, but not altogether unwelcome. The only time he hated the jeans was when his dick got hard, which was almost every time he saw or thought about Randi. The material had very little give, and for a man his size, an erection was highly uncomfortable pressing against the unforgiving fabric.

Hope had taken him shopping after they'd bought groceries, telling him he needed to loosen up and try to make himself more approachable with some casual clothing. He was willing to do just about anything to get Randi to communicate better with him, even if it meant giving up his usual attire. The items weren't as well made as his usual clothing, but if it meant getting Randi to notice him as something other than an asshole, he'd wear them.

He was just opening the office door when he heard an audible scream from upstairs.

Miranda!

A cold chill raced down his spine, and he sprinted up the steps like an Olympic champion, his heart racing as he imagined someone hurting her . . . or worse.

He came to an awkward, abrupt stop as he saw that she was still sleeping on the couch, but her body was flailing restlessly on the leather.

"I'm not a whore. I'm not a whore," she kept repeating in a muffled voice. "No. Please. I can't."

She was whimpering now, and the sound of her distress tore straight through Evan's heart. She was dreaming, but what in the hell was her nightmare about?

As if she'd experienced her mistress's bad dreams before, Lily approached Randi cautiously and started to lick her face.

"Nooooooo!" The tortured sound that escaped from Randi's lips was a combination of a scream and a plea.

Evan sucked breath into his lungs painfully as he moved forward just as Lily launched herself onto Randi's legs and her mistress sat up, panting. "Oh, God. Oh, God. Not again."

Evan waited for her to notice him, afraid of frightening her. She clutched her dog to her chest and fisted Lily's silky fur as she rested her forehead on top of the retriever's body.

"Lily," she said in a still-panicked, breathless voice, letting go of her death grip on her dog as she apparently recognized that she'd been dreaming.

Finally, he spoke quietly. "Are you okay?"

Randi continued stroking her dog absently as though it comforted her.

"Yes." Randi's voice sounded tremulous and anything *but* fine.

Unable to contain his fear, concern, and relentless desire to comfort her for another moment, Evan gently pulled the dog back to the floor and picked Randi up so he could sit and let her sprawl on his lap. Automatically, she wrapped her arms around his neck, and Evan rested her head on his shoulder while he stroked her silky, dark hair.

"What happened?" he asked soothingly. "I could hear you screaming from downstairs."

"Nightmare," she murmured into his sweater. "I'm sorry I disturbed you. I used to have them as a teenager, but I thought they were gone. I hadn't had one in years until Joan died. This is the second time it's happened since. I think maybe they were triggered because I'm alone again."

She's not alone. She has me.

He tried to curb the fierce longing to make her understand that she wasn't without somebody who cared just because her foster mother was gone now.

"What were you dreaming about?" Evan tried to keep his tone even, but he hated anything that frightened her, even if it was only a dream. "Why were you denying that you were a whore?"

"Long story," she said anxiously. "The dreams are left over from a long time ago. It's over."

"Talk to me, Randi. Please." Evan intentionally used her nickname, sensing that whatever was bothering her was attached to her childhood and maybe her mother. If her memories were this frightening, he vowed to never again call her by anything *other* than her nickname. "Tell me about your life before you came to Amesport."

"My mother did bad things. I did bad things," Randi told him in a warning voice.

"I don't give a shit what your mother did. You aren't your mother, and you were just a kid. Tell me," Evan cajoled.

"My mother was a hooker."

Evan could feel Randi's body shudder as she made the confession.

Randi continued in a rush, "She was a prostitute for as long as I can remember. She was only sixteen when I was born, and I never knew who my father was—probably one of her . . . clients. We had a small apartment near her corner, but I didn't see her very much. There were quite a few other prostitutes who lived in the same building, worked the same general area, and they took turns visiting me. Sometimes they brought me food. They were kind to me when they didn't have to be. I wasn't their kid."

Evan's grip tightened in Randi's hair, his entire body shuddering with anger as he thought about a child growing up in those kinds of conditions. "What happened?"

I have to stay calm. This is about her and not me. She needs me right now.

And damned if he didn't want her to need him.

"One of the ladies helped me register for school, and I went every day. I don't remember anything much before early grade school."

"Did your mother bring her men back to your apartment?"

"No. She'd leave, sometimes before I got home from school, and sometimes she wasn't home when I left in the morning."

Evan felt his temper flare even hotter, an unusual occurrence for him. Randi had basically raised herself, with the occasional help of some prostitutes? "How did you end up in Amesport? What were you dreaming about? Something that really happened?"

She nodded slowly against his shoulder. Her voice was unsteady as she continued. "When I was thirteen, my mother left and never came home. They found her body a week later. She was murdered, probably by one of her johns, but they never found the perpetrator."

Evan's anger ramped up another notch. "So you were alone?"

"When social services found out I existed, they took me into foster care."

Confused, he asked, "So you were adopted by the Tylers?"

"No. I was fostered to a family in Southern California. And then I ran away."

Evan knew there was something missing from her story. "What happened?" He knew she had a reason why she ran away. If she'd had any sense of stability after her chaotic childhood, she wouldn't have left.

"My foster father knew I was the daughter of a prostitute. He assumed I had the same skills as my mother," Randi told him quietly.

Evan felt a rage rise inside of him, a fury that he'd never experienced before. "He forced you? You were a child."

"My mother was a runaway. Some of the ladies start very young, usually a product of broken homes and abuse," Randi explained patiently. "He tried to shove his dick in my mouth. I had to fight my way out of the house. I left with nothing . . . not that I really had much as far as belongings were concerned anyway."

"They could have found you another home—"

"I was scared. I thought I was better off taking my chances on the streets than in foster care."

Evan could understand why. But it did nothing to calm the intensity of his fury for Randi and her previous circumstances as a child. "Tell me how you ended up here." He didn't want her to have to relive her past anymore. She might sound like she was over her childhood, but if she was still having nightmares, she was still holding on to some of the pain. If he could find the man who tried to violate her, he'd kill the bastard himself.

"I lived on the streets for a while, homeless. I stopped going to school. I did what I had to do to survive. One day, I was so hungry, so desperate, that I tried to steal a wallet from a tourist. The last thing I wanted to do was sell my body, but I knew I was getting close to going back to the ladies and begging them to take me in. I would have ended up doing whatever I needed to in order to survive." Randi's voice was tremulous as she recounted her desperation earlier in her life.

Evan took a deep breath, trying to focus on Randi instead of his own emotions. The thought of Randi coming so close to needing to sell her body to survive nearly made him come undone. "Did you succeed in getting the money you needed?" he asked, not giving a shit if she ripped off a hundred people to survive. She deserved a better life than what she'd been handed as a child . . . a life that sounded like a living hell.

"No." Her tone changed, her voice becoming melancholy and reflective. "The wallet I tried to steal belonged to Dennis Tyler."

"Your foster father?" Evan asked incredulously.

She nodded. "Dennis and Joan were on vacation for their anniversary. He caught me red-handed."

"He didn't turn you in to the police," Evan guessed, hoping he was right.

"Nope. He and Joan took me to the nearest restaurant and bought me something to eat. When they heard that I was homeless and what had happened to me, they brought me home with them to Amesport. Joan was a retired teacher, and she helped me catch up on my studies. It took me an entire summer of studying to be ready to start school here in the fall."

"But you did it," Evan replied, his admiration of her accomplishment clear in his voice. "How did Dennis and Joan manage the distance with foster care?"

"They lied," Randi explained bluntly. "They claimed to be distant relatives who had guardianship. Dennis was a retired principal at the school, and Joan was a teacher. They wanted to keep me here bad enough to do what they needed to do to get me into school." Randi's voice cracked, and tears started to fall down her cheeks. "Two people who had been upstanding citizens all their life lied and manufactured what they needed to keep a teenage kid from the streets. They didn't want to risk me going back into the system. They were already in their seventies at the time. None of us were sure what would happen if they told the truth and had to go through the legal system."

Evan was guessing probably nothing would have happened since she was an older child, and hard to adopt. Most likely, the Tylers could have adopted her if they'd pushed the system. But he imagined Randi would have had to go back to foster care at some time during the process since they took her illegally and out of state. He found himself being grateful for the Tylers' sacrifice and their lies. "How did you get their name?"

"I changed it legally once I was of age. They were the only parents I ever had, and I wanted to carry the same last name," Randi replied adamantly.

"I would have liked to have met them," Evan pondered, still pissed off that someone as special as the woman in his arms had grown up so rough. But he was in awe of her strength and her will to survive and thrive. How many kids like her ended up a respected teacher? Evan didn't have statistics, but he was guessing not very damn many.

Randi sighed. "You would have liked them. They were both very sensible people, but they gave me so much love," she answered wistfully.

"Why do you think the nightmares are back?" Evan barely got the question out, his outrage nearly making him mute at the moment.

"I think it's because Joan is gone. She was my rock for so long that I didn't realize how alone I'd feel without her. My foster parents gave me the education and the resources to live a better life, but I miss them so much," Randi said, sadness creeping into her voice.

Evan knew she wasn't without people who cared, but her loss was fueling her childhood insecurities. Although he'd never known the fear of not having a place to sleep or some food to eat, he understood that some fears were ingrained during those early years and could never completely be left behind. He was a perfect example to prove that theory.

It was no wonder she loved her food and ate like it was a religious experience. He guessed when you never knew where your next meal was coming from during your childhood, you savored every single thing you ate.

His chest tightened at the thought of Randi ever going hungry.

His gut wrenched as he thought about some filthy asshole trying to force her to perform sex acts when she was still a child.

I'll always protect her, make her feel safe.

She had *him* now, and if he held her close enough, maybe she'd feel more secure.

Wrapping his arms tightly around her waist, he vowed to stay with her as long as she'd let him, and he'd make damn sure she was secure.

Randi might not know it right now, but as long as he drew breath into his body, she'd never be afraid, alone, or lonely ever again.

Will she let me stay once she finds out I'm her email confidant?

Not wanting to risk the chance of losing her now, Evan rationalized that he needed to wait a little longer to tell her the truth.

CHAPTER 11

"What? You don't like cake?"

Randi looked at Evan with horror as he stared at the carrot cake on his plate like it was a venomous snake. First, he'd seemed unhappy that they were having spaghetti for dinner, mentioning it was loaded with carbs. But he'd eaten it like a man who was starving, and all of his complaints aside, Evan had managed to completely clean his plate. Now, he was eyeing the cake dubiously.

"I try to limit my sugar intake," Evan replied indifferently.

Randi took a large bite of her own cake, closing her eyes for just a moment as the taste of the rich cream-cheese frosting hit her taste buds. As she opened her eyes again, she stared at Evan like he was speaking a different language. She'd cheated on the spaghetti, doctoring up a ready-made sauce. But she'd made the cake completely from scratch. "Are you diabetic?" She'd never met a man who was in such spectacular shape watch every single thing he put into his mouth.

"No. I was a chubby kid. I was put on a stringent diet, and I haven't eaten much sugar since," he grumbled hesitantly.

His parents put him on a diet with absolutely no sweets? There were ways to encourage healthy food for children, but an occasional sweet wasn't going to make him overweight. "What did you eat?"

"Fish, lean meats, vegetables. The same things I eat now, for the most part."

"Were you really overweight?" It was almost an impossible diet for a kid to stick with, and she couldn't imagine being that drastic unless he had a very real problem.

Evan shrugged. "Not much. But I was getting chubby. In my father's eyes, I was fat. I didn't join the family for meals, and if I weighed in heavy, I didn't eat."

Randi's heart broke at the longing look in his eyes as he stared at the piece of cake on the plate in front of him. He was stuck in his own fear of eating anything outside of his normal. She'd already realized he was obsessively regimented in his routine. "Evan, you obviously work out, and you don't have an ounce of spare flesh on your body." She could attest to *that*. "It isn't going to kill you to live a little occasionally."

Getting up from her place at the large dining-room table next to him, she picked up his fork and slowly speared him a large bite of the cake. "Open."

He opened his mouth willingly, giving her the opportunity to feed him the cake. She watched as he chewed and swallowed, his eyes closed so he could savor the treat.

"Good?" she asked cautiously.

He chewed and swallowed before answering. "Fucking incredible."

Randi knew what it was like to experience great food after being deprived of it for so long. Maybe Evan had never had to scramble for food like she had, but he had definitely been forced to give up eating anything just for pleasure.

Making him push his chair back from the table as she seated herself on his lap, Randi took a bite of the cake herself. "Joan's recipe," she told him after she swallowed.

She offered him another bite, sharing the piece of cake with him. His eyes were lit with blue flames; his intense gaze stayed fixed on her face as he accepted her offering without hesitation. Randi smiled at him, feeling victorious because he so obviously wanted the sweet but was too afraid to break his rigid routine.

They ate in silence for a few moments before Evan took the empty plate and utensil from her hands and carelessly tossed both onto the table.

"That was fantastic. But now I desperately have to taste *you*," he snarled, his face contorting to a look of frenzied need.

An electric, piercing shiver ran down her spine as she felt herself hefted up into his arms as he stood. He didn't hesitate as he took the stairs, carrying her weight like it was nothing.

She wasn't going to pretend, not with Evan. She needed him right now just as fiercely as he needed her. Desire was growing hot in her belly, and her core was already tingling and saturated just from anticipating his touch.

"I need you," Randi admitted shakily as he lowered her to her feet.

Evan might be opinionated on almost everything, but he also accepted her for exactly who she was, ugly past and all. He hadn't batted an eyelash when she'd confessed that her mother had been a prostitute, and he hadn't shied away. Gently, sweetly, he'd tried to comfort her, make her feel safe again after her nightmare, and she'd never seen one single sign that he thought any less of her after her confession.

"I know, sweetheart. I need you, too. I need to show you that you're mine now," he growled. "Undress for me, or I'll end up ripping your pretty underwear to shreds."

His possessive, dominant words ramped up her desire as nothing else possibly could. It should have been frightening, and it probably would have been if it had come from anyone other than Evan. But right now, his words were a vocal declaration of the same need that was reverberating deep inside her soul.

She wanted to be his; she wanted him to belong to her. The emotions were primal and predatory, strangely feeling as natural as breathing at the moment.

Randi usually went for the more delicate and pretty pastels in her underwear choices rather than the sultry, sexy lingerie made to actually inspire lust, but Evan didn't seem to care. "They really aren't all that sexy," she answered, suddenly nervous.

It wasn't that she didn't trust Evan, but she'd never seen the wild look in his eyes that was now bared to her. He seemed . . . completely raw, and he was breathtaking when he was like this. She watched with her fingers on the zipper of her jeans as he steadily tore at his own clothing until he stood before her completely naked.

"Oh, God. You *are* beautiful," she whispered breathlessly, taking in every rippling muscle and what seemed like an enormous amount of bare skin, touchable skin. In complete daylight, she could see several faded scars on his shoulders and chest. "Turn around," she demanded as she shucked off her jeans, any self-consciousness she had experienced now gone.

"I'd rather not," Evan commented around his clenched jaw, his blue eyes flashing with anger and intense arousal.

Maybe she should have been afraid of his ferocity, but she wasn't. She knew his anger didn't lie with her, and he was man enough that he wasn't going to take it out on the wrong person. Evan was self-contained and cautious. What she was seeing right now wasn't something he showed to anyone. He was baring himself to her because he trusted her, at least a little. That knowledge spurred Randi on.

"Please," she begged, knowing that this was something Evan had to get through himself, another hurdle he needed to jump. Unfortunately, she suspected it would be much harder than eating sweets or wearing more casual clothing when he wasn't working.

She pulled her sweater over her head as she waited and held her breath.

He eyed her hungrily before slowly starting to turn around, and Randi released her breath in a rush.

The scars weren't horrible; they weren't even that noticeable at first glance. But as Randi moved closer, she traced every faded line across his back and butt, and noticed they marked the backs of his thighs as well. His heavy muscles convulsed beneath her fingers as she touched every mark.

Why? I don't understand why a parent has to beat a child. I know his father was a horrible man, but Hope never mentioned being beaten. I assumed he was just verbally abusive and treated them all like shit.

As the eldest male Sinclair, obviously the entire focus had been on Evan, and in some of the cruelest ways to a child.

Tears started to flow down her cheeks rapidly, but she ignored her own emotions. What had Evan's life been like as a child? He'd been barely fed, and apparently beaten so badly that the faint marks were still present years later. What kind of monster did that to a child? His father had separated Evan from the rest of the family to use as a tool for his own brutality.

"Bastard!" Randi said aloud, her voice raspy because of her tears. "If your father wasn't already dead, I'd cut his balls off and shove them down his throat." The more scars she found, the angrier she got. Her growing up had been tough, but not like this.

"Are you actually . . . upset for me?" Evan asked in a low, hoarse voice.

Yeah. Maybe he didn't know what it was like for someone to be outraged at what had happened to him, but she was absolutely standing up for the child he'd once been. "Yes."

"It was a long time ago," he replied calmly, strangely sounding like *he* wanted to comfort *her*.

Randi dropped to her knees and discovered every scar on his thighs and calves. "It doesn't matter. He was a damn monster. Did he do this to all of the kids?"

"No. Not to the same extent. But the mental abuse he heaped on everyone was worse than the physical."

Randi heard the hesitation in his voice as he answered, making her suspicious. "You did that on purpose. You let him beat the shit out of you so he didn't do it to the other kids." She knew she was right. Evan was a dedicated protector. He wouldn't have done anything else.

"I can't deny that it occurred to me that if I was his target of displeasure, he'd leave the others alone," he agreed reluctantly.

Of course it did. "And did it work?"

"For the most part. He was an asshole, and after I left home for college, he started picking on Grady more than he ever did before. I noticed it when I was home for Christmas, and I was going to have a discussion with him, but then he died."

She sensed relief in his tone, knowing that Evan had probably planned on more than just *discussing* his father's treatment of his younger brother. It would have been nice if Evan had gotten the opportunity to beat the crap out of his father, but it was better that the asshole had died. A physical confrontation between Evan and his father would have been difficult for the entire family.

"It's over now, Evan." She didn't want him to relive any of those memories again. "You're strong and gorgeous." Randi cupped his tight ass and brought her mouth to some of the faint lines at his lower back.

"Don't!" Evan protested, turning around and glaring down at her. "Don't feel sorry for me."

"I don't," she told him honestly, looking up into his intense glare. "I just . . . care." Evan would hate pity from anyone, which was probably why he'd never shared his past.

The expression on his face softened slightly. "Okay, then," he finally answered, sounding somewhat perplexed.

She brought her mouth to his ripped abs, using her tongue to trace the delineated muscles there.

The taut flesh of his stomach became impossibly harder as it flexed under her touch. Leaning back, she traced the sexy, dark, happy trail that led to one enormously rigid cock.

It's time.

This was a moment she couldn't let pass to put to rest some of the ghosts of her past, and show Evan that he was the most desirable man she'd ever met.

Slowly, she opened her mouth, flicking the bead of moisture off the mushroomed head of his member, savoring the taste of Evan.

It wasn't scary.

It wasn't repugnant.

It was divine.

All thoughts of her traumatic childhood experience fled as she experienced the forceful essence of Evan Sinclair. There was no mistaking the feel of him, the taste of him. Opening her mouth, she slid her tongue along the underside of his enormous cock, and wrapped her right hand around the base. He felt like hard steel covered in a silky softness that was impossible not to touch.

"Randi," Evan groaned. "Don't. You don't like it."

Her heart clenched as she heard his tortured words, his willingness to give up something that obviously felt so good, because of her fear. It elevated her own arousal to a level she'd never experienced before. Letting him pop out of her mouth momentarily, she answered, looking him directly in the eyes. "Maybe with you I do. Let me, Evan. It's pretty hot."

She watched him as her mouth enveloped him again, deeper this time. His head fell back and he closed his eyes in what appeared to be carnal bliss.

"You're killing me," he rasped.

Randi gained confidence quickly at a skill with which she had very little experience. Following Evan's vocal cues, she used her hand and mouth to taste him, mimic the act of sex by applying suction and using her tongue on the sensitive head of his cock.

His breathing was rough and ragged as she gently cupped his balls with one hand and splayed the other on his rock-hard ass to keep him close. The erotic, low, animalistic sounds escaping his mouth ravaged her senses and spoke to a portion of her soul that felt connected to him and the pain of his past.

She didn't flinch when he speared his hands through her hair and guided her mouth where he wanted it, and at the pace he seemed to need.

"I. Can't. Stop. It." His words sounded desperate and husky with need.

Don't stop it, Evan. For once in your life, let go.

Randi closed her eyes and savored the sensual connection she had with Evan at that moment, knowing he was about to find release.

"Fuck, baby! I'm going to come," Evan warned her.

Yes. Yes. Yes.

Randi was elated as she held on to him, even though he tried to push her away. His heated release flooded her throat, and she greedily accepted it, relishing the fact that she could bring this big, strong, proud man almost to his knees.

She took her time making sure she licked every drop of his orgasm from his cock, savoring his groans of approval.

Finally, he grasped her arms and pulled her to her feet.

"Why?" he asked hoarsely, his eyes as stormy as the sea right now.

She didn't pretend she didn't understand, because she did. "It felt right. You taste delicious." She licked her lips just to watch what would happen.

She wasn't disappointed. He picked her up bodily with a hungry look and dropped her on the bed.

"Did giving me head turn you on?" he asked seriously.

"More than I ever thought possible," Randi admitted.

He climbed onto the bed. "I'll fantasize about that beautiful mouth around my cock for the rest of my damn life," Evan said, partly in awe, but with a trace of self-deprecation.

Randi knew she'd remember everything they'd done together, the closeness they were experiencing. No sexual experience in her past had even come anywhere near the ecstasy she'd found with Evan. Being with him was dangerous and highly addictive.

"I need you," she whispered faintly, staring at Evan with a pleading look.

"You have me," he answered immediately.

"Show me more of what it's like to have mind-blowing sex?" she requested softly. "It's never been like this for me before," she revealed truthfully.

Evan let out a rusty chuckle. "And you think I'm an expert? It's never been like this for me, either. But I will admit that I practiced a lot. I think I was just waiting for you."

Her heart skittered as Evan reached for the front clasp of her lacy bra.

He stared at the garment as he gently removed it, pulling her arms from the straps before tossing it to the ground. "You're wrong, you know," he informed her. "The lingerie you wear is the sexiest I've ever seen. I love the soft colors and the delicacy of the lace. So sweet, but I know what's hidden underneath is even sweeter."

He laid her back on his pillow and knelt between her legs, his eyes devouring her. Leaning forward, he cupped her breasts. She wasn't well-endowed, and he could hold one orb in each hand.

"Perfect," he said gutturally.

She quivered as his thumbs traced her nipples, and she murmured his name as he slid into a position on top of her so he could take one of her nipples in his mouth. "Evan." She said his name with an erotic sigh.

Randi sifted her hands into his hair, arching her back as Evan bit gently on her left nipple and took his time soothing it with his tongue.

He moved back and forth, one breast to the other. Nipping. Soothing. Caressing.

"Evan, please," Randi pleaded when she felt like she couldn't take any more, loving the way he was making her feel, but needing more.

Gently, he put a finger to her lips and moved his big body to her side so he could touch her. "I have to watch you come," he told her in a voice rough with emotion.

Her pussy flooded, and her skin began to flush all over as his hand moved down her belly and slid between her thighs. Randi opened to him immediately, needing his touch desperately.

Delving beneath the elastic of her panties, he teased her clit with expert fingers, circling around it before giving her what she needed, and then starting all over again. Before she could climax, he'd back off and tease her again into a state of pure arousal. His mouth continued to erotically torture her breasts.

Randi thrashed her head, feeling like she was in torment and desperate to come. She closed her eyes, seeing a kaleidoscope of color flash beneath her eyelids. "Yes. Please, yes. Don't stop."

Evan replaced his mouth with his fingers teasing her nipples, putting his lips beside her ear. "Come for me, Randi. You look so beautiful when you're finding your release. I want to see it. I want to know it's me who put that beautiful look on your face," he said in a husky, seductive whisper, the heat of his breath wafting over her ear.

He was playing her body perfectly, superbly, sending an electric jolt right to her core. Her climax didn't come in a rush, because Evan didn't want it to. She tossed her head back and panted, feeling the slow approach of euphoria.

Her orgasm was different this time, her body tingling from her scalp to her toes as waves of sensual pleasure washed over her. It seemed to last forever; it wasn't long enough. Randi moaned uncontrollably as she let go, undulating her hips against his fingers.

"Beautiful," Evan said hoarsely. "You're so damn beautiful."

She felt like she was floating by the time her body recovered, Evan still stroking lightly between her saturated folds.

Her pussy convulsed in anticipation as he knelt between her legs. Wordlessly, he yanked her panties down her legs and tossed them on the floor. He flipped her onto her stomach, pulled her hips up, and buried his cock to the hilt.

Randi's channel stretched to accept him, her muscles protesting at first at the abrupt invasion at a different angle.

"Mine!" Evan growled possessively, his hands at her hips firmly holding her in place.

She gasped and moved to her hands and knees to accommodate Evan, her heart lurching as she realized that he was claiming her like a caveman.

It was the biggest turn-on she'd ever experienced. She wanted to be taken just like this: hard, demanding, animalistic, and wild as hell.

He started to move, his thrusts growing stronger and harder, his breathing ragged with arousal.

"You're mine. Say it," Evan demanded as he thrust into her again and again.

Randi was mute, silent because she was unable to voice the words. Her body was so agitated, ready to incinerate at any moment, and all she could do was push her hips back against him, begging wordlessly for his ferocious possession.

"Say it," he commanded again, this time slipping his hand between her thighs to tease her clit.

"Yes, dammit. Yes." Randi knew she was screaming, but her body was reaching a pinnacle that she desperately needed. Evan's feral, carnal claiming was driving her insane.

She needed to be closer. "Harder," she insisted, slamming her hips back as he entered her. "More."

He bent down and lightly bit the vulnerable nape of her neck where her hair had parted and fallen around her face.

Her climax came with blinding electricity that had her lowering her head and screaming into Evan's pillow.

"Don't," he demanded, lifting his mouth from the love bite and pulling her hair gently. "I want to hear your pleasure."

Her channel clamped down hard on his cock, which was pistoning into her at an almost impossible pace.

"Fuck. Randi." Evan released a strangled sound between a yell and groan before he relaxed above her, supporting himself on his arms as she sank completely down on the bed.

She almost purred when he moved to her side and pulled her against his damp body, cuddling her against him.

"Shit! I didn't use a condom." Evan's voice sounded uncharacteristically panicked.

Randi rolled slightly so she could see his face. Her heart sank when she saw the terrified look in his eyes. "I'm on birth control. You're safe." She'd started in college, and since it helped her periods, she'd stayed on the pill.

Noticing the look of relief on his face made her heart sink even further.

Of course he doesn't want to get the hooker's daughter knocked up. He's a billionaire. Too much at stake for him.

"I'm clean," he said in a rush. "I've been tested, and that's the first time I've had sex with any woman without a condom."

"You're safe with me," Randi replied flatly. "I've been checked out, too, and I haven't been with anybody since."

"I wasn't as concerned about that as I was about you getting pregnant," Evan shared blandly.

After what they had shared, hearing him say those words hurt. Logically, Randi understood his concern, but it slapped her back into reality.

This is nothing but a fling. Enjoy it, but don't get emotionally involved. It's sexual. You're both scratching an itch.

She moved to the side of the bed and got up, headed for the bathroom.

"Where are you going?" Evan asked gruffly, sounding unhappy.

"I think I'll take a bath in your enormous bathtub," she replied, reminding herself that she'd wanted to use it before she left.

"Want company?" he asked suggestively, his tone hopeful.

"I think I can handle it alone," she answered in a monotone voice, needing to hold it together until she made it out of the room.

He didn't answer, and Randi didn't expect him to.

Not a single tear leaked from her eyes until she closed and locked the bathroom door.

CHAPTER 12

The storm lost strength later that night, and Randi headed home the next morning, after Dante had called to let her know the power was back on at her house.

Restless even after his workout, Evan had headed over to Grady's house on foot, needing an outlet for his troubled state of mind.

"I don't know what I did wrong," he told his brothers as they all sat around Grady's table with a mug of coffee in front of each of them. He'd decided to confess everything about his relationship with Randi, hoping they could help. He'd risk all of them making jokes if he could get some information on the way a woman's mind worked. There was nothing he wanted more than to make Randi happy.

"Talk to her?" Grady suggested. "I'm beginning to learn that gifts don't really work with women when they're angry."

"He needs to figure out what he did wrong first," Jared observed, frowning as he tried to figure out the problem.

"What exactly did you say to her that pissed her off?" Dante asked curiously.

Evan looked around the table, and every one of his brothers' expressions was humorless. They were actually trying to be helpful . . . which surprised the hell out of him.

He'd been a little taken aback when all of his brothers had turned up at Grady's house soon after he arrived. Dante was dressed for work, but said he had time to kill before leaving since he'd worked straight through the crisis of the blizzard. Jared gave no real excuse for why he had wandered over.

Evan was willing to bet that Grady had called and asked his brothers to drop over because he was here, but he had no idea why.

But all of them seemed ready to give advice, so he didn't give a damn why they were all here.

"I don't even know what kind of flowers she likes, and I don't know what I did wrong. She just . . . changed." He'd thought about sending her flowers, and it annoyed him that he didn't know her favorites.

"What happened before she transformed?" Grady asked solemnly.

"We had incredible sex without a condom," Evan admitted reluctantly, hating to share anything personal between him and Randi with anyone. But he was desperate.

"And then what?" Dante queried after taking a slug of his coffee.

"I told her I was relieved that she was on the pill and wouldn't get pregnant." It was a normal response as far as Evan was concerned.

"No way!"

"Holy shit!"

Dante chimed in, "You might as well have told her you just wanted to get laid."

"Well, I did . . . kind of," Evan replied, squirming in his chair uncomfortably. "But only because I really like her and I'm attracted to her. But I don't ever want to have a child."

"Why?" Jared asked quietly. "Because of your disability?"

Evan's head shot up, his expression anxious. "Hope told you." He had no doubt where their enlightenment came from.

"She told us everything. You could have told us, Evan. Damn, I took enough crap from the old man. He must have made your life a living hell," Grady grumbled.

They had no idea just how bad it had been, and Evan wasn't going to apprise them of the details. "I lived. But the problem does seem to be hereditary."

"Your kid won't have our father," Dante reminded him. "He or she would have you." He hesitated before adding, "Randi loves kids. Maybe she doesn't want to have some of her own now, but hearing how relieved you were could have been mistaken for a lack of interest in anything other than sex. Did you explain?"

Evan shook his head slowly, contrite that he might have inadvertently given Randi the idea that she wouldn't have been a fit mother for any child he fathered. She'd completely misunderstood if that was the case. In reality, he was terrified of fathering a child with *any* woman, and he didn't want to talk about it. Trying to change the subject, he asked, "Any advice on what I can do to make her understand?"

"Grovel?" Jared suggested.

"Talk to her. Tell her the truth about everything," Grady remarked.

"Make her realize that you care about more than just getting laid," Dante replied sensibly. "You do care about her, right?"

Evan looked at Dante and nodded slowly. There was no reason to deny it anymore. Just thinking about the fact that he had obviously hurt Randi with his comments made his gut ache so much that he reached into his pocket and popped a few of his ever-ready antacids. He was getting to the point where he didn't go anywhere without them.

Yes, he'd wanted to fuck her, but there was far more to how he felt about her than just *that*. Emotions were tangled with his desire, and she hadn't understood his obvious distaste at the idea of fathering a child.

She didn't understand that it wasn't her; it was him.

Dante added, "Because if you aren't serious about her, a couple of the detectives have been asking about her. Every single guy at the station thinks she's hot."

Evan saw red and slammed his fist down on the table. "She's mine. Tell them to back the fuck off or I'll crush every one of them, officer of the law or not."

He flew completely off his rocker at the thought of Randi being with anyone but him, and his fury blinded him to the fact that he *never* lost his temper completely. Not that he would have given a damn even if he was rational enough to think about it.

His brothers just grinned.

"Did you see Elsie's article in the paper today, dear?"

Randi had popped into Natural Elements to see how Beatrice had weathered the blizzard. Obviously, she was doing fine. The elderly woman's enthusiasm was infectious.

"She's got an article out today?" Randi asked curiously as she looked at the eclectic collection of items for sale in the store. "I'm surprised, since the snow just stopped last night."

Beatrice's head bobbed excitedly. "Yep. She titled it 'Blockbuster Movie Star Coming to Amesport.'"

Randi laughed as she listened to the drama in Beatrice's voice as she relayed the title of Elsie's article.

"He's single," she reminded the self-proclaimed matchmaker with a wink. Julian Sinclair coming to Amesport really *was* a big deal because he'd become a box-office sensation, but Randi supposed his family was trying to keep his presence as quiet as possible. Elsie Renfrew—or Elsie the Informer, as most of them called her when she wasn't present—was Beatrice's bosom buddy, and still wrote for the Amesport newspaper. Randi wasn't sure how either one of them had known about the Sinclair cousins coming into Amesport, but somehow they had. No doubt they had finagled the information from one of the family. Beatrice and Elsie might look like two sweet little old ladies, but they were merciless when it came to getting the scoop on town gossip. Randi had known them both long enough to ignore their seemingly innocent probing questions.

"I know, dear, but he won't be single for long," Beatrice told her confidently. "His destiny is here."

Randi fingered the Apache tear in her pocket, thinking how wrong Beatrice had been in her prediction for her. The only man Randi really wanted was totally unavailable to a woman like her. Her anger with Evan was already diminishing. What had she expected? Had she wanted him to tell her that it didn't matter if she got pregnant? That wouldn't have been logical or reasonable. In truth, she didn't want to be a single mother, but she did want children someday.

She had gone into the sexual relationship knowing nothing more could ever happen with Evan. It was *her* that wanted something more; not *him*. She really had no right to expect any other reaction than one of relief. Randi knew she should feel the same way. Oddly, she didn't.

"You think he doesn't care about you?" Beatrice asked as she ran a feather duster over the shelves.

"I know he doesn't," Randi agreed, leaning back against the counter of the store.

"You're wrong," Beatrice chirped. "He hides a lot, but the truth will come out eventually."

"He's not for me, Beatrice."

"This isn't one of my errors. My spirit guides seem to be strong with the Sinclairs," Beatrice said firmly.

Randi smiled. She wasn't about to break the news that she thought Beatrice's spirit guides had dementia.

"I have to run," she told her warmly. "Lily is in the car."

She hadn't been home, so she was still carrying her dog around with her.

Beatrice turned and speared Randi with a pointed look. "Don't give up. He's worth the wait. He was always going to be a tough nut to crack."

Randi nodded even though she wasn't a believer in Beatrice's predictions. At least not this one. "What about the cousins?" she asked, wondering what Beatrice was likely to predict for them.

"They all belong here, and I've already had dreams about the first one."

Poor guys. The Sinclair cousins have no idea what's coming.

She highly doubted any of the cousins were going to move to Amesport. Micah was into extreme sports, Julian's place was in Hollywood, and Xander the bad boy had to be out painting a big city red to remain happy. Not a single one of them belonged here.

"Take care of yourself, Beatrice," Randi said fondly as she reached for the door.

"You too, honey, and remember what I said. You two were meant to be."

Shoving the door open, Randi called back, "Thanks, Beatrice."

Once outside, Randi sprinted to her vehicle with a shake of her head. Poor Beatrice was destined for failure on this prediction. She just didn't know it yet.

Later that afternoon, Randi had a tutoring session at the Center. School would start up again tomorrow, but she'd committed to an appointment, and she was glad Matt's mother hadn't canceled.

She'd been working with him on his reading, one of the third grader's problem areas.

"It doesn't make sense," the child complained, frustrated as he tried to read a passage in a storybook.

"It will," Randi encouraged. "You just have to keep trying. Sound the word out," she told him with a patient smile. "You'll get it."

Matt was smart, but unfortunately he needed more one-on-one time, something that she wasn't able to give him in class. She'd asked his parents to start sending him to her free tutoring sessions at the Center, and she made sure to carve out an afternoon where she could work with him alone.

Catching a brief movement out of the corner of her eye, Randi turned her head to see Evan watching her and Matt as they struggled through the book. His shoulder was comfortably propped against the doorframe, so he'd obviously been there for a while.

He was dressed in a power suit again, and his expression was darkly brooding. Putting his hands into the pockets of his wool coat, he strolled into the room as he spoke. "It will take him at least four times as long for word recognition. What he sees isn't the same as what other kids see. His brain is wired differently. Sometimes he won't be able to connect a word with an object or a meaning. Sarcasm might be hard to understand sometimes, and he might have problems finding the right words to say. Joking around might be something he can't always grasp, so he might be uncomfortable with it sometimes. But he can be just as accomplished as any other child."

Randi stared at Evan, dumbfounded at his words before the lightbulb went off in her head. There had been subtle signs: his need for extreme organization and rigid routine, him asking her to dial her own phone number instead of doing it himself, his quirk of sometimes taking things seriously that were actually teasing, and his drive and determination to succeed when he was already more accomplished than most men in the world.

Evan had way overcompensated for his disability.

"You're dyslexic?" It was almost an unnecessary question. After Evan had stated accurate facts and she'd pieced things together, she was certain of her conclusion.

He nodded slowly, never taking his turbulent eyes away from her face. "I am." He nodded his head toward Matt as he asked, "Did you know he is, too?"

She swallowed hard before answering. "Yes. I have a master's degree in education with a certification to teach children with learning disabilities."

Matt was looking up at Evan, his eyes wide. "You have the problems I have?" he asked curiously.

Evan sat next to Matt at the table, both of them seated across from Randi now.

"I do," he told the child honestly. "We're different, but that doesn't mean we can't be successful. Lots of famous people are dyslexic."

"I know," Matt chattered enthusiastically. "Randi told me. But it gets hard to read, and sometimes I get my numbers mixed up."

Evan nodded solemnly. "Your brain will figure it out in a different way. Just remember you're special and not stupid. You have ways of figuring things out that nobody else can."

Randi's hands were shaking as she closed the book they'd been reading and listened to the honest conversation Evan was having with Matt. It was hard to fathom that Evan had dyslexia, but after thinking about it for a moment as he chatted with Matt, it made sense.

He'd tried to make up for his weaknesses by riding hard on his strengths. He was anal at times because everything had to be perfectly organized for him to function optimally. Sometimes he really *didn't* understand when someone was teasing, so he said nothing at all. He'd probably never ignored her on purpose. Hadn't he mentioned that he didn't know what to say? So he hadn't said anything. If he'd never had much of a chance to be around people who joked around, it was natural that he still might not always be completely comfortable with someone who teased him.

Every child with dyslexia had their own path to success and learning. She was willing to bet Evan's road had been long and hard, with his background of abuse. But he'd still made it, still achieved a level of success that most people could only dream about.

Yes, he'd been *born* wealthy, but his partnerships in megasuccessful businesses almost from their inception had made him even richer.

"Mom's here," Matt exclaimed happily, shaking Randi out of her own thoughts.

Randi saw Matt's mom standing near the door with her son's jacket in her hand. Luckily, his mother was a caring parent who understood Matt's disability.

"Go," Evan told Matt as he clapped the child gently on the back. "And remember what I said."

Randi was sad that she'd missed part of the conversation because she had been lost in thought.

Matt nodded at Evan with a cheerful smile and an expression of hero worship on his face. Randi watched her pupil leave, and turned to Evan, uncertain what to say.

Finally she found her voice. "Why didn't you tell me?"

He shrugged. "I don't tell anyone."

"Why?"

"I know I'm not stupid, lazy, or slow, so why should it matter to anyone else?" Evan remarked, raising a questioning eyebrow at her.

"Is that what your father thought? He thought you were lazy and slow. Is that why he beat you?" Randi clenched her fists on the table, hoping to God he'd deny her suspicions.

He didn't.

"Yes. That's how it started," Evan explained, looking away from her probing eyes. "I was expected to excel in school. I was the Sinclair heir apparent. Anything else was unthinkable to him. I wasn't supposed to have defects." Evan released a long breath. "I was my father's greatest disappointment. I was slow to read and I had a problem with numbers, an inconceivable problem for a Sinclair. Sometimes I still do mix up numbers. I need my staff to make sure what's in my head is on paper properly. I dictate reports a lot so they can be properly put on paper to avoid mistakes."

The way he hid his disability when he should be proud of all he'd accomplished tugged at Randi's heart. She rose and moved around the table, hefting herself up to sit on the table right next to his chair. "How did you learn?" He still wasn't looking at her, and she wanted to weep for the boy he once was. Evan was brilliant, but he'd been made to feel less than smart by an insensitive idiot.

"After my father discovered that beating me senseless wasn't going to miraculously make me smarter, he got me a tutor. The teacher was a bastard, but it worked. Repetition and phonics helped; memorizing the words that connected to a tangible object or person was easier. Bigger concepts came later. I worked with a tutor every night of the week and on the weekends when I wasn't in school."

"You're amazing. You know that, right?" Randi reached out her hand and turned his head toward her.

"Not really. It was the way I was wired. I had to deal with it."

Evan was so nonchalant that her heart melted. It *had* hurt, and it had hurt badly when he was a child. Obviously, it had made him all the more determined to find a way to conquer his problems, and he had. Dyslexia was never cured, but he'd found his own way to understand.

She'd studied examples of how children with dyslexia saw written words or books, and how best to conquer the problems. It had opened her eyes to children with learning disabilities and made her want to be able to teach them to cope. Plenty of famous people were dyslexic, including some of the brightest and most creative minds in history.

"I disagree," she commented, trying to get him to look at her by keeping her palm on his face.

"So you teach children with learning disabilities?" he asked huskily, obviously trying to change the subject.

Randi shook her head. "No. I teach a regular class of third graders. I volunteer here for special needs. Amesport doesn't have an organized program for gifted or special-needs students."

"So you're overqualified?"

"Not really. I just can't use all of my skills in my current position. I don't mind volunteering here." Usually it was the best part of her day. "It makes me happy. Do you know what it's like to be happy, Evan?"

Randi wondered if he'd ever been able to step out of his comfort zone in the past. He considered himself a caretaker of his siblings, responsible for their happiness. But what about him? He had a brilliant mind that functioned uniquely, and he'd compensated by being solemn and ultra-organized. Okay . . . he was majorly anal, but he had a reason to be. His learning disability didn't explain his arrogance, but Randi figured that was all Evan. He'd gained confidence over the years, and he wasn't shy about sharing his lack of insecurity about his intelligence.

He got to his feet and finally looked at her, his nostrils flaring and his eyes flashing blue fire. "I think I do understand happiness. Maybe I didn't last week or last year, but I think I'm beginning to get the concept now."

Randi drew the hand she had on his face to his shoulder and met his intense gaze. "Why now?"

"Because I think I'm happy when I'm with you and watching you come," he growled, his hand moving at lightning speed to grip the back of her neck, so he could lower his mouth to hers.

CHAPTER 13

Randi lost herself completely in his kiss, the power of the embrace all-consuming and fierce. She steadied herself by gripping his powerful shoulders, and let her senses drown in Evan's dominant assault.

She lost all of her will to fight her untamable attraction to him. *This* was Evan. Powerful. Indescribably sexy. Completely irresistible when he was this out of control.

Panting as he tore his mouth from hers, Randi looked at him with wide eyes.

"Did I hurt you when I told you that I didn't want you to be pregnant?" he asked in a graveled voice.

She nodded slowly. "It's not that I wanted to be pregnant. It was just the fact that you were so horrified that it might happen with me."

"You know that dyslexia is hereditary. It runs in families. I was afraid for Grady when he had problems early in school, but his issues turned out to be completely different. And once I left for college, things got even tougher for him. I hated that."

It wasn't like it was Evan's fault that he'd had to go away to college, but she'd learned enough about him to know he took the problems of the world onto his broad shoulders. He didn't see it as a burden; it was simply his responsibility. "So?" Randi challenged. "Would you see any child of yours as defective if they had your condition?"

"Of course not," Evan denied vehemently. "But it isn't easy."

"Evan, you're not your father. He doesn't define you," she told him softly. "You'd be a good parent and your child would be special. Dyslexic children can learn, and they can be incredibly intelligent and creative like you. You talked to Matt brilliantly." Okay . . . she hadn't heard the whole conversation, but he'd made Matt happy.

He shook his head. "He told me he wanted to be a shark like me."

Randi chuckled at the child's reference to a popular television show. "Are you a shark?"

"No. I just look at things differently, and probably some luck has been involved. I am an investor, and I seem to be able to look outside the box to decide what will be successful and what won't. Sometimes it's a talent, but sometimes it's just a good gut instinct," he admitted slowly. "Besides, I have more money than the typical shark."

Randi wanted to laugh at his cocky mention of his superior bank balance, but she didn't. She needed to address the rest of his statement.

"You're brilliant." Randi was stating the obvious, but she didn't care. Even with the horrible trials that dyslexia brought to a child, the fact was that dyslexic children *were* wired differently, and it caused many of them to have creative talents others didn't have. Obviously, the disorder affected Evan by letting him see an entire picture of a prospective business instead of focusing on one or two negatives that could be resolved. He had a special gift of picking the right businesses, no matter how much he tried to explain it away.

"I'm business-smart," Evan corrected, apparently unwilling to believe he was brilliant. "And I have a natural instinct for what will fly and what won't. I've picked up companies that nobody else will touch and made them work."

"You sold your father's businesses?" Randi knew he had. Evan had liquidated when his father had died and distributed the Sinclair wealth to all of the children equally. Then, he'd proceeded to build another huge empire of his very own.

"They weren't really my father's. They were actually started by my grandfather. He was a wily old coot who could sniff out a good business from the other side of the world. I sold them all when my father died so I could divide the family fortune." He frowned as he continued, "To be honest, I *wanted* to get rid of them. I wanted to prove to myself that I could pick my own companies and make my own fortune. Obviously, I was lucky I had the money in the first place, but I've multiplied my initial inheritance several times over." He wasn't bragging; he was just stating a fact.

"What does it feel like to be that rich? I always wondered what it would be like to be wealthy," she asked curiously. It didn't matter to her that she wasn't rich and never would be, but she honestly wondered what it would be like not to follow a budget every month.

"Not so different than what anyone else feels, I imagine. We have the same concerns, the same fear of failure. We just have nicer cars, nicer houses, and more zeros in our net worth." Evan shot her a small grin.

"And does that make you happy? Is a lot of money ever enough?" Once a person was that rich, did how much they have really matter anymore?

"I told you what makes me happy, and it's not all about the money to me," he answered gruffly. "But I guess I've always wanted to prove that I could build something on my own. I wanted to accumulate more than my father."

She knew what he meant. He'd been proving himself for years, trying to be better than his father to prove himself worthy and negate the labels his father had given him as a child. "More money doesn't mean better," Randi explained. She was sure people could be wealthy and absolutely miserable. "There's much more to happiness than money."

"I think I'm figuring that out." He lifted a hand to her head and stroked over her hair gently. "I'm sorry I hurt you, Randi. It's never been my intention."

It didn't escape her notice that he was still thoughtfully using her nickname, not wanting to remind her of her childhood. His sensitivity touched her like nothing else could.

She understood his violent reaction now to the possibility of getting *anyone* pregnant. It wasn't exactly for the reasons she'd assumed. Honestly, it wasn't even rational. Just because he was dyslexic didn't mean his child would also have the learning disability. With his fortune, he could afford the finest schools to help his child, and dyslexic children were often at average or above-average intellect. But maybe in Evan's mind, he didn't want a child to suffer like he did. He didn't consciously realize that the way the problem was handled made all the difference. "You could have just told me." She gave him a fake punch to the shoulder. "I thought you were starting to like me," she teased.

"I think I more than just started," Evan said grimly. "Show me happy, Randi. I think you're the only one who can."

Her heart accelerated as she contemplated what he was asking. Evan thought in broad terms when he requested something he didn't quite understand. It hurt her heart to think he'd never really experienced a happiness that could help him understand contentment. "You have to trust me first."

"I do," he shot back immediately.

She grimaced, knowing she was committing herself to spending most of her free time the next few days with Evan. It was tempting, but dangerous. "It won't be all about sex," she warned him. Hell, she loved the sex as much as he did, but it wasn't *all* there was to being happy and content.

His face fell, and Randi bit her lip to keep from smiling. Jesus, it felt good to have a man want her *that* much, but it wasn't enough for

Evan. He needed to learn that he wasn't going to find what he was look-ing for by working every waking hour of the day. There was obviously little levity in what he did, or the people he worked with on a day-to-day basis.

"Okay," he agreed, sounding reluctant.

"It won't hurt a bit. I promise," she assured him with a smile, her heart aching that Evan trusted her enough to let down his arrogant guard with her.

"Then show me." He leaned forward and put his lips to her forehead.

His willingness to put his vulnerability into her hands had been her downfall. Randi was going to show Evan that there was more to life than just work and duty if it killed her . . . and judging by the sensual, hot look in his eyes, she decided that she just might not make it out of the whole experiment unscathed.

> *Dear M.,*
> *What's your favorite flower?*

Randi looked at the short email from her pen pal, wondering what prompted him to ask that question. They threw out weird questions to each other, but it was usually relevant to something they'd been discuss-ing at one time or another. This one was totally random.

Shaking her head at her laptop, she replied.

> *Dear S.,*
> *I love calla lilies. My foster mother used to*
> *plant some of the huge, white variety down*
> *by the creek on her property every spring.*
> *Calla lilies in general don't do well in the*
> *Maine climate, so she dug them up every*

year and preserved them inside for the win-
ter so she could replant them in the spring.

Randi had named her dog after the flowers, because their center was actually the same gold color as Lily's coat.

She had a momentary stabbing pain in her chest remembering that there would be no giant, white calla lilies by the creek this year. Joan had been too sick to preserve them, and Randi had never learned how.

It will be sad not to see the giant white flow-
ers by the creek this year.

Randi added the sentence to her previous message before S. could reply.

Dear M.,
Still hurting?

Randi answered honestly.

Dear S.,
I think I'll miss her and my foster father for
the rest of my life. It's been way over a month
now since she passed, but it still hurts so
much sometimes that I can hardly breathe. I
know I was lucky to have them in my life at
all, but our time was too short.

Randi pressed "Send," already knowing that her friend would understand. He always did.

Dear M.,
I wish I had the words to make everything
right, but I think time will help. I can't say
I've ever been standing in your shoes. I can
only imagine how much it would hurt to lose
someone I loved that much.

Randi sighed. S. always made her feel better somehow, maybe because he had an uncanny ability to empathize.

Dear S.,
I guess you'll just have to put up with my
sulking for a while.

She'd been pouring out her heart to him since her foster mother died.

Dear M.,
You're not sulking, you're grieving right now.
Is it helping to have a guy in your life?

Randi thought about his question for a moment. Evan wasn't really what she'd call the man in her life, but they'd shared more deeply buried secrets with each other than they had with anyone else. She'd never shared her secrets with a man she cared about except S., and he was a fantasy. He didn't know her background, and Randi had no idea what her email friend was like in person.

She was willing to bet Evan shared very little with anyone.

Dear S.,
I think it does help, even though it's nothing

permanent. It takes my mind off my own
sorrow.

Thinking of the challenges Evan had been through made her determined to teach him how to be content and live in the moment for just a little while. Her mission did help to lessen her grief.

> *Dear M.,*
> *It could become permanent. You never know.*

She wrote two words back quickly.

> *Dear S.,*
> *It won't.*

He typed back one word.

> *Dear M.,*
> *Why?*

There were a lot of reasons, but the fact that Evan was leaving was the biggest one.

> *Dear S.,*
> *He won't be around long. We'll spend some*
> *time together this week and then he'll be*
> *gone.*
> *How are things with the new woman in*
> *your life? I think I'm a little bit jealous.*

It was winter in Amesport, not the best time to be showing Evan how to have fun. But she'd manage something.

> Dear M.,
> Don't be jealous. I had you first, and I think I
> really like her because she's a lot like you.

Randi was slightly taken aback by his words. S. didn't really know her, yet he did. She'd shared so much of her thoughts, feelings, and emotions with him, even though they'd never met in person. In some ways she was envious of the unknown woman. If S. liked this female, he'd pursue her. If he went after her, he'd get her. Randi had never met him, but someone as intelligent, thoughtful, and insightful was undoubtedly a great guy. He'd never run away from *her*, and that was saying something since she'd done nothing but pour her heart out to him since Joan's passing.

> Dear S.,
> I'm happy for you. She's a lucky woman.

The two of them signed off after a few more exchanges.

She wandered into the kitchen, wondering what to cook. Too tired to really fuss with anything, she emptied food into Lily's bowl and nuked herself a huge bowl of nacho cheese and took out the chips. Chuckling as she stood at her kitchen counter, she could only imagine what Evan would say about her dinner.

Evan.

What in the world had possessed her to accept his challenge to help him know happiness? What in the world did she know about being an upbeat person right now, anyway? She was a mess, a woman who was still in mourning with a piece of her soul missing.

I've been happy. I just need to remember how it was before I lost the last person who would love me like a daughter forever.

Maybe if she was very lucky, she and Evan could help heal each other. She could get her joy back, and Evan could find it for the first time.

She didn't regret reaffirming that she'd go to Hope's party with him, when she'd seen him earlier at the Center while tutoring Matt. It would be the last night she'd spend with him before he climbed into his expensive airplane and flew halfway across the world for another possible business deal.

Don't think about him leaving. Just think about tomorrow. Live for now.

She ate a few more chips, dunking them in the massive bowl of warm, creamy nacho cheese.

Since she had no choice but to live for the moment, she wasn't going to fight it. Thinking about the fact that Evan was leaving soon wasn't going to ruin her chance of making him see that life was about so much more than work.

If anyone deserved a little bit of happiness, it was Evan Sinclair.

Pushing her negative thoughts from her mind, Randi contemplated exactly how to teach a man who knew nothing but work how to be happy.

CHAPTER 14

The next evening, Micah Sinclair found himself sitting at Sullivan's Steak and Seafood wondering what in the hell he was doing there. He was alone, sitting at a corner table, completely obsessed with watching Tessa Sullivan.

And so he did just that. He watched her.

Obsessively.

Compulsively.

Constantly.

He watched as she moved around the room with the grace of a dancer, disappointed that she wasn't the person who took his order. Instead, it had been an angry-looking man not much older than him, his hair almost the same color as Tessa's.

You're a pathetic loser, Sinclair. Get up and leave.

Micah had reminded himself several times that he wasn't here by chance, and that he was actually stalking Tessa, but he couldn't help himself. When he'd found her gone, he'd needed to reassure himself that she'd gotten home safe. Yeah, maybe he could have gotten her number from Hope, or asked her to text Tessa rather than just showing up at the restaurant himself.

He hadn't.

Because he wanted to see her in person again.

He'd gone to Sullivan's just to see her, and ended up eating the best lobster roll he'd ever had. The place might look like a dump, but the food was phenomenal.

He was still nursing a beer when he saw the guy who'd delivered his order making his way to his table.

"You good?" he asked as he stopped at Micah's table. And damned if the guy wasn't blocking his view of Tessa now.

Micah raised his hand. "I'm stuffed. Thanks."

"Here's your check," the waiter answered, practically slamming the paper down on the table.

Micah nodded and grabbed the ticket, wondering why the big guy seemed to have suddenly become less friendly. That was saying something, because he hadn't exactly been much fun in the first place. "Thanks."

"You've been watching Tessa all night. Don't even think about it, man." The stranger's face grew threatening and annoyed.

"She's an attractive woman," Micah replied sensibly.

"And she happens to be my sister. Stay the hell away from her. She's been through a lot in the past several years. She doesn't need a Sinclair to screw with her head." The burly man crossed his arms and shot Micah a dangerous look, one that said if Micah fucked with his sister, he'd kill him.

"You know who I am?" Micah asked, surprised.

"Yes, I know. I recognize you. I've seen some of your work, and I've used your equipment in the past."

"I don't mean her any harm. I'm just looking," Micah said calmly. "She makes it difficult *not* to look."

"Well look in another direction. She's deaf, handicapped," Liam growled protectively.

"Being deaf isn't really a handicap for her. She seems to cope quite well," Micah observed, not liking the fact that her brother seemed to think his sister was less desirable just because she couldn't hear. "You must be Liam Sullivan, one of the owners of this place, right? Has the place been here long? The food was good." He tried to make casual conversation to get the man off his back.

"Since my grandfather's time," Liam admitted. "It's not the ambiance that makes the restaurant. People come back for the food." Liam hesitated for a moment before he asked, "Are you trying to change the subject?"

Actually, Micah was trying to forget about the fact that he was a certifiable stalker. "Yes. Look, I find your sister attractive. That's all there is to it. I wouldn't want to upset her."

Liam gave Micah a warning glance. "Stop looking. She's not going to end up being a notch on your bedpost or anywhere else, for that matter."

Micah thought about telling the man that he didn't keep track of the women he slept with by carving a notch on his expensive bed, but he didn't think Liam would appreciate the comment.

"Since when do you run your sister's dating life?" Micah asked evenly, standing up to go pay his bill. He did need to leave. He had work to accomplish, and sitting here stalking a deaf woman was pretty damn pathetic.

"Since I'm the only one around to protect her anymore." Liam shoved Micah's shoulder with a closed fist. "You're trouble, and the last thing Tessa needs is any emotional issues right now. She has enough to deal with at the moment."

Micah put some distance between himself and Liam. "Don't touch me, asshole. You profess concern for your sister? How do you think she'd feel if we started going a few rounds in the middle of her restaurant?" Micah wasn't afraid of Liam. He knew he could kick his ass if he needed to, but he didn't want to. The guy was Tessa's brother, even if he was an overprotective prick. Micah didn't want to go there.

"You think you'd win?" Liam asked with a smirk.

"I know so," Micah replied arrogantly. Liam might outsize him by a few inches and pounds, but Micah was fast and had the skills to go along with his speed.

"Cocky bastard," Liam mumbled.

"Don't worry; I'm leaving. But I won't promise I'll never come back." Micah put on his jacket and zipped it up.

"Just make sure you keep your eyes pointed in another direction," Liam warned ominously.

Micah wasn't certain he could promise Liam that he wouldn't gawk at Tessa if given the opportunity, so he remained silent.

"I'll take that," Liam said anxiously as he snatched the bill and the credit card Micah had pulled from his wallet.

Clearly the guy wanted to make sure that Micah had absolutely no opportunity to talk to his sister. Liam was pretty obvious in his enthusiasm to see the back of him, at least for tonight.

Micah smirked as he strolled to the front of the restaurant to watch Liam hastily take payment.

"I'm not going to tell you to come back and see us soon," Liam stated in an unhappy tone.

Micah took back his card and returned it to his wallet. "No need. Good food and an ass like your sister's will always bring me back," he told Liam with a cocky smile and turned to leave the restaurant. Most likely, he wouldn't be back, but he wasn't going to give Liam the satisfaction of admitting it. He would have liked to have seen the look on Liam's face, but he suppressed the urge to turn around again.

"Bastard," Liam muttered angrily.

Micah chuckled as he walked out of the steakhouse and back into the cold.

Randi parked her car on the side of the road in the cemetery, doubtful anybody would care. She was the only living soul in the place.

Pulling a shovel out of the car, she watched as Lily slipped out and scampered through the snow and over to exactly the place where Randi was headed: her foster parents' tombstones.

It had become a ritual for her to come clear a path to the stones since Joan had passed away. For some reason she always felt better once the stones weren't buried in snow like they'd been forgotten.

She locked the SUV even though it probably wasn't necessary and started her trek toward the area where Dennis and Joan had been laid to rest side by side.

The reverent silence was broken by Lily's excited bark.

The moment she stepped off the sidewalk to trudge through the snow to the markers, Randi knew something was off. Amazed, she walked over the dead grass on a path that had been cleared directly toward Dennis's and Joan's stones.

Somebody was here.

Randi realized it wasn't the family of another loved one who had done it. The cleared area led directly to where Lily was standing, excitedly sniffing the ground. Not a speck of snow marred the writing on the marble remembrance markers, her foster parents' names and dates of birth and death completely revealed.

"What the hell?" Randi mumbled to herself, resting a gloved hand on top of Lily's head. "You recognize a scent, girl?" she asked her curiously. The dog's nose was off the ground and she was now sitting and looking up at Randi with her head cocked to one side.

Why would anyone clear a path to her foster parents' gravestones, and then proceed to carefully remove any snow from their markers? Nobody came here except her, and occasionally Beatrice and Elsie. The elderly women went to graves to leave flowers for deceased loved ones and friends on some of the major holidays.

But it wasn't a holiday.

And Randi knew it wasn't Beatrice and Elsie who had shoveled the heavy snow.

A flash of color caught her eye, and she bent over to retrieve an object that was situated between the two stones.

She rose with a perfect single calla lily between her fingers. Randi's mouth opened and closed with surprise as she read the small handwritten tag attached to the flower. There were only two words: *Thank You!*

Clutching the flower, Randi sat down hard on the snowbank beside the path that had been created by some massive shoveling. Her ass was cold, but she didn't notice. She was too busy trying to understand what was happening.

Lily cuddled up to her side, quiet as she laid her furry head against Randi's shoulder.

"Who would do this? And why?" Randi whispered, turning the perfect bloom around with her fingers. It was a smaller calla lily, and it had splotches of a color that reminded her of a ripe plum on the inside of the white flower. In the middle was the signature tiny gold bud that matched Lily's golden fur coat.

It was still beautiful, which told her it hadn't been out in the cold for very long.

"Impossible," Randi marveled, still confused. There was no way somebody had just happened to find this flower in town. The local florist didn't carry calla lilies. They were rarely seen in her area, and definitely not in the winter.

Fingering the small tag around the flower, she wondered who was thanking Dennis and Joan . . . and why? If anybody should be thanking them, it was her. They'd rescued her from a hopeless life and made her feel like a real person for the first time in her life.

Her eyes misted and tears began to trickle slowly down her face. Even though it could be a little creepy that an unknown someone else had visited their graves, it wasn't. Whoever had dropped this off and cleared the site had once been touched by Dennis and Joan's kindness . . . just like her.

Maybe it was an old student of her foster mother's, or a student at Dennis's school. The couple had done so many kind things in their lives; they deserved to be remembered.

Randi wrapped her arms around her dog as Lily started licking at her face, lapping at her tears. "I miss them, Lily. I miss them so damn much." Giving up the fight, Randi lowered her head and sobbed against Lily's silky fur, keeping the calla lily clutched in her fist.

She cried for the loss of a mother and father, even though they hadn't shared the same blood.

She cried for the sacrifices they'd made just to keep her with them.

She cried because she'd never completely mourned their loss because it was so hard to let them go.

Finally, she stopped, and memories of the two people she'd loved the most in life drifted through her mind.

They'll never really be gone, because I'll keep the memories alive and both of them in my heart forever. They showed me what it was like to truly be happy and loved. Both of them would hate it if I stayed sad when I think about them.

"They wanted me to be happy, Lily. That's why they lied to keep me here in Amesport," Randi murmured quietly to her dog as she lifted her head from Lily's fur.

Swiping away the rest of the tears from her face with her glove, Randi walked back to her car and removed a pretty red rose from the backseat. She took the calla lily and wrapped the two flowers together with the tag the other visitor had provided and walked back to the two stones.

Gingerly, she dropped the entwined flowers back between the two graves, her heart much lighter than when she'd arrived.

She didn't know who had dropped off the calla lily and cleaned the path and markers, but she and that person had a connection, an abiding love for two of the kindest people who had ever existed.

"I hope I can make you both proud," Randi whispered, determined to make their every sacrifice really count. "I'll try my best."

Lily whined softly, as though she agreed with Randi.

She patted the dog on the head. "Come on, girl. Let's go home."

The canine sprinted in front of her to the SUV. Randi followed slowly, thinking about some of the happy memories she'd created with Dennis and Joan. She'd have those peaceful times in her heart forever even as she began to let go of her sadness.

Finally, the healing would begin.

CHAPTER 15

"Evan looks so much happier," Mara Sinclair shared with Randi as the women put food away and loaded the dishwasher in Hope's kitchen. "I've been so worried about him."

Randi wrapped the remainder of the chocolate cake that she'd made and placed it carefully in the refrigerator. "Was he that bad?" she asked curiously.

Hope snorted as she wiped the stovetop. "Yes," she answered simply.

One of Randi's attempts to make Evan happy had been to gather his entire family in the same place for dinner. Some moments had been painful to watch since she could see Evan's struggle not to pull away from them because the habit was ingrained, but he was doing well. She had told him that so much happiness came from the people who loved him, so she'd arranged to have a family dinner at Hope's home.

The ladies had kicked the men out of the kitchen even though they'd tried to help clean up. Poor Hope was afraid for the safety of her dinnerware. Not that it had taken that much arm-twisting to make the guys retreat to the living room, but they'd grumbled goodheartedly anyway.

With Randi, Emily, Hope, Sarah, and Mara in the kitchen, they'd made short work of cleaning up.

"I can't believe he actually ate my lasagna and garlic bread. He even went for dessert," Mara contemplated, her voice sounding happily surprised.

"He didn't just eat it. Evan enjoyed it," Emily said, a smile on her face. "It was so nice to see him eat for a change."

Randi grinned. "I'm slowly trying to introduce him to the joys of eating things that aren't good for him. His diet was boring and bland. It's not like he's going to get fat. He works out."

"Thank God he's eating like a normal guy," Mara replied. "I just wish we had known sooner what he went through as a child. I can't imagine having dyslexia with a father like theirs." She shuddered visibly. "It had to have been a nightmare for him."

Randi knew exactly how Evan's childhood had affected him all the way into adulthood. "He was beaten pretty badly. You can still see the scars."

The kitchen went absolutely silent, all of the women suddenly staring at Randi.

"Oh, my God. Grady told me his father didn't beat him," Emily said in a somber tone.

"Jared said the same," Mara related.

"Dante, too," Sarah added.

"Our father was an asshole and verbally abusive. If he didn't have something bad to say, he ignored us completely for the most part," Hope explained. "But as far as I know, he didn't ever beat any of us." She looked directly at Randi. "Is it true? Did Evan really get beaten? Why wouldn't he tell me that part?"

Randi knew exactly why Evan had never told . . . now. She should have kept quiet. Evan putting himself out there as his father's target for physical abuse had kept his other siblings from getting beaten. Even though she thought his siblings should know everything, she shouldn't be the one to break that news. "I assumed you all knew. He said he told you about his childhood."

"We didn't know that part," Hope mentioned mournfully.

"Maybe he doesn't want you to know. It's in the past, and I think Evan is trying to find his place in the family and in the world. I'd appreciate it if you didn't tell anybody else," Randi said, her voice slightly pleading.

All the women nodded their heads.

"We won't mention it. I want Evan to feel comfortable. But I still don't understand. God, my father was an asshole!" Hope exclaimed, sounding angry for Evan. "It's a wonder that Evan turned out to be so successful."

Randi shrugged. "It's not really surprising. Dyslexic children can be very creative and extremely intelligent. Lots of famous people are thought to have been dyslexic: Alexander Graham Bell, Albert Einstein, Pierre Curie, Picasso, Ansel Adams, Richard Branson, and Thomas Edison." She paused to take a breath. "And there are so many more."

"Evan is just as smart as any other genius," Mara confirmed. "How did he learn?"

Randi sighed. "He learned by working so damn hard. It takes a lot of repetition, and learning to understand things in a different way. He had to learn the concept of phonics before he could actually apply it to reading. For Evan, dyslexia was one learning problem in a sea of strengths that he possesses. Time and perseverance helped him learn to read and write when he was struggling. Every child is different and has different levels of difficulty. Now we have reading programs that help, and audiobooks are a great tool if kids can read along with the audio."

"What makes him so uptight?" Hope asked inquisitively.

"He's anal," Randi admitted. "But I think in his mind everything around him has to be running optimally for him to be functional. No highs and lows. No ups or downs. No shades of gray. It keeps him organized and focused. The problem with Evan is he's never had time to be spontaneous or undisciplined. It's not healthy for him now, even though it was probably his coping mechanism earlier in life. He's always wanted to prove to your father that he can run his business well, be successful. Unfortunately, I think he's still trying to prove something even though your father is gone."

"We want to help. What can we do?" Mara asked anxiously.

"Just care about him and realize that he isn't wired the same way as everybody else. He's not going to change so much that he'll never be an arrogant jerk sometimes, but he's trying. He wants to be part of the family. Now that you're all grown up and happy, he's not quite sure where he belongs." Evan could protest all he wanted, but he *did* want to be loved.

"He belongs with the rest of us," Mara said forcefully. "I don't care if he's arrogant. All of the Sinclair men are arrogant in their own way, but their hearts are good. I just want Evan to be happy, and so does everyone else."

The women nodded their heads enthusiastically.

"It will just take time," Randi admitted.

"We aren't going anywhere," Hope said emphatically.

Randi smiled, knowing the four tigresses in the room would grab onto Evan and never let go. The Sinclairs loved their family, and Randi knew they'd help him find out exactly where he fit in. He would eventually realize he really was loved.

"Are you going to tell us what's happening between you two?" Sarah asked bluntly.

Randi flushed, turning her face away from the other women on the pretense of wiping the countertops. "Nothing. He'll leave right after the party. He said he's got an important meeting on Monday morning. We're just trying to be . . . friends." *That sounded safe enough.* "We got off to a bad start, but I think I'm starting to understand and like him a little," she added.

"I know that's bullshit," Hope answered. "I can see how he looks at you, and how he watches you constantly. But thank you for trying to help my brother."

"I'm not doing much, really. I'm just trying to get him to relax a little and enjoy life." Randi sighed.

"Well, he is more relaxed, and he looks like all he wants is to take you home and jump your bones," Mara observed.

Randi couldn't deny that she and Evan had off-the-charts chemistry, so she remained silent. She'd probably been just as guilty of watching Evan like a woman who just wanted to strip him naked and devour him.

Hope came to Randi's rescue. "Shall we join the guys? I think they've been deprived of our company for far too long."

Randi breathed a sigh of relief as they all left the kitchen to go join their men.

The next evening, Randi wanted to laugh as she watched Evan trying to meditate. It was clear this night was going to be a challenge.

Since Evan had brought her supplies to his house during the storm, she'd cooked at his place tonight, and he had eaten like a horse, including dessert.

After spending the night with his family the night before, Evan had insisted on her staying with him on the Peninsula and letting him take her home early in the morning so she could get dressed for school.

He'd rocked her world as soon as they'd walked through the door last night, and Evan had promptly announced he was "happy" the moment she had her first climax.

She'd laughed, both exasperated and amused that Evan only appeared to be "happy" when he was making her come.

Tonight, she was determined to show him that not all happiness or being content revolved around earth-shattering sex.

So far, she seemed to be failing miserably.

"You need to close your eyes and concentrate on your breathing," Randi instructed as she sat cross-legged on his living-room floor. She'd brought a few items of clothing, including the pair of yoga pants and the tattered T-shirt she was wearing. "Center on your breathing and be an observer. You can acknowledge your thoughts, but don't react to them. Just treat them as if they're random information that isn't connected to you."

"Not possible," Evan grumbled as he sat across from her in a pair of gray sweatpants and a navy tank top.

"Close your eyes," she prompted.

"Can't," he insisted.

"Why?"

"My thoughts aren't something I can ignore, and my dick is hard. It's been that way since I saw you come downstairs in those yoga pants," he grunted unhappily.

Randi laughed, wondering what in the world he saw in her that was attractive right now. The yoga attire had been washed so many times that the pink material was faded to a very light pastel color, and she'd pulled her hair back into a ponytail. In her mind, she wasn't exactly an enticing sight.

The man sitting across from her was a different story. Evan looked impossibly tempting, his hair slightly mussed, the muscles in his arms and chest rippling every time he moved.

All she'd need to do was lean forward and lick every inch of his exposed skin, then she could . . .

Stop. This is about Evan. I want to teach him to relax! I can keep my hormones under control for an hour. Okay . . . maybe thirty minutes.

Randi slammed her eyes closed and swallowed, unable to stop her reaction to the hot look he was giving her, like he wanted to devour her as another helping of dessert. "Close your eyes," she demanded. "I told you this wasn't going to be all about sex."

It was the last evening she had to spend with him other than the ball. Tomorrow night she had a tutoring session. She and Evan would attend Hope's party together and then he'd be gone.

I can do this. I can spend one night with Evan without wanting him to do me.

She felt his heated breath on her ear before he spoke huskily. "It isn't all about sex, Randi. With you, it never has been and it never will be."

She shivered as she felt his lips nuzzle her ear, but she didn't open her eyes. "Then what is it?" she whispered shakily.

"I don't have to explain it to you. You already know. You want this as much as I do," he said with a low growl as he wrapped a strong hand behind her neck. "I need to do everything in my power to make sure you never forget how this feels, to make you remember that you're mine. Everything about just being with you makes me happy."

It was all about the connection, the addictive euphoria of having him claim her like it was the most natural thing in the world. Like she could ever forget Evan? She knew *that* would never happen.

"The man who tried to assault you is dead," Evan told her unhappily, as though he was disappointed he couldn't make Randi's tormenter suffer. "He died of a heart attack several years ago."

"You tried to find him?" Randi asked, her eyes opening wide in disbelief.

"Of course. If the asshole wasn't already dead, he was going to wish he was when I found him," Evan answered, his voice vibrating with anger.

"You tracked him down for me?" She had no doubt Evan had been seeking revenge for an incident that happened years ago. Randi knew he wasn't capable of cold-blooded murder, but there were plenty of other ways for a billionaire to completely destroy somebody's life.

"There's nothing I wouldn't do for you," Evan answered in a grave voice. "If the bastard was still molesting children, he needed to be stopped."

Randi was relieved the man was dead. "How did you find out?"

"There are very few things I can't do," Evan answered cockily.

She squealed as her back hit the floor with Evan looming over her, his expression fierce. She asked breathlessly, "So this is what really makes you happy?"

"It makes me fucking ecstatic," he grumbled as his head swooped down to capture her mouth with his.

Randi wrapped her arms around his neck, trembling as their heated skin made contact.

Screw the meditation. I need this more. Evan makes me crazy, and I can't concentrate.

Randi separated her mouth from Evan's with a determined turn of her head and pushed against his shoulders. "Up," she grunted as she found herself pushing against what felt like a rock wall. Evan was heavy and muscular, definitely strong enough that she couldn't move unless he let her.

He did.

Immediately.

Helping her move to a sitting position, he looked at her, confused. "Are you okay?"

Desire still simmered in the pool of his gorgeous blue eyes, but it was mixed with concern.

Randi reached for the bottom of his tank top and yanked, causing him to raise his arms to remove it. She tossed it over her shoulder as she told him sternly, "I promised myself I'd teach you to loosen the reins on your control when you aren't working." Reaching for the hem of her own T-shirt, she whipped it over her head and sent it in the same direction as Evan's garment.

She was braless, and her nipples were pebbled and sensitive, which was probably the reason Evan's eyes kept returning to her chest.

"Are we going to meditate naked?" Evan asked calmly, his gaze questioning as his eyes scanned her naked breasts hungrily. "If so, I'm definitely doomed to fail."

"Nope," Randi answered firmly. "We're just going to do it differently."

She pushed Evan onto his back and he went willingly. "Is this your naughty teacher persona?" Evan said huskily. "If it is, it's pretty hot."

Biting her lip to keep from laughing at his comment, Randi stood and started sliding her yoga pants slowly downward. "Since you can't seem to be happy unless you're getting laid, maybe you can let go of control this way." She kicked aside the thin, stretchy pants and her panties, leaving her completely naked. She looked down at him and licked her lips nervously.

Evan was a dominant male, and was obsessive about making her climax. Would he tolerate her taking complete control? Would he trust her enough?

"Do you trust me?" Randi asked him as she went to her knees and slowly pulled the drawstring on his sweatpants.

"Yes," he answered quickly, sincerely.

He lifted his ass as she pulled at his boxers, cooperating to get himself as naked as she was at the moment.

"Good." She nodded at him as she swung her leg over his body. "Then let me have control this time. All you have to do is think of nothing except sensation."

His cock had been rock hard as she'd divested him of his clothing. Her core spasmed in anticipation as she grasped his shoulders and finally met his fiery gaze.

"Why?" he asked huskily, looking like he was struggling with the idea of doing almost nothing.

"Because I want you to," she answered simply, letting her saturated core slide against the long length of his cock.

Rocking her hips, she used Evan's hard member to rub against her slick clit, a low moan escaping her lips as she felt the friction against the sensitive bundle of nerves.

"Okay." Evan didn't sound happy, but he was watching her face as though he was mesmerized by her every movement.

She could feel his eyes on her as she reached up and stripped her hair from its confinement, allowing the silky strands to fall in a messy heap around her shoulders. "Close your eyes," she requested, her voice deep and aroused as she continued to move her hips against him.

"I want to see you come—"

Randi pressed two fingers against his lips to silence him. "You'll know when it's time. Just concentrate on clearing your mind of everything except the feel of us together."

He pressed his eyes closed, but muttered unhappily, "Like I could think about anything else?"

Randi smiled because she knew Evan couldn't see her. She knew that he fretted about making her happy and making her climax whenever they were together. She didn't think he realized that it was going to happen naturally. He didn't have to think about it, because he was Evan. She could get off just from thinking about him.

She leaned forward and grazed her lips along his neck. "You're so damn gorgeous, Evan. Everything about you turns me on," she whispered softly, giving herself permission to be the aggressor, and with a man this dominant, it was pretty intoxicating.

He let out a low growl as she nipped at his earlobe.

"Fuck! Have some mercy, woman," Evan rasped. "Fuck me. Now."

Okay . . . maybe he wasn't able to be completely submissive to her, but it was enough. She speared one of her hands into his hair and pulled his ear against her lips. "I plan on it, big guy. I want to ride both of us to a cataclysmic orgasm. I've wanted that since the moment I first saw you."

"You can start anytime," Evan replied desperately. "Jesus, you feel so damn good, Randi." He lifted his arms and stroked his hands slowly down her back and cupped her ass. "There isn't another woman who feels and smells like you do."

She could sense Evan's anguish, the difficulty he was having not taking what he wanted and needed. But he didn't. He trusted her.

"There isn't a man quite like you, either," she confided as she lightly, teasingly brushed her lips against his.

Lifting her hips, she positioned Evan at the opening of her channel and started to slowly slide down his length.

"Oh, fuck, yeah!" Evan groaned, arching his back to help her.

Randi was ready to ride him into oblivion. In fact, she couldn't wait a moment longer. Sinking down on him, she buried his cock completely inside her, letting out a satisfied moan as she did.

She started a slow, sensual grind, but Evan was having none of it. Granted, he didn't open his eyes once, but he grasped her hips and held her in place as he pounded up into her . . . over and over again.

In the end, it was Randi who got lost in sensation, focusing only on the feel of Evan permeating her entire being and stealing the breath from her body as they worked toward a common goal: a stunning, fireworks-seeing, sweaty climax.

Supporting herself on his shoulders, she met Evan stroke for stroke, slamming down on him as he thrust his hips up, creating a fullness and a volatile joining that drove her crazy.

"It's going to happen," she panted as she felt her impending orgasm.

"I know."

Looking down, she noticed his eyes were open and watching her before the massive waves of her climax hit her. Evan grasped her hands and held her upright as her channel clenched down on his cock, milking him of his own release as she threw her head back and screamed his name.

He groaned and thrust into her one more time before staying buried deep inside her as he came.

Randi collapsed on top of Evan still holding his hands. He untangled their fingers and wrapped his strong arms around her back, keeping her plastered against him.

When they finally caught their breath, Evan muttered against her ear, "You're right. Meditation *is* stimulating to the body and mind. I think it should be practiced at least a few times a day."

Randi actually giggled. It wasn't often that Evan made a joke, but he seemed to be doing it more frequently in the last few days. "That was what I would call a much-modified version of what I wanted to teach you," she scolded.

"I think I like the modified version," Evan decided as he stroked her hair. "I'm feeling very relaxed."

Randi leaned up so she could look at him. "You don't really want to meditate for real, do you?"

"I thought you wanted me to find happiness. Right now, I'm happy. I'm ecstatic whenever I'm with you, no matter what we're doing."

Randi's heart stuttered as she saw the serious look in his beautiful eyes. The truth was . . . so was she.

Don't do this to yourself, Randi. Don't fall for Evan Sinclair. Even if he cares about you, he never wants to have a child, and you know you love kids. It might feel good right now, but the two of you together forever isn't an option. He's leaving, and you'll still be here in Amesport teaching.

Unable to utter an answer, Randi just buried her head against Evan's neck and savored the unique scent of him and the feel of his body close to hers.

Right now, she didn't want to think about what would happen in the future. Right now was all she had.

CHAPTER 16

Randi tried to shake off the strange residual emotions following her visit to the Amesport cemetery on the way home that day.

It felt odd that somebody else was apparently visiting her foster parents' graves on a daily basis. The path was still clear, even though they'd had some light snow since she'd last been there, and the calla lily and the rose were still entwined and lying between the markers. The problem was . . . they were perfect. There was no way they were the same flowers. The two she'd put together would be frozen and dead. The only explanation was that somebody was there daily, moving the snow and leaving new flowers on the graves.

Strangely, they had duplicated what she'd done by re-entwining the two flowers and leaving them there daily with the same tag with only two words: *Thank You!*

As she opened her email, Randi wondered at the identity of the unknown person.

One time hadn't really made her think about it, but now that it seemed to be happening every day, it was making her curious as to what her foster parents had done for whoever was apparently honoring them.

A note from S. distracted her from her musings.

Dear M.,
Just checking in to see how you're doing.
How's your new relationship? Have you
changed your mind about making it into
something permanent?

Randi smiled sadly at the note from S. She'd already given up on writing to him only from the Center. He knew plenty about her, enough to find her if he so desired. Somehow, she knew he'd never intrude on her life unless she wanted to meet him. Besides, he had a woman of his own now.

Dear S.,
No. No change. He has to leave tomorrow
morning. Important business.

He replied.

Dear M.,
You okay with that?

She wasn't okay at all, but it was reality, and she always knew her relationship with Evan could never be more than temporary. She answered.

Dear S.,
Yeah. I'm fine. I always knew it could never
be anything more than a brief interlude. I can
never fall in love with a man like him.
*   How are things with your new relation-*
ship? Why aren't you out? It's a date night.

Randi knew she was lying, but she could hardly tell S. that she was already in love with Evan Sinclair and that her heart was slowly shattering into tiny little pieces because he was leaving tomorrow. Evan might not be S.'s immediate supervisor, but he was the big boss in the scheme of things. Although she trusted S. with her own secrets, she couldn't talk to him much about Evan.

She waited, tapping her fingers on the desk in anticipation of a reply. He never took this length of time to answer when they were in conversation.

She needed to get dressed and ready for Hope's party. She'd had a lunch planned with her female friends today, so she hadn't had time to see Evan earlier. Besides, she would have felt guilty taking up what little time he had to spend with his cousin Julian. The famous actor had just flown in from California late last night.

More time passed before she got a short reply from S.

I have to get going.

Randi frowned at his response, afraid that she might have hurt his feelings because she didn't want to talk about Evan. Maybe he saw her lack of communication as a snub. She sent a final one-line email, not sure how to explain why she couldn't share her feelings with him.

Have a great weekend.

She signed out of her email, a sense of loss overwhelming her as she closed the laptop. Somehow, she was losing her connection with S., and tonight was going to be the last time she ever saw Evan. Oh, he'd be back someday for his family, but Randi knew she could never be with him again intimately.

She was way too emotionally invested in this whole affair with Evan, and it hurt. The best thing she could do was try to forget what had happened in the past with Evan and move on. She did want to have children someday. Her love for kids had been her entire reason for going into teaching and trying to make a difference in their lives.

I'll forget him eventually. The emptiness I feel right now will go away.

Evan had shown up at the Center last night after her tutoring session with Matt, giving the child his personal email address so they could keep in touch. The gesture had almost brought Randi to tears. The thought of a man as busy and important as Evan giving a kid his contact information to hear about his progress was so damn touching that she'd wanted to cry. The sincerity in Evan's expression, and his personal interest in a little boy who had the same disorder he had was just so damn . . . sweet.

Afterward, she and Evan had gone for coffee at Brew Magic. Randi could still hear his voice saying that he was happy just because he had a chance to see her. They hadn't done anything except talk about their day, but it had seemed almost as intimate as sex.

Evan had seemed disappointed when he had to leave their impromptu meeting to go see Julian, who was just about to arrive in Amesport.

I'm totally, completely, and undeniably addicted to him. I was just as sad to see him go last night.

Conflicted, Randi got up to head to her bedroom to get ready for Hope's ball. Because she was going with Evan, she wished tonight could last forever, but the pragmatic woman in her knew it was going to end.

She looked at her computer, thinking about the distance that seemed to be growing between her and S. Randi was glad he had a woman in his real life, but she missed their uncomplicated conversations, too.

No Evan.

No S. to console her anymore.

"It's going to be lonely," Randi murmured to Lily as she stroked the dog's head, wondering why in the world a streetwise woman like

her had been stupid enough to fall head over heels in love with Evan
Sinclair.

"I'm worried about Evan," Mara Sinclair shared with her husband,
Jared, as she looked at herself in the mirror and changed her earrings.
She was almost ready to leave for Hope's ball, but she had a bad feeling
about how things were going to end for Evan after tonight.

Jared stood above her, adjusting his bow tie. "Why?" he asked
curiously.

Mara's breath caught as she looked up and saw her husband's handsome reflection in the mirror. She still wasn't used to being married to
such an amazingly gorgeous man. Sighing as she picked up her lipstick,
she didn't ask herself why they had fallen for each other so hard or so
completely. She was just grateful for that love every single day.

"All of us are worried," Mara confessed. She, Hope, Sarah, and
Emily had shared their concern during their coffee time. "He's in love
with Randi. I know he is. What happens when he leaves?" Would he
retreat inside himself again, lose all the progress he had made in coming
out of his defensive shell? Mara was pretty certain that Randi was the
reason for the change in Evan. And he *had* changed. She was doubtful
he'd ever lose his know-it-all arrogance. That was just part of Evan. But
he *was* different, less guarded, more connected to the family. She didn't
want him to lose that now.

"I know he's in love with her," Jared answered nonchalantly. "I'm
just not certain *he* knows it yet. It's pretty evident to Grady, Dante, and
me because we've been where he is right now. After the way he stuck
his nose into my relationship with you, I shouldn't feel sorry for the
asshole, but I do."

Mara turned and punched him lightly in the stomach. "That's a
terrible thing to say. You love Evan and you know it."

"I love you more," he answered promptly. "I love you more and more every single day."

Mara's heart melted. There wasn't a single day that Jared didn't declare that he loved her more today than yesterday. "You love your siblings, too."

Jared shrugged. "I do love them, and yes, Evan saved my life. But I'm not going to meddle in his business."

Mara smiled, knowing that Jared would absolutely intervene with Evan if necessary, as she took a final look at herself in the mirror and stood up. She didn't look bad for a plain, ordinary woman. She'd never be a stunner like Randi, or as eye-catching as Sarah, but the way that Jared looked at her was all that mattered.

Jared whistled as he caught her around the waist. "You're gorgeous."

Mara wrapped her arms around his neck. "You don't look so bad yourself, handsome." She paused before looking up at him, meeting his gaze. "You know you *will* interfere if Evan is miserable. He deserves to be happy."

Jared's expression changed to one of regret as he answered, "I owe Evan my life and my happiness now. But I don't think anyone knows what to do. None of us really knows how Randi feels, and Evan holds everything in a place where no one can see that he's suffering. I'm hoping they'll resolve this on their own."

"She loves him," Mara said confidently. "She wouldn't be sleeping with him if she didn't. She hasn't been with anyone since college. I tried to pry some information out of her during our lunch today, but she wasn't talking."

Randi had arrived to their women-only lunch late that day, after the others had finished talking about how concerned they were for Evan.

Mara was just as concerned about Randi. If she loved Evan, which Mara was pretty sure she did, his departure was going to break her heart. Randi had been through so much in her life. She deserved to be loved by a good man.

"She's sleeping with him?" Jared asked with a false tone of shock.

Mara rolled her eyes. Her husband knew damn well that Randi and Evan had been hot and heavy with each other. "I don't know what to do, either. Randi lost Joan so recently; I don't think she's quite recovered from that. Her relationship with Evan could hurt her badly."

Jared stroked her cheek and said softly, "Hey, sweetheart, don't worry so much. We don't know that they won't work everything out for themselves."

"I don't have a good feeling about it," Mara replied sadly. "Evan hasn't been here long enough to completely lose his guard, and he went through such a lot. I guess I'm worried he'll leave before he realizes how he really feels."

"He's learning fast." Jared wrapped his arms around her waist again and stroked her back. "Dante pressed him just a little about whether or not he was interested. He told Evan if it wasn't serious, he wanted to introduce Randi to some friends of his at the station. I thought Evan was going to have a heart attack or a stroke."

Mara raised an eyebrow. "So Dante was baiting him just like Evan did to you?"

"That was different. Evan did it personally," Jared grumbled.

Mara laughed. "Why do I have a feeling you enjoyed it just a little?" she asked as she recovered.

"I did," Jared admitted unabashedly. "But that doesn't mean I don't want to see him happy. Hell, I feel guilty about not knowing about his problems. I feel like a selfish bastard. I know Hope, Grady, and Dante do, too."

Mara lifted her palm to Jared's cheek gently. He'd suffered enough guilt in his past, and she didn't want him taking on blame that he didn't need to carry. "You didn't know. Nobody did. Evan wanted it that way. You know he's protective of all of you in his own way." The eldest Sinclair was hyperprotective, but he'd probably never admit it.

"I wish I would have known, but I know it isn't my fault. Because of you, Mara, I'm done carrying baggage," he told her fiercely. "If I need to, I'll do what I have to do to make my stubborn brother face his own ghosts from the past and learn how much better it is to be happy."

She smiled at him, proud of how far Jared had come at being brutally honest about everything in his life. "I know you will."

"I wonder how Randi took the news that Evan was her secret email buddy. Did she say?" Jared was curious.

"She didn't mention it," Mara answered thoughtfully, wondering herself how Randi had felt when she found out that she'd been talking to Evan all this time. "I'm sure she was shocked. Hope mentioned that they'd been anonymous friends for over a year, but Randi thought it was an employee of the Sinclair Fund."

"Would it matter to her?" Jared queried, his expression concerned. "Do you think she'd be pissed?"

"I'm not sure. I don't know exactly how they related to each other, but she won't be happy that he lied all this time."

"He said he didn't exactly lie. He just didn't correct her whenever she mentioned him being an employee of our fund." He hesitated before adding, "And he might have acknowledged it as the truth once or twice."

Mara gave Jared an admonishing look. "He lied."

"They agreed not to share identities," Jared argued.

"He's Evan Sinclair. He could have told her the truth once they got to know each other. I doubt that Randi blatantly lied to him."

"It's over. She knows now, and she's obviously forgiven him," Jared said confidently. "Hope told him to come clean and see what happened from that point on."

Mara nodded. "I hope everything goes okay tonight. I hope I'm dressed okay. The party didn't start out to be formal, but once Hope started calling it a ball, everyone seemed to think they needed to dress for a fancy do." Her sister-in-law was still calling it a come-as-you-are event, but she knew the attendees were excited to put on their best dress and have a good time. "The ballroom looks beautiful. We all stopped to do a last-minute check before we came home."

Jared pulled her closer. "You look beautiful, Mara. Can't you tell?"

She shuddered as his rock-hard erection connected with her body. "You always think I look beautiful," she told him in a teasing voice.

"That's because you always do," he answered immediately, his hands moving down to caress her ass through the silky fabric of the blue cocktail dress.

Mara sighed as he moved closer, getting drunk off his scent and the deep timbre of his voice. Jared invariably affected her that way. Just that quickly, he could set her body on fire with a desire so strong that it was unstoppable.

"I love you," she told him softly, looking into his adoring eyes.

"I love you, too, sweetheart," he rasped, lowering his mouth to hers as he threaded his hands through her hair, undoing her hard work in trying to tame it into an upswept, more sophisticated style.

Any regret she had about her spoiled hair dissolved as she melted into Jared's embrace.

They were going to be late for the ball, but even that thought was erased from her mind.

A few seconds later, all she could think about was Jared.

CHAPTER 17

I can never fall in love with a man like him.

Evan could still picture those words from Randi, written in her email, over and over again. Of course, she hadn't been talking about some unknown male. If so, Evan would have been pretty damn happy knowing she was blowing off another guy. However, knowing it had been *him* she was referring to made him almost certifiable.

Evan rarely got angry, and he still couldn't figure out why he was so pissed off. After all, did he really think a woman like Randi was going to fall in love with a defective man like him? He was an unromantic, anal type of fucked-up man, focused more on business than anything else in his life.

I'm still trying to prove myself worthy of her friendship, much less her love.

Hell, it didn't matter, and it didn't relieve the burning pain in his chest when he thought about the fact that she had written that she could never love a man like him.

I'll make her love me. She will love me.

Evan wondered if that was even possible, but he didn't accept defeat well at all. Maybe this wasn't about business, but it had become just as damned important to him.

It's more important.

Even as the thought slipped into his mind unconsciously, he admitted it was true. For the first time in his life, someone other than his family took precedence over his portfolio.

"What's your driver's name?"

Evan straightened the cuffs of his tuxedo—which didn't really need fixing—as Randi's voice jolted him from his rampant thoughts. He was seated next to her in the backseat of the Rolls, on their way to the ball.

She was dressed in a beautiful red cocktail dress that showed off every one of her curves and revealed way too much of her flawless skin, as far as he was concerned. He could have done without the low-cut back and the plunging neckline. It wasn't that he didn't want to see her in the dress she was wearing; he'd just prefer that nobody else did.

Mine!

It had taken everything he had not to lock her inside of her house with him and keep her there. His dick had been hard from the moment she'd smiled at him when she opened the door.

Her killer smile got to him. *Every. Damn. Time.*

Finally, he answered her question. "His name is Stokes."

"What's his first name?" she asked in an insistent whisper, obviously not wanting the older man to hear.

"I have no idea," he answered honestly. Evan rarely knew the first name of *any* of his employees.

"He's a new driver?"

"He's been with me for years," he corrected.

"And you don't know his first name? Does he have a wife and children?" she whispered adamantly.

"I don't concern myself with my employees' personal business. If I did, I'd never get anything done."

Evan knew he was in trouble from the moment he saw the disapproval on her face. "That's not true and you know it. He's a personal employee. He takes care of *you*. Maybe it's true that you need to be impersonal with some people, but not the people you let into your personal life."

Evan shrugged. Truth was, he didn't let anybody into his personal life. Hell, he'd never really *had* a personal life. It was always all about business.

Stokes drove the car.

Evan worked in the backseat until he reached his destination.

They didn't exchange personal comments.

He watched as Randi leaned over the front seat. "What's your first name, Stokes?"

To give Stokes credit, Evan noticed that his driver seemed completely unflustered. "Gerald, madam. My family calls me Jerry."

"Are you married?" Randi questioned conversationally.

"Yes, madam. The wife and I just celebrated our fiftieth wedding anniversary," Stokes told Randi in a stoic voice.

"Children? Grandchildren?" Randi prompted.

"Three wonderful children, six grandkids, and now three great-grandbabies so far," Stokes answered, his voice warming as he spoke about his family.

"You didn't want to retire?" Randi shifted positions so she could lean closer to the driver from the backseat.

Evan hated that.

"No, madam. I lost my job when I was almost retirement age. Mr. Sinclair was kind enough to give an old man a chance instead of hiring a younger body. I needed the work then. My daughter was sick and needed help. He made it possible for me to help her with a more-than-fair income as his driver. I'll be a loyal employee until the day I can't drive anymore," Stokes answered, his voice a little more emotional as he spoke of his employer and his past.

Evan fidgeted uncomfortably in his seat, wondering why he never knew about Stokes and his family. It wasn't that his driver wasn't willing to talk. Evan realized he'd just never bothered to ask.

He made a vow to find out if Stokes was financially set for the rest of his life. The man usually traveled everywhere with his car, always there at Evan's beck and call. If he had family, maybe it was time for him to enjoy some kind of retirement.

"I hired you because you were qualified. I've kept you on because you're one of the best employees I've ever had," Evan stated loud enough to be heard by Stokes.

"Thank you, sir," the driver replied humbly, his voice filled with pride. "We've reached your destination."

Evan looked out the window to see that they were parked right in front of the Center. People were filing into the building slowly, all dressed for a party.

"It's an open party, Jerry," Randi said brightly. "Would you like to come in and get something to eat?"

Stokes turned around and smiled at her. It was the first time Evan had ever seen his driver actually smile.

Stokes shook his head. "No . . . but thank you, madam. I'll just pop over to that little restaurant with the lobster rolls. Great food there."

"Sullivan's," Randi answered with a kind smile and a nod. "Have a nice dinner."

Evan waited as his driver got out and opened the door for him. He stood and said quietly to Stokes, "Talk to me when you're ready to retire. I'll make sure you're well taken care of, Stokes."

His driver nodded. "I know that, sir. Thank you." He paused before adding, "That's one sweet girl you have there. She's a keeper."

"I plan on keeping her," Evan answered fiercely. "She just doesn't know it yet."

He saw Stokes smile in the dim light. "Very good, sir."

Evan moved to the other side of the vehicle, but Randi was already out of the car and headed straight toward him. She seemed totally unconcerned that she had to open her own car door. Most of the women he knew would have sat and waited for somebody to do it for them.

Not his woman. He needed to be faster if he wanted to keep up with her.

Randi had been independent most of her life, and she knew nothing about the rituals of the super-rich.

That was one of the things Evan liked about her. Randi was unpretentious and as real as a woman could get.

She just found out more about my employee in two minutes than I have in all the years Stokes has worked for me.

He offered his arm as she reached him, and he dismissed Stokes to go have his dinner.

"It wasn't that painful, right?" Randi asked quietly as they walked arm in arm to the front entrance of the Center.

"What?"

"Learning something about your employees. He idolizes you."

"I pay his salary," Evan replied solemnly. "But you're right. I'm glad I know his situation. I can set him up for retirement as soon as he's ready."

Randi nodded. "There's nothing wrong with caring, Evan."

He didn't reply. Obviously there *was* a problem with caring. He wanted Randi, but she only wanted him for the short time he was here.

For the first time, he *did* care, and it fucking hurt that she didn't.

I can never love a man like him.

It was going to take a long time for Evan to forget seeing those words, and exactly how he felt when he thought about them.

Micah had seen her the minute she walked into the ballroom. There was no way he could miss her.

"Are you headed out tomorrow?" Julian asked him as he wolfed down another plate of food from the buffet.

"Yeah. I have to go. I have early meetings Monday morning," Micah replied.

Micah liked Amesport, and he didn't like the thought of actually leaving. He hadn't been back to Sullivan's since his run-in with Liam, but he'd been tempted.

"Me too. I have an interview in Los Angeles," Julian admitted.

"Good. Then I can have my jet back. You can get your own now, you know," Micah told him testily, still watching Tessa move around the room gracefully.

"I know," Julian replied with a grin. "But I never really went any-where before. I didn't have to."

Julian could have always afforded to buy any private jet he chose. He might have been a "nobody" in Hollywood until he hit the big time just recently, but he was still a very rich Sinclair.

The orchestra kicked up the volume a few notches, obviously ready for people to start dancing.

"I'll be back," Micah told Julian without looking away from Tessa.

If his brother answered, Micah didn't hear it. He was determined to make his way to the beautiful female across the room before some-one else did.

He approached her as she was talking with two elderly women, one of them dressed in deep violet, the other in a rather flamboyant hot pink.

As he got closer, he heard Tessa speak. "Beatrice, I appreciate the present, but you know I don't believe in miracles."

The woman in bright pink beamed back at Tessa. "It's your turn, dear. Your destiny."

"She knows," the woman in purple said excitedly. "Beatrice saw it clearly."

"You'll hear him, but not in the way you might expect," Beatrice told Tessa, patting her on the cheek. "You'll need to listen with every-thing in you to understand what he's trying to tell you."

"Hello." Micah finally spoke, touching Tessa on the shoulder so she knew he was behind her.

"Micah Sinclair," Beatrice said, staring at him with a radiant expression. "I've been looking for you. I'm Beatrice, and this is Elsie." She waved toward her friend.

Tessa turned to read his lips.

"Why were you looking for me?" he asked, confused. He'd never seen either of the women before.

Beatrice extended her hand and Micah automatically reached for the item she held out to him. He looked curiously at the stone that dropped into his hand, turning it over and over. "I can't accept this. I don't even know you." He had no idea why an elderly woman he didn't know had just given him a rock.

"No, but I know you, young man. That's your destiny." Beatrice waved toward his fingers.

"I don't understand. I just came over to ask Tessa to dance." He looked at the two women, perplexed.

"I'll dance," Tessa squeaked, taking his hand in hers and making their escape. "Thank you, ladies. It was nice to see you both."

Micah dropped the rock into his pocket and lifted his hand at the two ladies in a farewell gesture. Tessa started dragging him away like she was running from a fire.

What in the hell had just happened?

As she came to a halt in the middle of the dance floor, Micah asked, "Are they crazy?"

"No. But they're both very eccentric. Beatrice is the town matchmaker and resident psychic, and Elsie writes the gossip for the paper. They're harmless, but I needed to be rescued. Thank you."

He looked down at Tessa. "Can you really dance?"

She shrugged. "I don't know. I haven't tried since I lost my hearing. Can you lead?"

"Of course," he replied immediately. "I'm good at most things that require physical participation." He winked at her.

She rolled her eyes. "Show me."

Micah clasped one of her hands and put his other arm around her waist. "This is a waltz."

She nodded at him and kept her eyes on his face.

Surprisingly, she was a very graceful dancer, better than anybody he'd ever danced with before. She followed him easily, and she felt incredible in his arms.

He stared down at her and remarked, "You're very good."

"Thanks," she answered politely.

Micah was surprised when she winked back at him and then laid her head against his shoulder. He continued to lead her, and she followed him every step of the way.

Neither of them spoke as their bodies communicated without words . . . and they danced.

CHAPTER 18

Evan's fists clenched at his sides as his eyes tracked Randi on the dance floor. An hour after they'd arrived, she'd agreed to a dance with Liam, and Evan wasn't dealing well with anybody holding Randi except him.

I should have asked her to dance first. I should have kept her on the floor all night.

Unfortunately, he'd done neither one of those things, so he was standing alone in a corner, one shoulder propped against the wall, trying especially hard not to bash his fist into it.

He gritted his teeth as he saw Randi tip her head up and smile at Liam, apparently enjoying both the dance and his company. He almost stepped forward as the guy had the audacity to move his hand over her bare back.

His forward progress was stopped by a rather large body that stepped in front of him.

"You look like you need this." Jared handed him a glass filled with ice and what Evan assumed was alcohol.

"I don't drink," he replied irritably, stepping around his brother to move toward Randi again.

"Maybe you should tonight," Jared suggested smoothly, grasping the back of Evan's tuxedo so he didn't move forward. "Don't do it, Evan. He's a decent sort of guy."

"He's touching her," Evan rasped angrily.

Jared stepped in front of Evan again and pushed him back against the wall. "Have a drink and relax. Tessa tried to set up Liam and Randi, but Liam got sick. I'm sure he just wanted to apologize for leaving her high and dry. She's not interested in him."

Evan downed the entire glass of liquid in one gulp and handed it back to Jared. It took superhuman effort not to cough as the alcohol burned all the way down his throat to his gut. "Did you just poison me?" he asked in a painfully hoarse voice.

"Scotch on the rocks. It's a good year and brand. You'll get used to it. It's kind of an acquired taste," Jared remarked with a mischievous grin as he handed Evan a second glass that he'd snagged from a passing waiter. "Drink it slow," he warned.

Evan scowled at the glass in his hand. "How do you know that she's not interested? She's smiling at him."

"Generally, if a guy asks a woman to dance it's not really appropriate *not* to smile. Just calm the hell down. It's just a dance," Jared advised. He paused to take a sip of his own drink before adding, "Damn, you have it bad for her."

Evan took an unconscious swig from his glass, his mind elsewhere as the liquid burned its way to his stomach. The fiery heat didn't even make him flinch. "You're blocking my view," he growled.

"I know," Jared answered calmly, shoving a hand in the pocket of his tuxedo pants and looking like he was making himself comfortable. "Believe me, it's better this way. The song will be over in another minute or two."

"I hate feeling this way," Evan admitted. His control was slowly slipping, and he knew he was acting irrationally, but he didn't give a shit.

"Now you know how I felt when I thought my own brother was interested in my woman," Jared reminded him harshly.

"I didn't dance with her," Evan pointed out.

"No, but you did touch her, pick her up, and hold her," Jared remarked casually. "And you did take an interest in her."

"Because I actually liked Mara," Evan snapped. "And you were acting like a jackass."

"Kind of like you're acting right now?" Jared prompted.

"Yes," he growled, realizing just how Jared had felt when Evan had tried to make him see sense by hinting that he might be interested in Mara himself. "Okay, I'm sorry. I didn't know how it felt back then."

"Apology accepted," Jared replied calmly. "I'm thinking that karma is a bitch right now for you."

Evan took another sip from his drink. "Pretty much," he grunted as he swiped a hand across his face. He was starting to relax, but he was sweating. It had to be the effects of the alcohol. He didn't usually imbibe, and the drink was obviously starting to hit him pretty hard.

"You okay, Evan?" Jared asked in a milder, more concerned tone.

For the first time in his life, Evan answered the question honestly. "No. No, I don't think I *am* okay." His voice was raw with emotion, and his chest ached with a pain he'd never experienced before. So many feelings began to bombard him all at once that he wasn't certain which ones to react to first. "I love her," he added, his vulnerability open for Jared to see, but it didn't seem to matter.

"I know." Jared's answer was benevolent. "But it's not the end of the world, Evan. It's the beginning of something so good that you'll wake up every morning happy to just see her face when you open your eyes."

"I won't be seeing her. I'm leaving tomorrow, and she can't love me," he snarled back. Maybe his younger brothers' relationships had worked out, but Evan couldn't *make* Randi love him no matter how much he wished he could.

"Then don't go," Jared suggested.

"I have an important meeting in San Francisco on Monday, a company I've been trying to acquire controlling ownership on for a long time. I think they're ready, because they need capital to grow. If I'm not there to snap up the company, somebody else will," he answered automatically.

"So let them." Jared was blunt. "Evan, there comes a point where the money doesn't matter anymore. We have so much that we couldn't spend it in a dozen lifetimes."

"It's not about the money. It's about being better, being successful. The old man never thought I'd do it, but I can." Evan was breathing heavily as he downed the rest of the drink and tossed the glass on a table beside him.

"You already have," Jared answered furiously. "You don't have a damn thing to prove to anybody anymore, Evan. That battle is over and won. It only still exists in your own head."

"Is everything okay?" a feminine voice interrupted.

Jared stepped aside, revealing Randi and her dance partner. "Fine," he said amiably. "Evan and I were just discussing . . . business."

"Would you like to dance another one, Randi?" Liam asked politely, his hand resting on her bare back.

"No, she wouldn't," Evan growled, his temper finally snapping.

He stepped forward and grabbed the front of Liam's starched white shirt that he was wearing with a gray suit and tie. "Take your hands off her," he rasped, his rage now beyond being contained.

Jared reached out and pulled Randi to the side, causing Liam to lose any connection with her. "Stop it, Evan. People are starting to stare," Jared advised.

Evan didn't give a shit whether the entire world was watching. He stood toe-to-toe with his rival, a homicidal look on his face. Without letting go of Liam's shirt, he said in a low, dangerous voice, "Don't look at her. Don't think about touching her. Don't ever even imagine yourself with her or your ass is mine."

Jared jerked Evan backward, forcing him to let go of Liam. "Randi, can you take Evan somewhere to cool off? He's . . . overheated. I'll talk to Liam."

Randi grasped Evan's arm and whispered fiercely, "What in the hell was that about?" She started to lead him away from the crowded ballroom.

Evan followed . . . well . . . just because he'd follow her anywhere.

He let her lead him down the hallway and away from the ballroom, stepping into a smaller room some distance away from the crowd.

She closed the door and locked it behind her, and then pushed him into a padded chair that seemed much too small for him.

"What in the hell just happened?" she asked, sounding more puzzled than angry.

"I didn't like the way he was touching you." Evan's response was angry.

"We were dancing," she answered reasonably and propped her hands on her hips.

"I know. I hated it." His answer was blunt as he struggled to regain his usual control.

"Then *you* should have asked me to dance," she said softly. "You are my date."

"That's another thing I never did right for a Sinclair. I suck at dancing," he confessed. "I wish I would have done it anyway. I don't do it perfectly, so I rarely dance. Would you have cared?"

Randi's expression softened as she looked down at him. "No. I wouldn't have minded at all. In fact, it would make you more human. Nobody is perfect at everything. *You* don't have to be perfect at *everything*, Evan. You're already disgustingly close."

Then why can't you love me? Why can't you love a man like me?

He wanted desperately to ask her, but the answer was obvious. Love just . . . was. There was no explanation for it, no way to rationalize it, and no way to pick the perfect partner and feel those kinds of emotions.

He was starting to understand that love wasn't a choice, it just happened. He definitely never thought it would happen to him.

"I think you owe Liam an apology," Randi remarked matter-of-factly. "He was being charming and polite."

"He wasn't charming." Evan's response was disgruntled. "He wants to get you naked."

"How would you know?" she asked.

"Because I want the same damn thing. I recognize the look, but he's not nearly as pathetically desperate as I am for that right now." He stood and grasped her around the waist. "I want it every time I see you or hear your voice. I want it when you smile at me. I want it every fucking minute of the day. If I'm not with you, I want to be." His breathing labored, he added, "I. Need. You."

Evan shuddered as Randi wrapped her arms around his neck and placed her soft cheek against his slightly whiskered jaw. "I need you, too. I'm not interested in Liam, Evan." She sniffed and then asked him quietly, "Is this the alcohol talking? I can smell it. Have you been drinking?"

"Two drinks. I'm not drunk, Randi. I'm emotional, something that never happens to me."

"Jealous?" she questioned.

"Yes," he answered promptly, honestly. "I don't want any man touching you except me."

"You're leaving early in the morning. We can't be this intense right now," Randi warned him in a husky voice.

"Right now is what we have," Evan said angrily, unable to process the thought of leaving her side, much less putting any more distance between the two of them. He'd lose it entirely.

He watched as the gold in her beautiful eyes seemed to erupt into tiny, sparkling particles. She gazed up at him with a look of longing that made Evan feel like he'd been punched in the gut.

"Then fuck me, Evan. Here. Now. One last time," she begged breathlessly. "I know we can't have a relationship, but you're right. We have right now. I've learned that sometimes that's all a person will ever have."

He wanted forever, but he needed her so desperately that he'd figure that all out later. He looked around quickly, realizing they were in a powder room, and the door beyond probably led to the toilets. He knew from previous visits that there were plenty of restrooms at the Center, but this was obviously one that Grady had redone to be nicer, plusher.

There were small, elegant chairs lined in front of a long line of mirrors, probably so women could do whatever it was that women did to freshen up.

Too far gone to really care where they were, he reached behind her and double-checked the lock on the door to make sure it was secure, and then he stalked her. "It's going to end up hard and fast, Randi. Possibly even rough. I don't have even an ounce of control right now when it comes to you," he warned her in a dangerous voice.

"I don't care," she answered emphatically, letting him pin her against the makeup counter.

Evan removed his tuxedo jacket roughly, yanking it from his body and turning it inside out in his haste to get it off him so he had more freedom of movement. He needed his body to be as unrestrained as his mind was at the moment.

He dropped the jacket on the floor, feeling relieved once it was gone. His gut tightened and his cock pulsated with the need to be inside Randi as he looked down at her vulnerable expression.

"Are you scared?" he asked gruffly.

She shook her head. "No. Not of you. But I'm afraid of the way I feel."

Her statement made a million questions flitter through Evan's mind.

How do you feel?

Do you feel like you're losing your sanity as much as I do?

How do you expect me to leave when I want more than anything to stay?

All of those unanswered questions fled from his brain as Randi tore off his bow tie and tugged hard at his shirt, scattering buttons onto the carpeted floor.

When she touched his bare skin, he forgot about them completely as the feral, carnal emotions he'd been experiencing became his elemental focus.

When Randi curled a hand behind his neck and tugged his mouth down to hers, Evan Sinclair, master of the art of control, finally lost it completely.

CHAPTER 19

If Randi wasn't so lost, she might have pondered that if she looked back on this night later, she'd admit that it was Evan's vulnerability that had finally gotten to her.

His anger, the fear and pain she could see in his expression, and his willingness to expose himself tore at her heart. She could see his need in those beautiful eyes of his, and the war he was waging with his emotions was her undoing.

I love him.

There was no uncertainty, no hesitation anymore. She wanted Evan Sinclair and all of his unguarded fierceness more than she needed the oxygen she breathed.

He ravaged her mouth like she was the only woman he ever wanted to kiss, but she needed so much more. She wanted to climb inside him until she couldn't get any closer to him.

Need slithered inside her belly, moving straight to her core, as she wrapped her arms around his neck and held on for dear life.

"Evan, please," she begged as his mouth left hers, trailing a rough path with his tongue down the sensitive skin of her neck. "Fuck me."

All her defenses were stripped away. She wanted and needed him.

"You. Are. Mine," he told her in a demanding voice as he pulled the silky material of her gown up to her waist.

Randi moaned aloud as Evan's fingers pressed insistently between their bodies and beneath the scant covering of the thong she was wearing beneath the dress. She had worn the most daring set of lingerie she'd ever owned underneath her gown, needing to feel like the sexiest woman alive for just one more night.

"Christ, what are you wearing?" Evan's voice was needy and hungry.

She didn't answer; she panted as she leaned back on the counter, letting Evan look until he growled.

Randi trembled as he yanked the dress over her head, helping him as she shrugged it off and let it drop to the floor. She hadn't worn a bra since the dress had a low back, and she could just imagine what she looked like in the red thong panties, her heels, and silky stockings held up by a garter belt. "They're new. I bought them for our last night together."

It was a bold move for her, a woman who liked lacy, pretty underwear rather than what she was wearing now.

Evan traced the outline of her folds through her saturated panties. Grasping her roughly by the waist, he sat her up on the counter. "I'll buy you more," he said in a harsh voice.

Before Randi could react, he gave a hard tug on the flimsy material and the panties came apart.

His mouth was between her thighs almost instantly, as he placed her legs on his shoulders.

The feel of his hot, hungry mouth on her bare pussy was a shock to her senses, especially since he didn't start slow. He devoured. He tasted. He licked until Randi was chanting his name. "Evan. Oh God, Evan."

His fierce possession of her was exhilarating. He held open her folds and buried his face in her pussy, feasting on her ravenously, greedily. He didn't tease. He was a man driven to make her come, and his laser focus on the task was mind-blowing.

"Yes," she moaned, fisting his hair and pulling his face flush against her needy core. "More."

Evan could be as rough as possible, and it still might not be enough. She needed to come, and she needed it right now.

His tongue rolled exquisitely over her clit, forcefully and commandingly. There was no real finesse. There was only passion, desire, and raw, carnal need.

"Yes. Please. Now." She whimpered her plea, grinding her pussy against his face, demanding that he make her climax.

And suddenly, devastatingly, she did, with a blinding-hot intensity that made her scream. "Evan!"

Pulsating waves washed over her in assaulting forcefulness, making it impossible for her to do anything but ride along with them. Evan rose and tore at his tuxedo pants, freeing his massive, hard cock in record time.

Randi barely had time to draw breath before Evan was inside her. He claimed her savagely, need riding him.

She coveted his possessive, caveman-like claiming, *needing* it to make her feel alive. Wrapping her arms around his neck, she clung to him. Her channel was still squeezing him from her first orgasm.

"Christ. You feel like a dream, but I know you're real," Evan said gravely, his voice vibrating with passion.

"Harder." Randi needed more.

He yanked her off the slick countertop, and she nearly wailed aloud as he pulled himself out of her. Flipping her around, he took her hands and placed them on the counter as he moved behind her. "This will be hard, but I can't control myself right now."

"I need you out of control," she agreed.

He drove his cock home, burying himself so deeply that Randi moaned.

"You're mine," Evan insisted in a feral groan as he pulled his cock almost totally out of her channel and drove it back in again.

Randi gasped at Evan's carnal claiming, needing something to hold, something to keep her from flying away on a violent wave of elemental desire. Gripping the marble countertop tightly, she pushed back as Evan surged forward, and a feeling of satisfaction enveloped her at the sound of their bodies slamming together.

It was too much.

It wasn't enough.

Randi wanted to hold Evan inside her as deeply as he could possibly get. That was the moment she realized that he owned her: heart, body, and soul. She wanted more; she wanted everything from him.

"Don't hold back," she begged him with a moan, her body writhing.

"I can't," he admitted, sounding tortured as his grip on her hips tightened hard enough that she'd probably have bruises come morning. "Admit that you're mine, Randi. Say it or I'm going to lose my damn mind."

"I love you," she blurted out helplessly, unable to keep her emotions under control. Every movement, every ragged breath she took was focused only on Evan at the moment, and she had to tell him how she felt.

"Fuck," Evan rasped, pummeling into her with a strength that left her mindless. "What did you just say?"

"I love you," she bellowed out loud, the words echoing in the tiny space.

She exploded the moment Evan moved one of his hands to the front of her body and stroked a thumb over her engorged clit. Her head dropped to the counter as her body was assaulted by pulsations that had her heart racing and her entire body trembling in climax.

"Don't look down." Evan grasped her hair and pulled her head up. "I need to see you."

She probably wouldn't have lifted her head if Evan hadn't been supporting it by his hold on her hair. He threaded his fingers through the tresses, and their eyes met in the mirror as she saw herself in the throes of an orgasm.

Desperate.

Needy.

So entirely pleasured that at the moment, she didn't even know her own name.

"You make me feel so good, it's almost painful," she moaned as she stared into a pair of blue eyes filled with torment and confusion.

Their gazes locked and held until Evan gave one final thrust and leaned his head back in ecstasy as she milked him of his own release.

He wrapped his arms around her and pulled her back against his body as they both panted for breath, finally pulling her into the too-small chair and letting her collapse onto his lap as his cock slid from its position inside her.

"Tell me why, Randi," Evan demanded as he recovered his composure.

She clung to him, her arms around his neck to retain her position on his lap. "What?" She had no idea what he was talking about.

"Tell me why you said you could never love a man like me. Those words nearly killed me. Why did you say that?" He stroked her hair like she was the most precious female on earth.

Randi tried to make her brain functional again, his questions sinking in as she slowly regained coherent thought. She hadn't said that, had she? "I never said that."

I can never love a man like him.

Her brain started working, and she shook her head at the conclusion it was making.

It wasn't possible, but yet . . . She'd never said those words to Evan; she'd made that comment in writing to S.

Somehow it all made sense. Actually, hadn't S. started encouraging her relationship with Evan, even asking her to give him a chance after he'd warned her away?

S. had changed since she'd started a relationship with Evan—now that she really thought about it. He asked a lot about her relationship, and was almost prompting her to give Evan a chance, a man he'd never met. His behavior was exactly the opposite of his normal and constant cautiousness.

She stood, feeling naked figuratively as well as physically. Snatching her dress from the floor, she donned it mechanically, pulling down the silky material of her gown to cover her scanty remaining lingerie hastily.

Her stomach lurched as she thought about some of the conversations they'd had, and the fact that S. now had a woman in his life. The Sinclair Fund was Evan's business, so it wasn't a stretch that it could be him, that it had always been *him*.

Her heart started to bleed as she thought about the fact that if he was S., he hadn't told her, had actually lied to her. He'd used the relationship to his advantage, and to hell with how she felt. They were incongruent actions from the Evan she'd come to know and love.

Maybe I only thought I knew him.

"I didn't say those words to you. I wrote them to a man I thought was a friend, a man I trusted." She took a deep breath and asked quietly, "Are *you* that man?"

Randi wasn't looking at him directly but she saw him give an affirmative jerk of his head from the corner of her eye as he stood up. "Yes," he admitted huskily.

"The calla lily on Dennis and Joan's graves. It was you?" She already knew the answer. Gut instinct told her that it was true. Maybe she was able to blow it off before, but that made sense to her now, too. Evan Sinclair was probably one of the only men who could get anything he wanted, even a perfect calla lily every day in the dead of winter in Maine.

"Yes." Evan zipped his pants and reached for his shirt and tie. "I did it every day to thank them."

"What were you thanking them for?" Her mind was spinning, and she was still trying to wrap her head around the idea that S. and Evan were one and the same man.

As he jammed his arms into his shirt, he replied, "I was thanking them for saving you when I couldn't. I'm grateful you're here, that you're healthy and strong. I'm grateful that they gave you a home. Most of all, I'm grateful they saved you for me." He shouldered into his jacket and put his tie in the pocket.

Randi felt completely destroyed and betrayed by the two men who meant the most to her. "You lied to me. When did you know who I was?"

"The day I brought you supplies and you lost power. Hope told me that you had recently lost your foster mother, and everything fell into place. I should have told you that day, but I couldn't."

Okay . . . so maybe he hadn't known for very long, but he'd known before they'd ever been intimate. He should have told her before anything ever happened between them. "There was nothing stopping you from telling me," she told him furiously, angry now that the initial shock of his confession had worn off. "You played me." He'd used his status as a trusted friend to get information from her.

"I didn't do it on purpose," he grumbled as he strode forward and gripped her by the shoulders. "Why did you say you couldn't love me if you do?"

She shook off his hands, not wanting him to touch her. He'd betrayed her, and his dishonesty and the way he'd toyed with her emotions infuriated her.

"I didn't say I *didn't* love you. I said I *can't* love you because of my past and the problems it might cause. You're a billionaire who travels and I'm a teacher who stays in the same place. Don't worry. I'll get over it. The fact that you're a liar and that you deceived me will help me get over you that much faster," she answered hotly.

Evan grabbed her shoulders again. "You'll never get over me. I'll never get over you," he growled, sounding enraged. "I've never gotten over you. I feel the same damn way every time I see you. I wasn't as shocked as I should have been to learn that you were the woman I was corresponding with, either. I should have known that two different women could never hold my interest in the same way. I have to wonder if deep down inside, you knew who I was, too."

"I didn't know," Randi denied emphatically. "I thought you were my friend." The loss of both men was practically ripping her heart from her chest.

"I am your friend. I'm also your lover," Evan replied flatly.

"You're nothing," Randi answered, thinking about all of the times he'd played with her feelings. "Was any of it real?"

"All of it," Evan said in a graveled voice. "And don't say I'm nothing to you. You just told me you loved me."

She pulled away from him to look at his face, unable to decipher exactly what was real and what wasn't. He'd lied to her from the very beginning, agreeing that he was just an employee. Then he'd bullshitted her again, not telling her the truth even after he knew who she was. "I don't really know you, do I?" she asked angrily. "How can I love a man who doesn't exist?" The question made her nauseous. How could she have been so stupid?

"You do love me, dammit!" Evan answered sharply. "You said you did."

"That was before I knew that you were a manipulative liar." Randi unlocked the door as tears rolled down her face, the pain of his duplicitous actions gripping her heart and tearing it to shreds.

Gasping for breath, she knew she needed to get out of the tiny room, create some distance between her and Evan. She had to think, needed to understand. Opening the door, she quickly fled, wondering if she'd ever be able to get over the excruciating pain of Evan's betrayal.

Male voices sounded behind her as she ran toward the entrance to the Center, but she couldn't make out who they were or what was said. Honestly, she didn't care.

I have to get out of here.

Escape was the only thing she could think of right now.

The harshly cold temperatures hit her the moment she ran out the front door, her gown offering little protection from the elements.

"Madam, are you all right?" The male voice came from beside her.

She saw Stokes as she turned her head to the side. "No. I'm not okay," she told the elderly man as she angrily swiped the tears from her face. "I need to get home."

"I'll take you." The driver took her arm gently and led her to the Rolls.

"Evan will want you," she protested.

"For once in his life, Mr. Sinclair can wait," Stokes answered firmly, helping her to the vehicle sitting right out front.

Distraught, Randi didn't argue. She needed to leave this place, she needed to think, and she needed to put space between herself and the man who had just rocked her world in a good way . . . and a devastating one. She jumped into the rear seat of the luxury vehicle as soon as the driver opened the back door for her.

Stokes set the car in motion almost immediately, leaving her huddled in the seat behind him—bewildered, crying, and feeling as though her heart would never be whole again.

CHAPTER 20

"What the hell happened?" Micah grilled Evan about the scene he'd stumbled upon at the Center.

Completely confused, he eyed Evan curiously. It never looked good when a disheveled woman came sobbing out of a bathroom with an unkempt man right behind her. Oh, not that he thought Evan had done something wrong, but when it came to Randi, it was quite possible for him to actually do something stupid.

"I told her the truth about being the guy she was writing to," Evan admitted glumly.

"I thought she already knew. Hope told you to tell her right away."

"I . . . didn't." Evan was chugging down whiskey like it was bottled water.

Shit! No wonder Randi was pissed off. Micah wondered what had motivated Evan not to follow his sister's advice.

"Why didn't you tell her?" Julian asked curiously as he motioned to the bartender for another beer.

As soon as he'd prevented Evan from making more of a scene in the Center by keeping him from chasing after a sobbing Randi, Micah had grabbed Julian and the three of them had left to go somewhere quieter.

That destination ended up being Shamrock's Pub. It was a small, quiet bar and grill on Main Street, not far from the Center, and there were only a few other people in the entire place. Micah was betting that it was so slow here because of the party. Half of the town was probably there, and it wasn't tourist season.

Evan looked at Julian suspiciously.

"I filled him in," Micah confessed calmly, not feeling the least bit guilty because he'd told Julian all about Evan's past and his attachment to Miranda Tyler. After all, it was *family* business.

"I was fucking afraid to tell her," Evan rasped, jerking at his collar, only to have the buttonless shirt he was now wearing open wider. "It's hot in here."

It wasn't warm at all in the bar, but Micah suspected it was the whiskey that Evan was slugging down causing his hot flashes. "Hope told you to tell her," Micah reminded him.

"I couldn't. I was afraid she'd dump me. And I was getting more uncensored information as her friend on the Internet than I was in person."

"You talked about yourself to her via email? And she didn't know it was you, but you knew exactly who she was?" Julian asked, obviously trying to verify what he was hearing.

"Yes." Evan slumped back in his chair.

"You're an asshole," Micah and Julian said in tandem.

Evan threw both of them a furious look from across the wooden table. "I thought you said you were going to help me."

"That was before we knew you did something so stupid. Jesus, Evan. Why couldn't you just listen to Hope? She might be your sister, but she's also a female. You betrayed Randi's trust. There's no getting around that." Micah wondered how someone as smart as Evan could be so clueless when it came to relationships.

I may not be an expert, but I know better than to lie to a woman. They always find out the truth, and it's never good when they do.

Micah had never been in Evan's predicament. In fact, he'd been the one who had been shafted. He'd tried a serious relationship once, and his supposed fiancée had ended up sleeping with, and eventually marrying, his best friend. He hadn't tried having another exclusive relationship since.

Evan slammed his empty glass on the table. "I know I kept the truth from her. But I was going to tell her."

Micah looked at Julian and caught him grinning. "Don't piss him off," he warned. "He's already going off the deep end." He spoke just loud enough for Julian to hear him.

"I know. I can't help myself. I can hardly believe *this* is *our* Evan," Julian said in a low voice, still smirking as he looked across the table at his cousin. "He doesn't get rattled about anything, but right now he looks completely destroyed. I feel sorry for him, but it's really just a little bit scary to see him looking this way. And it's all happening because of a female." Julian shook his head.

Micah knew what Julian was thinking, but he also knew Evan was hurting . . . bad. The guy *did* look like somebody had taken him to hell and back, and that was so *not* like Evan. He rarely had a lock of hair out of place, and he wore his custom suits without a single wrinkle. It was pretty shocking to see that a woman had reduced him to his current state.

Turning back in Evan's direction, Micah questioned, "When were you going to tell her? She probably thinks you were playing her."

"That's what *she* said," Evan agreed, nodding his head.

Bingo! That *was* a problem. Once you burned a female by lying, she never forgot about it. Micah knew Evan hadn't intended to be deceptive, but it had looked that way because he was totally clueless.

The female bartender interrupted their conversation, taking Julian's empty bottle and putting down a fresh napkin with a full beer on top.

"Thanks, Red," Julian told her with a wink.

Micah recognized her. If he remembered correctly, her name was Kristin Moore. He'd met her at both Dante's and Jared's weddings. "I know you. I thought you were a medical assistant at Sarah's office," he said, wondering why she was bartending here.

The curvy redhead nodded at him curtly, and then glared at Julian. "My name is Kristin, not *Red*. I hate that nickname, and if you say it again, I'll show you the door. But not before I put your balls in your throat, superstar," she told him irritably, then turned to Micah with a kinder gaze. "I do work for Sarah, but my parents wanted to go to the ball. I'm filling in for them tonight. I work here in the evenings fairly often."

"Cinderella couldn't make it to the ball," Julian teased, unable to resist.

"I didn't want to go," she answered defensively.

"Of course you did," he shot back. "It's the event of the winter season here in Amesport."

"Not for me, hotshot." Kristin's voice was cold, and her eyes were shooting icicles in his direction. "I don't need a bunch of perfect Hollywood models to be happy."

Micah was fairly certain the two of them had met before. Kristin was Mara's best friend, and she had been at Dante's wedding. She'd been at Jared's wedding, too, but her broken leg had still been healing. "How's your leg?" he asked, trying to dissipate the tension he could feel flowing between his brother and the feisty bartender.

He could feel the angst flowing between them, and because he was sitting right between the two, Micah was directly in the line of fire. What in the hell had happened between the two of them to make them so antagonistic toward each other? Julian was a smartass on the surface, but it was all a cover, his Hollywood way of dealing with the ton of rejection and lack of callbacks in the early days of his career.

Kristin was outgoing and incredibly blunt. From what little he knew of her, she didn't take shit from anyone.

She was attractive, but not in any blatant way. She was slightly plump by Hollywood standards, and her flame-colored hair was pulled up in a ponytail. He could see some stray freckles on her face, so she was obviously not wearing much makeup. Kristin was the girl-next-door kind of pretty, not the supermodel type of bombshell that Julian was usually escorting around these days.

The two were bound to rub against each other. Julian acted like a jackass sometimes until a person got to really know him, and Kristin obviously didn't take any of his crap.

Micah smiled at Kristin, thinking it was interesting that she was obviously unimpressed by Julian's fame and success. He was an A-lister now, the actor everybody wanted for their next film.

The redhead didn't seem to give a damn who he was at all.

"My leg is healed now. Thanks for asking." She shot Micah a genuine smile, and he couldn't help but grin back at her. She might not be conventionally attractive, but he thought she was much more appealing than any of the women his brother had been dating. Obviously Julian thought so, too. He was certainly baiting her enough to find her interesting.

"I'm glad you're better," Micah said honestly, finding her more and more attractive as she became happier and less guarded.

"Can I get you anything else?" she asked politely, looking from him to Evan.

She completely ignored Julian, a fact that made Micah want to laugh as he noticed his brother's irritated look out of the corner of his eye.

"No, thanks. We have to leave soon," he told her kindly.

"I've probably had enough," Evan grumbled, squinting at his half-empty glass with a frown.

"You've had plenty," Micah agreed emphatically. He was slightly worried that he and Julian were going to have to carry Evan out of the bar if he didn't stop.

He'd never seen his cousin take a drink in his entire life. Evan was bound to be a lightweight when it came to alcohol, even though he was a big guy.

Kristin winked at Micah. "He's cut off. He's starting to tilt in his chair." She moved to Evan and straightened his body with her hip. "Need help with him?"

"No. We're good. We aren't driving." Micah had limited his drinking, but Stokes was now waiting for all of them out front. He'd take them all home.

Kristin nodded and walked away. The fact that Julian watched her all the way back to the bar didn't escape Micah's notice.

"I need to go talk to her," Evan said as he sat up and slumped on the table, his voice maudlin and somewhat slurred.

"Not tonight, buddy. You need to give her some time for all of this to sink in. How long did you say you were writing to each other?" Micah asked curiously.

"Over a year," Evan said grudgingly. "She got me with a smartass email. I've been addicted to her ever since."

"How is it that neither one of you knew who the other really was?"

"I tried to track her earlier in our correspondence. All I could find out was that it was coming from the Center. After that, I stopped trying. We agreed not to share identities. To her I was just some random guy. I wasn't a billionaire from one of the most well-known families in the world. I kind of liked that. But I did want to meet her. I don't think she wanted to meet me." Evan stabilized his upper body by resting his arms on the table, his body staying upright. "Now that I think about it, I should have known it was her."

"Why?" Micah asked.

"Because she got to me both ways, via email and in person," Evan replied, his voice getting more and more garbled.

"If you knew very little about each other, what did you talk about?" Julian asked, his expression more serious now.

"Everything and nothing," Evan answered after a short contemplation. "We didn't talk in specifics. It was all about how we felt about certain things. Very little of our conversation related to work or other people. Her foster mother died not long ago, and she mostly talked about her and how it felt to lose someone she loved so much."

"You were there for her." Micah's words were a statement rather than a question. His respect for Evan kicked up a notch knowing that he'd just been there for Randi when she needed to vent.

"She was there for me, too," Evan replied as he finally looked directly at Micah. "She changed the way I looked at life sometimes, made me not take everything so seriously."

Jesus! Evan looked so damn broken that it tore Micah up inside. He'd already been through so much, and Evan had always made his family his priority. He deserved something for himself. He hoped to God that Randi would finally realize that Evan hadn't meant to deceive her. His cousin just sucked at intimate relationships.

"We'll figure something out," Micah told him firmly.

"I have to talk to her." Evan sounded desperate.

"Not tonight," Micah said, shaking his head. An idea sprang to his mind as he contemplated how to get Randi to realize that Evan really loved her. "I think you should consider writing to her. It was how your relationship started. Maybe you can say things easier that way."

"Good idea," Julian agreed. "That way she can't slam the door in your face."

"She probably won't read it," Evan rumbled.

"She'll read it. Women are funny that way. If you send an email, she'll have to read it," Micah told him solemnly.

"I need her," Evan informed his cousins fiercely. "I'm not sure what I'll do if she won't talk to me."

"She will. Eventually." Julian's voice was supportive now.

Micah was pretty certain that his brother understood the gravity of the situation now that Julian had seen how torn up Evan really was.

"What are your plans for tomorrow? I thought you had to be in San Francisco."

Evan shook his head. "I'm not leaving until she talks to me. I don't care how long it takes."

"You could stand to lose a pretty big deal," Micah warned, familiar with the company Evan was trying to buy into with controlling interest. It definitely had big possibilities.

"There's always more deals," Evan answered bitterly. "It doesn't matter to me."

Those were words he never thought would come out of Evan's mouth. Micah looked at Julian, who shrugged like he was equally confused before asking Evan, "Can I borrow your jet tomorrow? I need to get to Los Angeles, and Micah is going to New York."

"I don't care," Evan agreed readily. "I'm not going anywhere for a while."

Micah had planned on having his pilot drop him off in New York and then fly on to get Julian back to Hollywood. But if Evan wasn't using his own plane, Julian could get back faster as he wouldn't have to make the trip to New York first.

"Thanks," Julian muttered.

"We need to get home. We have an early morning tomorrow," Micah said. He stood and grabbed his tuxedo jacket off the back of the wooden chair.

"I need to write to Randi," Evan said hoarsely as he stood unsteadily.

"Leave it until tomorrow, Evan." Julian's voice was sincere as he rose and put on his own formal jacket. "I've got the tip."

Micah wasn't sure how much Julian left for Kristin, but judging by the wad of bills bulging from under the napkin holding the empty beer bottle, he was assuming it was plenty.

"Let's go, Evan," Micah prompted his cousin.

"I'd like to talk to Hope," Evan notified Micah, his words starting to slur even more as he downed the rest of his drink and stood up.

"I doubt she's still at the party. She was showing Davy off around at the Center, and she's probably in bed by now. It's getting late." They'd been at Shamrock's for a while. Micah was pretty certain that the party had already wound down.

Evan frowned. "I can't wake her up. She's tired anyway because she's up a lot with the baby."

Micah spotted Evan as he weaved toward the door. He finally grasped him by the collar and steered him in the right direction.

"Thank you for coming. Have a good night," Kristin called from the bar.

Micah raised his hand in acknowledgment, but he noticed that Julian just turned around and shot her a false smile.

"She's a nice woman," Micah commented as he assisted Evan into the car.

"She's a major bitch," Julian retorted, grinning.

"I like her," Micah argued, not seeing Julian's grin because he was busy trying to get his drunken cousin situated in the vehicle.

Julian sighed. "I like her, too."

Micah rolled his eyes, wondering how his brother would act if he really *didn't* like a woman, because he'd been a real prick to Kristin. He didn't show his interest in a good way. "Then quit acting like an asshole when you see her."

Julian shrugged. "I can't. I have too much fun watching her eyes change color when she's pissed off."

It was interesting that Julian even noticed. Micah waved for him to get into the car before climbing in himself.

He lingered for a moment, wondering if Tessa had noticed that he was gone. Picturing her face as they'd danced made his cock stiffen. He saw her face in his mind as she smiled up at him, and he swore she looked familiar, like it was a face he'd seen somewhere before. But he didn't think he'd actually been introduced to her. He would have remembered her.

His fingers curled around the crystal Beatrice had given him. For some reason, he'd kept it, even though he shouldn't have accepted any kind of a gift from an elderly woman he didn't know.

Problem was, there was no redemption for him, and no woman waiting for him to claim her. He was as free as a bird, traveling from place to place looking for a new extreme. Micah loved his life just the way it was right now.

He let go of the stone and jerked his hand from his pocket as he slid into the car.

Not able to completely forget Tessa's beautiful, delicate face, Micah tried to focus his attention away from her and on Evan so they could figure out a way to get him his woman back.

Nevertheless, when Micah boarded his own jet the next morning, he did wonder how long it would be before he'd see her face again in the future.

He hoped it wouldn't be long.

CHAPTER 21

The next morning, Evan sat in front of his computer in his downstairs office, wondering how in the hell he was going to write to Randi. It had always been so easy before, so natural, that he never thought about what to say. It was so much different now, and there was so much at stake.

His stomach rolled as he took another slug of his coffee. He'd already swallowed some pills to make his head stop banging. While the headache was slowly improving, the coffee he was swilling wasn't helping his gut.

He popped a few antacids into his mouth and threw the roll back into the drawer.

No wonder I never drink. I feel like crap.

Ignoring his discomfort, he stared at the blank email in front of him with a scowl. Granted, he had known Randi wouldn't be happy that he hadn't shared who he really was with her, but he didn't know she'd feel betrayed. All he'd wanted was a little more time. It nearly killed him that his actions had made her sad and distrustful. He'd rather die than to see her in pain, emotionally or physically.

What am I going to do if she doesn't forgive me?

"Not an option," Evan growled to himself as he placed his fingers on the keys. He'd gone from elation to the depths of despair last night. She'd told him she loved him, and then she'd left him. "She still loves me," he muttered. "I need to make her understand that I didn't intend to hurt her."

No. I was just being a selfish prick. I didn't think about how my secret would affect her, how she would feel because I didn't share the discovery with her immediately.

Putting himself in her place, he would have probably been annoyed, too, but he would have gotten over it. He would have eventually ended up being pretty damn happy that the two women who fascinated him were one and the same.

Problem was, he hadn't been certain she'd feel the same way.

I can never love a man like him . . .

Dammit . . . why had she written those words? There was nothing that would have stopped him from claiming her for a lifetime if he'd known that she loved him. He didn't care what background she came from or what obstacles they had to overcome to be together.

I love you.

Had those words been real, or just a momentary thought when she was in the throes of a good climax? If she had meant it, did she *still* love him?

Evan was starting to hate himself because he was wracked with insecurities. He wasn't a man who dealt well with failure, anxiety, indecision, or self-doubt.

"To hell with this," he said aloud, talking to himself. He wished Lily were here. At least the canine would cock her head and pretend to be listening to him. She pretty much agreed with everything he said—that was the way he chose to interpret her actions, anyway. "I'll keep writing to Randi until she listens."

He'd had a brief conversation with Hope that morning to explain why he, Micah, and Julian had gone missing before the festivities had ended. He'd confessed that he hadn't taken her advice. After a long lecture, she agreed that writing to Randi and giving her some space was the best option.

I'm writing, but I know it won't be long before I show up on her doorstep. I can't stay away.

Evan was wrestling with himself to not go directly to her house and demand that she belong to him forever.

"She's mine. She was always meant to be mine. There's never been anyone else for me," he grumbled angrily, knowing he'd blown his one chance at real happiness. He knew what happy was now; it was Randi.

Maybe he'd known since the day he couldn't resist replying to her smartass email over a year ago, but he just hadn't been able to admit it. He hadn't been lying when he told her that, maybe subconsciously, he'd always hoped she was his mystery woman. He'd blown off the idea months ago because of the way she signed her emails and the fact that he didn't know Randi had a foster mother. They had never spoken to each other enough for him to know much about her life in person. But somewhere deep inside, Evan didn't think the possibility had ever left his heart—even if it didn't make sense to his conscious mind.

Evan was discovering that not everything was based in reality; some feelings just happened . . .

> *Dear M.,*
> *Have you ever wanted something so badly*
> *that you did something stupid to get it?*

"Please be home. Please read my email. Please understand me," Evan whispered desperately before shooting the email into cyberspace, hoping she'd do all three of those things before he lost his mind.

I'm not checking my email. I'm not checking my email.

Randi patted Lily on the head, consuming a large sandwich as she chanted the mantra in her mind. She'd already done her run for the day, gone through her yoga routine, and then meditated.

It hadn't helped.

She was still fighting the urge to check her email and see if Evan had written. It was late morning, so she had no doubt he was already gone. She'd nearly broken down in tears as she'd watched the two private jets climb in the sky early this morning during her run. It had been cold and clear when she'd woken up, so she'd decided to forgo the treadmill and do a cold-weather run instead. It had felt good to be outdoors, and she'd been exhilarated until she heard the roar of jet engines flying low overhead, meaning a private jet had taken off from the small airport outside of town. Actually, two planes had taken off within minutes, and Randi knew it was Evan and Micah because Julian didn't have a jet, and none of the other Sinclairs had plans to go anywhere.

I knew he was leaving. It shouldn't have hurt that badly. I wonder if he thought about me.

Most of her anger was gone, had disappeared as she thought about all of her conversations with both S. and Evan. The initial shock had worn off once she'd determined his actions had been more careless than intentional.

I'm not checking my email. I'm not checking my email.

Of course, she *could* get on the computer. She just didn't have any reason to log in to her email for the Center.

Randi sighed as she dumped the rest of her sandwich in the garbage, suddenly not very hungry. She'd spent last night mostly awake and restless, trying to figure out who the real Evan Sinclair was. Granted, she'd been hurt initially, and it hurt even more that he was gone now. After almost an entire night of tossing and turning, reliving a lot of the things he'd said to her, she wondered if his motivation had really been to make her a fool. Everything they'd shared, online and offline, had felt so *real*.

She walked into her foster parents' former bedroom slowly, finally sitting down after going back and forth for what seemed like a thousand times and then leaving without turning the computer on.

Oh, for God's sake, just look. It doesn't matter anymore. He's gone.

The desire to know if he had tried to contact her before he left was killing her. He hadn't texted or called, so this was her one last hope.

If he didn't write, I can start moving on, start trying to forget. If he didn't at least try to explain himself, he's not worth all of the moping I'm doing right now.

Randi flipped on the computer and proceeded to bring up her email for the Center, holding her breath.

She felt pathetic as she waited, pinning so much hope on some kind of explanation. Maybe she should have listened to him last night, but her immediate reaction had been one of betrayal. She'd been feeling vulnerable and wounded because she'd told him she loved him and then . . . bam! The news that he'd known for quite some time that she was his mystery friend had broadsided her.

Finally, the mailbox came up and she released a shaky breath as she saw that there *was* an email from him, and he was using the exact same email address that he'd always used to write to her.

> Dear M.,
> Have you ever wanted something so badly
> that you did something stupid to get it?

Randi stared at the one-liner for a moment, trying to figure out why he was still using the same style and her mystery name to ask her a question. Checking the date, she noticed it had been sent less than an hour earlier. Contemplating the question, she knew it was about the two of them. What stupid thing had he done?

Dear S.,

She started her reply knowing she was going to play along. She wanted answers too badly not to. She didn't want to go through the rest of her life not knowing why he hadn't come clean with her. She continued.

> *No, I don't think I have. I'm not certain I've ever wanted anything badly enough that it required doing something stupid. Was it illegal?*

She shot the reply into cyberspace, hoping he was going to explain. Not expecting a reply while he was in the air, she was surprised to see an answer come back in a matter of minutes.

> *M.,*
> *It wasn't illegal, but it should be. I hurt you, and that is unacceptable to me. You're the last person on earth I'd want to hurt, but I did because I was stupid. I'm so sorry, Randi.*

Tears started to flow down her cheeks as she saw his apology. Breaking all pretense, she wrote back.

> *Evan,*
> *Why didn't you tell me? I have to know.*

She assumed the S was short for Sinclair. He'd used a businesslike initial just like she did when she'd first started writing to him, using the first initial of her real name. They were beyond that now, and she wasn't going to hide behind an initial that she rarely used.

Her heated conversation with Evan the night before flowed through her memories, especially the part about the possibility that deep down inside she'd always known that S. might be Evan. Although she'd never acknowledged it, or even really thought about the possibility consciously, maybe there was a part of her that wished they could be the same man. Maybe that was one of the biggest reasons she hadn't wanted to meet him in person—because she suspected she'd never feel the same chemistry for another man that she felt with Evan. If she'd met S. and the chemistry wasn't there, she'd lose a friend who had come to mean a lot to her.

Evan had mentioned that he wasn't all that surprised when he realized she was M. Was she really all that surprised now that Evan was really her mystery man? She'd always been drawn to both of them in different ways, yet the connection was similar. Now that she put them together, it was hard not to realize that they were the same person. They'd had time to get to know each other through emails, but the connection was strong for two people who had never met face-to-face. Her physical connection with Evan in person had been immediate and intense. Both of them were powerful bonds like she'd never experienced before. So was it really so surreal that they were one and the same man? Probably . . . not.

Did I secretly always hope that S. was really Evan? Is that why I never wanted to meet him? Did I want to keep the fantasy alive that I'd be just as attracted to him in person as I was via email?

Now, she could answer with certainty that she *did* want them to be the same man. It was highly possible that she'd always wanted that, but had been afraid of disappointment when she discovered they weren't.

It took a few minutes, but Evan finally answered.

Randi,
I could easily say that I don't know why I did
it, or that I just hadn't gotten around to tell-
ing you yet, but that wouldn't be the truth.
The truth is that I was afraid of losing you.
What if you didn't want me to be your mys-
tery friend? What if he was more important
than our physical relationship? I was trying
to figure out how I'd deal with that, but I
couldn't. I guess I was a coward, and I was
trying to find out how you felt about me
by continuing to be S. for a while. It never
occurred to me that it might hurt you. I was
going to tell you before we went to the ball,
but when you said you couldn't love a man
like me in your email, it nearly destroyed me.
I guess I felt like there was no point in con-
fessing after that.

Her tears flowed faster as she read the response again through blurred vision. If it had been any other man except Evan, she might hesitate before she believed what he was saying. But this *was* Evan, and he was special. His brain was wired a little differently, and his experience with true relationships was almost nonexistent. She believed him.

She typed back.

Evan,
Why does it matter to you what I said? We've
always both known that our relationship
couldn't go anywhere. I have a life here, and

you're constantly traveling. I never meant to fall in love with you. It just happened. Maybe I shouldn't have told you, but I couldn't hold it inside me anymore. But I didn't expect the words to matter, and I didn't expect anything for saying them. I've just learned that life is too short not to tell somebody you love them if you really do.

Randi sighed as she sent the message, her hands still shaking from the knowledge that her feelings had been *that* important to a man like Evan.

He wrote back quickly.

Randi,
Maybe I've never had a woman who made me want to stay in the same place before. Perhaps I've been chasing goals that I've already achieved. I wanted to be better than my father, and it's been my priority for years. I guess when you meet the right woman, your priorities change completely. I challenged you to make me happy. You do. You're the only person who can. It doesn't matter what we're doing. If I'm with you, I'm a happy man.

She read the message quickly, realizing that he was saying he wanted more. Although she wanted the same thing desperately, it just wasn't possible. She started to sob as she typed back a quick reply.

Evan,
Being together permanently isn't practical.
I'm a prostitute's daughter, Evan. I was a
street kid. You're a very powerful man, and
people would love to get that kind of gossip
to make your life miserable. I can't do that to
you, no matter how much I care.

After she sent her reply, Randi knew she should sign off. Her emotions were drained, and she had her answer. It was more surprising than she'd ever imagined. Evan cared about her so much he had been afraid he couldn't measure up in person to the man he'd been while she was writing to him. For such a complicated man, his emotions were simple. He had been afraid to tell, terrified of being rejected.

Evan shot back an email moments later.

Randi,
Bullshit! Do you think I give a flying fuck
about what other people think? Your past
has made you who you are, and I love every-
thing about you. I'd change your childhood if
I could, but only because nobody was there
for you except your foster parents. Contem-
plating all of the things that could have hap-
pened to you rips my heart out every time I
think about it.

"Evan loves me," Randi told Lily, stroking the golden head that was currently plopped in her lap. Lily's ears seemed to prick up as though she recognized Evan's name, her nose twitched interestedly, and her tail thumped a couple of times before she laid her head back down.

Randi's heart started beating so hard and fast that it was pounding in her ears. She wrote back.

> Evan,
> We can talk next time you're in town. Maybe we just need some time to think about this before we jump into anything stupid. Since you're already on the way to your meeting in San Francisco, we can spend some time thinking about if we can manage to work this out.

Randi felt like she needed to give Evan an out, an opportunity to think about who he was getting seriously involved with before he made declarations he might regret. Distance and time wouldn't change the way she felt about him; she'd just miss him more.

"Did you seriously think I was going anywhere? I'm going to convince you to marry me before you have a chance to think about what a jerk you're committing yourself to—even if I have to drag your gorgeous ass up the aisle."

The masculine voice behind her made Randi gasp and swing around in her chair. There at the door to the bedroom was the man of her dreams, his shoulder propped against the doorframe, the cell phone he'd been using to communicate with her in his hand, and a stubborn look in his eyes. "Hello, my mystery friend," he said in a husky, seductive voice. "I'm glad we could finally meet in person."

Randi's heart melted and her tears started all over again.

CHAPTER 22

"What are you doing here?" Randi's vision was blurred from crying, but her tears were of joy rather than pain. "Your meeting—"

"Wasn't important to me," Evan finished for her. "Sweetheart, what do I have to do to make you understand that nothing means a damn thing without you?"

"Will they reschedule?" She knew Evan had wanted this deal pretty badly.

He shrugged. "I don't know. I didn't ask, and it doesn't matter. All I want is to hear that you forgive me for being an asshole."

Randi knew Evan was serious. He'd blown off a huge deal just because he cared about her. "Your plane left. I saw it take off when I was running this morning."

"It was Julian. He had to get back to California, so I let him use the jet since I'm not going anywhere in the near future."

She swallowed hard. "You're not?"

"No."

He looked exhausted, his expression weary. He hadn't shaved this morning, and his jawline was dark. "Are you okay?" she asked, concerned.

"No. I got drunk for the first time last night, and I didn't sleep. All I could think about was you and how much I love you." He pushed upright, tossed his phone carelessly on a small table, and came slowly toward her, his eyes a stormy sea of desire, possessiveness, and intensity.

Randi stood up as Lily circled Evan excitedly, whining for attention. Evan stroked the dog's head, making her go into fits of ecstasy.

"Did you say that you loved me?" Randi asked, not able to take her eyes off Evan's face.

"It's either love or madness. I'm thinking it must be love that produces some type of insanity. I've watched Hope and all of my brothers go through the same thing. I never knew I could feel like this," he told her in a raw, hoarse voice, finally getting close enough to wrap his arms around her.

Coming from Evan, the declaration was enchanting and magical. He sounded tortured and relieved at the same time. Randi wrapped her arms around his neck and held him tightly, riding the wave of emotions along with him as they clutched each other like they never wanted to let go.

"I love you, Evan, so much that it hurts," she admitted as she sobbed into the gorgeous sweater he was wearing. He looked amazing in a pair of jeans and jade wool. It made her wish she was dressed in something nicer than jeans and an old college sweatshirt.

She knew she was a mess, but Evan didn't seem to care. He just held her tighter, swept her up in his arms, and carried her out to the living room. He sat on the couch and cuddled her on his lap.

"Don't cry. I don't want it to hurt because you love me." His voice was pleading and husky with emotion.

"They're happy tears," she rushed to explain. "It doesn't hurt. It feels wonderful."

"Then marry me, Randi. I want you to feel wonderful for the rest of your life, and I'll give you whatever you want to make you stay that way. God knows you've shown me a happiness I never knew existed. I need you."

Tilting her head, she looked into his eyes and saw her future. "I don't need *things* to make me happy, Evan. I just need you." He didn't realize it yet, but she needed him just as much as he needed her. Fate had brought him into her life at a time when she'd really needed to not feel so alone. Destiny had brought her something special, a man she loved—heart, body, and soul.

"We have to talk about marriage," Randi said cautiously. She wanted to say *yes* with every fiber of her being, but it was a big step for both of them.

"No talk," he growled. "Say yes or I'll lose it," he warned her dangerously.

She straddled his lap and wrapped her arms around his neck. "What happens if I don't?" she asked curiously.

His hand wrapped around her nape and he jerked her head down to his mouth before she could even blink. "I fuck you senseless until you don't have the strength to say no anymore," he rasped, grasping her hair as he held her head so he could kiss her.

She melted into him as his heated mouth ravaged her lips and her senses. He tasted delicious, masculine and exactly like Evan. She kissed him back, unable to resist rubbing her wet denim-clad core against his hard erection.

Heat spiraled through her body as Evan thrust his tongue into her mouth, taking what he wanted and giving her what she so desperately needed.

He didn't stop ravaging her with his possessive embrace as he stood up and pinned her against the wall. "Clothes. Off," he grunted bossily as he yanked his mouth from hers, his eyes like liquid blue flames as he met her gaze and let her feet touch the ground.

Randi felt another flood of wet heat gush between her thighs at his dominance as he swept her sweatshirt over her head. He divested her of her bra, dropping it on the floor without a second thought. He pulled his sweater over his head and it fell on the carpet along with the growing pile of clothing. Her jeans and panties joined the collection a moment later.

"Jesus, you're beautiful." Evan's voice was reverent and raspy as he stared at her completely nude body.

Randi knew that he meant it. It didn't matter that she wasn't really a big-breasted beauty who spent hours in a spa or beauty salon. To him, she *was* attractive, and that was all that mattered.

To her, Evan was perfection, and she trailed her palms down his bare, muscular chest. "I've always thought you were the hottest guy I'd ever met." Her voice was a needy whisper. She had to have him inside her before she started begging.

"Always?" He lifted an arrogant brow.

"Yes. Ever since the first time I met you at Emily's wedding." She cried out as he cupped her breasts, his fingers teasing her nipples relentlessly.

"Marry me," he insisted again.

"Evan, we can talk about it," she whimpered.

"No talking. I need a *yes* from you." His hands moved slowly down her belly until they reached her pussy. He stroked his fingers lightly between her folds, sliding slowly through her wet heat.

"Oh, God." She clenched his shoulders, her legs starting to get weak as he sought and found her clit. "Fuck me, Evan. Now."

"You're so wet, sweetheart," Evan crooned in a low, sultry voice as he removed his fingers and deliberately put them to his lips and sucked her juices from the digits. "Your taste is addicting. Did you know that? I want my head between your thighs every time I look at you."

Randi's legs gave out as she watched him lick and suck every bit of her essence from his fingers like it was nectar. Evan wrapped his arm around her waist and lowered her gently down until she was on her back, lying next to the pile of clothes.

He shucked his remaining clothing before following her to the floor and kneeling between her parted thighs. "I can't wait right now," he told her in a demanding, graveled voice. "Tell me, Randi, because I don't think I can hold off any longer before I bury my cock inside you and fuck you until you come."

The look on his face was fierce and dangerous as he towered over her, but Randi didn't feel anything except a thrill of excitement at his loss of control. "Then do it," she dared him, moving her hand down her belly as he watched and sliding her fingers through her own slick warmth. "I can't wait either."

She met his eyes with a challenge as she stroked her clit, moaning softly as her body vibrated with longing. Lifting her other hand, she stroked and pinched her nipples, making her own body rise into an even hotter state of arousal. She knew she was pushing his buttons, but she didn't care.

It should have been awkward to masturbate in front of Evan, but it wasn't. She wanted him to lose it, and he needed to learn that he wasn't going to always get his way by teasing her until she broke.

Some things required a logical, rational conversation.

"Does it feel good?" Evan asked huskily, his eyes following every one of her motions.

"Oh, yes," she moaned, watching his heated eyes as she put more pressure on the tiny bundle of nerves between her saturated folds. "I wish you were inside me right now. I'd love to feel your cock filling my emptiness."

"I just want to see you come," Evan replied, sounding completely fascinated.

He stripped her of all of her intentions with his reaction. Jesus, he *did* just want to see her pleasured. He had started out by insisting on her promise to marry him, but his desire to see her happy had just trumped his own wants and needs.

Evan Sinclair was the most complicated man Randi had ever met, and the only one who could make her crazy and so damned touched at the same time.

"I love you so much," she moaned, the look of pleasure on his face as he watched her take herself to climax arousing her almost unbearably.

"I love you, too, baby. Make yourself come," he encouraged, his eyes now glued to her face.

The fact that he was watching her with laser focus was so erotic that Randi found herself tumbling over the edge as she pinched and stroked her clit harder and harder.

Her back arched as she moaned, her body pulsating as her head moved from side to side.

She screamed as Evan pushed her thighs apart, pinned her hands over her head, and entered her with one smooth thrust. The feeling of him filling her on the heels of her self-induced climax was almost more than she could bear.

"That was one of the hottest things I've ever experienced," Evan rumbled above her. "But I was getting jealous of your own hands."

"Nothing feels as good as this," Randi purred as she wrapped her legs around his waist. "Fuck me, Evan. I need you."

She heard a desperate, low groan fall from his lips as he pumped into her again. "I love you, Randi. Don't ever doubt that. There's never been anyone for me but you. There never will be."

Believing him wasn't a problem. She felt the same way, and she knew she couldn't be feeling all of this alone. "Feels so good," she panted. "More. Please."

He gave her what she wanted, releasing her hands and putting one of her legs over his shoulder to change his angle of entry. His massive cock rubbed against her clit with every hard thrust of his hips, pushing her higher and higher.

Randi watched his face as she felt another orgasm starting to build. Evan was a miracle to her, a man she considered out of reach to a woman like her. Little did she know how very real he was, or that he had a heart as big as the ocean beneath his arrogant façade.

"I love you, Evan," she cried out as she felt her climax thundering over her, her emotions tumbling along with the waves of rapture.

She raised her hips, meeting his thrusts with her heart skittering and her body vibrating in ecstasy.

Evan let her leg drop from his shoulder and he found her mouth with his, absorbing her screams of pleasure as he ravaged her with a kiss of deep possession and urgent demand. She wrapped her arms around his neck and returned his embrace with the same fiery passion, as her fingernails dug into the skin of his back with a grip so strong she knew she was marking him.

He pulled his mouth from hers and bit at her bottom lip. "Fuck, yes!" he exclaimed with a low groan that was almost a howl as she continued clutching at his back, endless pulsations gripping at his cock.

Her climax had milked him of his own release, and the two of them clung to each other in a hot, sweaty mess as they both tried to catch their breath.

"Mine!" Evan growled. "You'll always be mine, Randi."

She shuddered at his animalistic tone and covetous, carnal words. Strangely, his claiming felt more like a vow, his commitment to be there for her for the rest of their lives.

He rolled, pulling her with him so she was sprawled on top of him. Randi sighed, knowing it was just one of many of Evan's moves to protect her and keep her from taking his weight on top of her, even though she'd welcome it.

"Yes," she said simply in a breathless voice.

"Yes?" Evan asked hopefully.

"Yes, I'll marry you." She'd do everything in her power to make Evan happier than he'd ever been in his life. He deserved to love and to be loved more than any man she'd ever met. Randi knew nobody would ever love this complicated man more than she would, and nobody would ever understand him better than she could. He'd probably never lose his veneer of sophistication and arrogance, but it didn't matter. She knew the kind of heart that was underneath all of that.

"What convinced you?" he asked, sounding elated.

"Not your teasing tactics," she admonished him.

"Then what was it? I'd like to know for future reference," he told her jokingly.

She put a gentle palm to his whiskered jaw and told him honestly, "Because there's never been anyone else for me but you, either."

The look of relief on his face spoke volumes as he covered her palm with his larger hand and lowered his forehead to rest against hers.

"Thank fuck," he whispered fiercely, as though she was the most precious thing he'd ever been given in his entire life.

Knowing the pain that Evan had suffered and the burdens he'd carried for so long all alone, Randi held him close to her and promised herself that this man of hers would never be alone with any future troubles ever again.

"I love you, baby," he said huskily.

Randi sighed happily, wondering if she might just believe in a little bit of Beatrice's magic after all.

EPILOGUE

A Few Months Later . . .

"What are we doing here?" Randi asked curiously as Evan led her around the back of her parents' house.

It hadn't been an easy decision for her to put the home up for sale, but they'd been living together at Evan's place because the two of them couldn't bear to be apart. The old home needed a new owner, and another family to find happiness in the house again. Randi hated that it was sitting empty. It looked . . . lonely.

Spring had arrived in Amesport, and Randi knew the house would probably sell during the late spring or summer, so she was fairly surprised when Evan had suggested they take a drive to her old home.

"I wanted to carry on the tradition for one more year," he answered solemnly as he clasped her hand and led her into the fields past the backyard.

"What tradition?" Now she was really confused.

"This one." He stopped and waved his hand toward the creek that ran through the property.

Randi stopped moving and covered her mouth with her free hand. "Oh, my God."

There, beside the small, rapidly flowing stream, were more white calla lilies than Randi could possibly count. They were already blooming, the warm weather in the late spring probably aiding their condition. Evan had obviously had them brought here and transplanted. Just because he thought it would make her happy.

The tall lilies were gorgeous all along the edge of the creek, but the thought of the trouble he had gone to in arranging for the flowers to be imported and planted on a property that was already up for sale was amazing.

"Don't you like them? I thought they were the same variety you talked about." Evan sounded calm but concerned.

"They're exactly the same. How do I thank you for something like this?" She threw herself into his arms and hugged him, so damned grateful that she had this man in her life.

The closeness they'd experienced over the last few months had been almost frightening, and each day she'd fallen just a little more in love with Evan. She was in so deeply now that she knew she'd never escape. Not that she wanted to.

There wasn't a day that went by that Evan didn't do something to melt her heart, and the rift between the Sinclair siblings was finally healing. What had once been a broken family was now whole.

"I have a few ideas," he said in a husky, suggestive voice.

Randi laughed happily, squeezing him tighter. Evan had learned to have some levity in his life in the few months they'd been together. Seeing him smile at her still made her heart lighter. "I'm sure you do," she answered teasingly.

She turned in his arms to just let the sight of the lilies sink into her soul. Evan wrapped his arms around her waist, and Randi rested the back of her head on his shoulder. "It's beautiful. Joan would have loved this."

"Are you sure you want to sell?" Evan asked cautiously. "It's not like you'll need the money. You are marrying one of the richest men in the world, you know."

Randi smiled, knowing when Evan said things like that, he was just stating a fact. "I'm sure. Unless you plan on canceling the wedding."

They were getting married in a month. Evan had wanted the ceremony to be sooner, but he'd also wanted it to be perfect. He was being a pain in the ass about the arrangements, but Randi didn't care. She found it fascinating that he was willing to help with the planning, and was more thorough than she and her female friends.

"Over my dead body," Evan vowed. "It seems like we've waited forever."

It had actually not been more than a few months, but it had seemed like a long time to her, too.

She glanced down at the beautiful platinum-and-diamond ring on her finger, sighing as she wondered how long it would take her to get used to having Evan bringing her a new gift every day.

His gift closest to her heart was his vow to find a plot of land to build a small school for kids with special learning needs. She'd broken down in tears as he'd explained that he didn't want any child to suffer the same way he had.

Their biggest hurdle, the fact that Evan didn't want biological children, had been resolved. They agreed on adoption if he didn't feel comfortable having children of his own within a few years. He'd touched her heart when he said that any kid they had didn't need his DNA for him to love them. Randi didn't mind if they adopted because she felt the same way, but she was pretty certain that Evan was starting to understand that any offspring he had with dyslexia would be just fine. They'd both help the child learn from an early age, and she had no doubt Evan would be a fantastic father.

"I still don't know what to say. This is incredible." Randi felt so at peace as she gazed at the collection of lilies.

Lily flopped down at Evan's feet, happy to be with him whenever she could. Lily had bonded with him the same way she had with Randi. In return, Evan seemed to adore her, and he still snuck her occasional sneaky pieces of steak. Luckily, not enough to stink up the house.

"Say you love me," Evan suggested.

"I love you," she obediently replied. He never got tired of hearing the words, and neither did she. "Are you going to keep putting flowers on Dennis and Joan's graves?" Evan still went to the cemetery every day. There was no snow to clear at this time of year, but Evan made it a point to keep the gravesite tidy and place fresh flowers there every day.

He shrugged. "Whenever possible. So far that's been every day."

Reaching for her hand, Evan entwined their fingers as they walked slowly away from the stream together.

"Beatrice was right, you know," Randi mentioned casually.

"I know," Evan grumbled. "I find that kind of frightening, since she gave Micah a crystal when he was here for Hope's party."

"You don't want him to be happy?" Randi asked curiously.

"I can't see him settling down. He's into extreme sports, and there aren't many women who can manage to be with a guy who does the crazy shit he does," Evan replied. "But yes, I would like to see him happy. Xander is going off the deep end again, and Julian is busy on his latest movie. A lot falls on Micah's shoulders."

"I wonder who has the other stone. Does he know?"

"Nope. He didn't mention it," Evan answered. "She'd have to be an amazing woman to put up with him."

Randi laughed, amused by Evan's assumption that he was any less arrogant or demanding than Micah. He didn't travel much anymore, sending out some of his higher-level employees to check out possible new deals. He might still have to go away sometimes, but they were learning to compromise. Honestly, Evan didn't seem the least bit eager to leave Amesport. He seemed quite happy to run his business from his home office and hang out with his family, although he still hadn't quite learned how *not* to try to tell them what to do. However, it was pretty funny to hear him refer to his eldest cousin as being less likely than *him* to settle down.

"I'm sure she will be. Beatrice has been one hundred percent right regarding her predictions for the Sinclairs." She'd even been correct that Randi would be closing one part of her life when Joan died and starting another. She was at peace now with her foster mother's death, even though she missed her every single day.

Stokes was waiting for them, standing beside the Rolls as they rounded the corner of the house. The man wore a smile most of the time now, and he'd become more like part of the family instead of just an employee. Still, he refused to retire, claiming he still had a few years of driving left in him.

"Are you okay?" Evan asked Randi quietly as he pulled her to a stop before they reached the car.

"I'm fine." She smiled at him. "Thank you for doing this. I hope whoever owns the home next time will keep up the tradition." If they didn't, that was okay, too. It would be someone else's home, someone else's preferences. Randi's place now was with the man she loved, and she was beyond happy just to be marrying someone she knew would cherish her for a lifetime.

"I hope they do, too, sweetheart," Evan said, dropping a kiss on her temple. "Let's go home."

"I'm cooking spaghetti," she warned him.

"Good. I'll need a workout tonight." He smirked.

Evan ate anything and everything she cooked, and he enjoyed every meal. Surprisingly, he'd started to help her in the kitchen, and cooking dinner had become one of their favorite times of the day because they did it together. "Let's go home," she finally repeated, taking a look back at the house as they strolled to the car. Her life had changed irrevocably since Evan, but she'd never forget the two people who'd saved her from a horrible life on the streets. They would both live on through her memories forever.

"Ready?" Evan questioned.

"I'm ready." She nodded emphatically. Not only was she ready, but she was excited to start a new chapter in her life, her life with Evan.

They walked hand in hand to the car, both of them ecstatically happy that their whole new life together was about to begin.

THE END

AUTHOR'S NOTE

It's estimated that between 10 and nearly 20 percent of children have a learning-based reading disability. Most of them are dyslexic. If you have a child who has problems reading, please have them tested. Early detection can help a child start to learn in different ways and start finding their inner creativity and their own unique talents.

ACKNOWLEDGMENTS

My sincere thanks to all of the Montlake team, especially my editor, Maria Gomez, who has always made writing this series such a pleasure. A huge thank-you to my employees and my street team, Jan's Gems, who are always so willing to make my burdens lighter so I can bury myself in my office and write. As always . . . you ladies rock!

-Jan

ABOUT THE AUTHOR

Photo © 2013 Carrie Herzog

New York Times and *USA Today* bestselling romance author J.S. Scott is an avid reader. While she loves all types of books and literature, romance has always been her genre of choice. Because she writes what she loves to read, she excels at both contemporary and paranormal romances. Most of her books are steamy and generally feature a to-die-for alpha male, and all have a satisfying happily-ever-after ending. She just can't seem to write them any other way!

Jan loves to connect with readers.

You can visit her at:

Website: http://www.authorjsscott.com

Facebook: http://www.facebook.com/authorjsscott

You can also tweet @AuthorJSScott

For updates on new releases, sales, and giveaways, please sign up for Jan's newsletter by going to: http://eepurl.com/KhsSD.

5/16